Monstrous Beauty

Monstrous Beauty

ELIZABETH FAMA

FARRAR STRAUS GIROUX

New York

The author gratefully acknowledges the research help of John Kemp, Buddy Tripp, Bill Rudder, and Kerri Helme (all of Plimoth Plantation), Christine Cook (Plymouth genealogy), and Adam Cifu (medical); and the editorial insights of Beth Potter, Sara Crowe, Susan Fine, Kate Hannigan, Linda Hoffman Kimball, and Carol Fisher Saller

Farrar Straus Giroux Books for Young Readers
175 Fifth Avenue, New York 10010

macteenbooks.com

Library of Congress Cataloging-in-Publication Data
Fama, Elizabeth.
    Monstrous beauty / Elizabeth Fama. — 1st ed.
      p. cm.
    Summary: In alternating chapters, tells of the mermaid Syrenka's love for Ezra in 1872 that leads to a series of horrific murders, and present-day Hester's encounter with a ghost that reveals her connection to the murders and to Syrenka.
    ISBN 978-0-374-37366-5 (hardcover)
    ISBN 978-1-4299-5546-1 (e-book)
    [1. Mermaids—Fiction. 2. Ghosts—Fiction. 3. Murder—Fiction. 4. Supernatural—Fiction. 5. Massachusetts—Fiction. 6. Massachusetts—History—19th century—Fiction.] I. Title.

PZ7.F1984Mon 2012
[Fic]—dc23

2011031668

For Eric Fama Cochrane and Sally Fama Cochrane,
who joyfully riffed this entire story into being
while I listened in wonder

And for my parents, Gene and Sally Fama,
who taught me that family is everything

Monstrous Beauty

Prologue

1522

Syrenka wanted Pukanokick.

She watched him but never spoke to him. She never dared to approach or reveal herself. A year of stealth had taught her his language, his habits, his dreams, his ways. The more she knew, the more she loved. The more she loved, the more she ached.

The sachem's eldest son did not go unnoticed by the women of his tribe. A quiet keegsqua watched him, too. Syrenka noticed the way she smiled at him, the way she brought her work to the shore while Pukanokick burned and scraped his first dugout canoe. And why shouldn't the keegsqua want him? His glossy black hair glinted blue in the morning sun, his skin beaded with sweat, his eyes shone as he worked with single-minded passion on the boat. Syrenka read the keegsqua's shy silence for the desperate proclamation that it really was: the girl wanted Pukanokick, too; she wanted a smile that was meant only for her; she wanted to know his deepest thoughts; she wanted to see him lift beautiful sons onto his shoulders and hug their warm, bare feet to his chest; she wanted to grow old with him. She wanted him to save her from emptiness.

Syrenka's smoldering ache ignited into a fire. She spent all of her time near the shore now, and ignored her sister's beseeching to join her below, where it was safe, where she was supposed to be. Where she could not tolerate being.

On the day Pukanokick finished the boat, his younger brother and his mother's brother helped him drag the charred dugout to the edge of the water. They watched as he paddled it out, and they leaped and shouted with pride to see how true it glided and how stable it was, even in the heavy chop of that day, even when he stood and deliberately tried to tip it. One corner of the keegsqua's plump lips lifted silently with joy, while she pretended to bore holes into stone sinkers. Syrenka studied them all from behind an algae-green rock.

But early the next day, the keegsqua was gone. Pukanokick's brother and his mother's brother were gone. Pukanokick was alone when Syrenka became entangled in his fishing net. Swimming a short distance from the dugout, she was distracted by the rhythm of his body as he plunged the paddle in the dark water, lifting his weight off his knees, stroking a heartbeat into the quiet morning. She forgot that he had set a net the evening before—it was cleverly anchored with rocks and suspended with cattail bundles—until the fiber mesh collapsed around her and her own surprised thrashing caught her fin fast.

Working quickly, she was almost free by the time he had turned his boat and eased it over the net. She was curled upon herself, tugging at her dark tail with her thick white hair in a bloom around her, when she felt the cool shadow of the dugout move across her skin. She looked up and her eyes caught his—they were brown-black, the color of a chestnut tumbling in the surf. Her own eyes would alarm him, she knew. She saw him take in a breath. He did not reach for his club, although he could have. He did not reach for his bow. He watched.

She attended to the net and her tail. She lifted her arm and slashed at the remaining strands with the fin on her wrist, cutting herself loose. She looked back up and slowly rose from the deep, shoulder hunched and face to the side.

Her cheek broke the surface first. He didn't recoil. She smiled, careful not to show her teeth.

"Kwe," she said, in his own Wampanoag.

"Kwe," he whispered.

She tried to keep her voice smooth and quiet, unthreatening. "I am sorry. I broke your net."

He shook his head almost imperceptibly from side to side. He wasn't angry. She saw him swallow.

"This is the finest mishoon I have ever seen," she said, sliding her fingertips along the hull of the boat as she swam its length.

"Thank you," he said. And then he seemed to remember something. Perhaps that he had a club, and a bow, and that he was the sachem's eldest son.

"Who are you?" he demanded.

"I am Syrenka. You are Pukanokick."

"How do you know my name?"

She had never been this close to him. The muscles in his forearm extended as he unclenched his fist. She followed his arm to his shoulder, to his angular jaw, to his broad nose and then his unwavering eyes.

"I have seen you. Fishing. I hear others call you. I follow you. I listen."

5

"Why do you follow me?"

She stroked the edge of the boat. "You are not ready for the answer."

He stood up, balancing easily in his dugout. "I am."

She whipped her tail below her, rising out of the water like a dolphin—but carefully and steadily so as not to splash him—until she was eye to eye with him. She reached out with her hand and stroked his cheek. He did not flinch. He allowed her touch.

"Noo'kas says I must give you time. You must grow accustomed to me. You are yet too young," she recited.

"I am a man." But his breath caught as she traced the line of his jaw. He lifted his chin. "Who is this Noo'kas to question that?"

"Noo'kas is the mother of the sea. I must obey."

Pukanokick's eyes widened. "Squauanit. You mean Squauanit thinks I'm not yet a man?—the sea hag who brought the storm that killed my mother's father?"

"Shhhh," she said, putting her fingers on his lips. Her nails were long and sharp, but she was gentle.

She sank down into the water again and swam away.

"Come back!" She barely heard the muffled shout. She stopped, astonished. She felt her skin tingle with hope.

She turned and swam underneath the dugout. Back and forth, with his shadow above her as he knelt in the boat. She needed time to consider. To be calm. To choose wisely.

He waited. She gathered strength from his patience.

She rose to the surface.

"You are right. Noo'kas is a hag. She has become ugly as the seasons circle endlessly. She will live forever, but she will never be beautiful again. She missed her time. What does she know? I will decide myself."

Pukanokick rested his forearms on the edge of the dugout and leaned his head over the side so that his black hair nearly grazed the water. He asked her his question again, but softly this time.

"Why do you follow me?"

She brought her face close. "I follow you because I love you."

She brushed her lips against his. Warm breath escaped his mouth. He put his arms around her and kissed her. His lips were nearly hot on her skin, but firm and gentle. She felt a hunger for his touch that she could no longer hold back.

The dugout did not tip, but Pukanokick lost his balance. He fell into the bay, clutched in Syrenka's embrace. She released him instantly. But of course he knew how to swim—she had seen it many times—and he came up laughing. She joined him. He kissed her again, and they sank under the water together. She saw him detach his buckskin leggings from the belt at his hips. He swam up for a breath.

Syrenka surfaced and saw the sunrise, spilling pinks and purples and blues into the sky, as if for the first time.

Pukanokick touched her cheek. "I want to be bare-skinned in the water, as you are."

She sank under again and tried to undo the belt of his breechclout, but it was foreign to her. His hands pushed hers away and fumbled with it while she pulled down on his leggings to remove them. She brought him deeper and deeper as she tugged.

Lost in concentration, she misunderstood his struggles. She

thought he was wriggling to pull out of the leggings. She did not see the bubbles that escaped his mouth in clouds. She did not remember the passage of human time. She forgot her strength.

Finally, triumphantly, she peeled the first pant from his right leg. When she looked up, she realized with an agonizing start that his head swayed against his chest slowly in the swells, and his body floated lifeless.

She screamed underwater, a high-pitched wail with a rapid burst of clicks that caused the sea life around her to scatter. It was as Noo'kas had foreseen. She had dared to love, and she had lost everything.

Chapter 1

THE WIND WHIPPED Hester's hair around her face. She shoved it behind her ears and closed her eyes for a second, taking a deep breath of sea air—faintly like salt, faintly like cucumbers. The ocean filled her with joy and longing, all at once. It was strangely, achingly bittersweet.

She had gone on dozens of Captain Dave whale-watch adventures over the last seventeen years: her best friend's father was Captain Dave Angeln himself, and her own dad—a researcher at Woods Hole—often used the trips to collect data and observe mammalian life in the bay. When she was a child she had loved clambering up on the ship's rails, her father gripping the back of her shirt in his fist, and scouring the horizon for the telltale spouts that she was almost always the first to see. She still thrilled at skimming alongside a massive humpback, its slick body and watchful eye hinting at secrets from beneath the surface.

She stole a glance at Peter, a bullhorn hanging in his right hand, his left hand shielding the late spring sun from his eyes. She could see just the side of his face: a high cheekbone, black glasses, a thick eyebrow, weather-beaten blond hair like bristles of a brush, lips pursed in easy concentration. He was looking for whales. His eyes passed right over her as he turned, scanning the bay. In a moment he lifted the bullhorn to his mouth.

"Awright, folks, we've got a spray on the horizon off the port bow," he announced cheerfully. "For you landlubbers that's the left side as you face forward, near the front of the boat." The tourists rushed to see, chattering and aiming their cameras. A father hoisted his son onto his shoulders.

"There it is again—eleven o'clock," Peter said. "Ah! There may be two of them."

The crowd oohed with delight and pointed eager fingers. Peter announced, "The captain is going to take us in that direction— toward the southwest corner of Stellwagen Bank. It'll be a few minutes, but with any luck we'll get a much closer look at those animals."

He lowered the bullhorn and caught Hester's eye, smiling. He yelled against the wind, "You're slipping, hawkeye."

"No fair, I was distracted by something," she called back.

"Oh, yeah, by what?"

She opened her mouth but nothing came out. The truth was, she had been distracted by him. She had dropped her guard. How could she have let that happen? She felt her ears heat up.

A girl with a pixie haircut and a nose piercing rose from her seat and tapped Peter's shoulder. He turned away from Hester to answer the girl's question. Hester examined her; she was boyishly pretty with a heart-shaped face and cherry red lipstick. She wore tight black pants and a gray cashmere sweater with a red silk scarf. The girl's eyes fairly sparkled as she spoke to him, and her broad smile revealed perfect teeth. Hester felt a little weight press on her chest, and then she felt irritated by the sensation.

Peter took off his Captain Dave's windbreaker as he talked and Hester tilted her head with a new discovery: his shoulders were broader now. Had she already known that? She'd been friends with him for so long that half the time in her mind's eye he was a bony six-year-old, hanging on to a swimming ring for dear life at the beach, craning his neck to keep the water from splashing his face, while she recklessly dove under him again and again, just to unnerve him. He was such a funny little chicken back then, she thought. She caught her eyes sweeping over his shoulders and his back again and she forced herself to look away.

She had no business admiring him, or spying on him when he was with other girls.

She pulled a necklace out of her collar—a rounded gold heart with softly brushed edges, on a delicate, short chain. She pushed the heart hard to her lip until the pressure against her tooth made her wince. She reminded herself of the history of the necklace: her dying mother had bequeathed it to her when she was only four days old, and her grandmother had given it to her mother under the same circumstance. According to a story passed down through the generations, the original owner was Hester's great-great-great-grandmother, a woman named Marijn Ontstaan, who had died of "languishment" or something equally nebulous less than a week after her own child was born.

What a burden that little heart represented for her family, Hester thought, dropping it back under her collar: a legacy of premature death, passed on to innocent new life. It was also a warning, she had decided years ago, against love and its cozy associates: sex and marriage. Other people could dare to love—Peter and the pixie girl, for instance—people who wouldn't lose everything if they did.

She looked back at the two of them. Peter was showing the girl a specimen of a baleen plate from a whale. From his gestures Hester knew he was describing the filter-feeding process of the whale and telling her that the baleen combs were made of keratin, like fingernails, rather than bone. She had heard him explain it to tourists a thousand times: wholly approachable, never impatient, always sharing a sense of discovery with them. But now his head was so close to the girl's, they were almost touching. And then they lingered like that; a beat too long. He was neglecting the other passengers, wasn't he? He wasn't tracking the sprays of the whales for the captain, as he usually did. The girl brushed her hand over the baleen sample and then grinned as she ran her fingertips over his hair, comparing the two. He received her touch without flinching—maybe even playfully?

Hester needed to lift the weight from her chest. She moved to the back of the boat, to the other side of the captain's cabin, away from them. She looked out across the water and allowed the feeling of longing to wash over her, spill into the crevices of her soul, and fill her completely.

Chapter 2

1872

Ezra left the stationer's shop with a lightness that felt suspiciously like joy, if he was remembering joy correctly. He pulled out his pocket watch to check the time. It was ten minutes before low tide. Perfect. He found himself smiling; the little muscles around his mouth had miraculously not forgotten how. In his other hand was a parcel—the object that promised to lift him just a little out of his misery.

He had taken a leave from his second year at Harvard nine months ago. It was temporary, he'd told the dean, perhaps a month at the most. His father couldn't shake a bad cold, the housekeeper had written—it was nothing that hot toddies, warm blankets, and the doting of an only son would not cure. But Mrs. Banks's optimism had already turned to shadowed eyes and a furrowed brow by the time Ezra's coach arrived. He had watched his father suffer six and a half months of fever, spasms, and the shakes, until pain and despair whispered the unthinkable into truth: death would be more merciful than life. Ezra watched it arrive with anguished relief.

As a boy he had played in tide pools, devoured books, imagined undersea worlds, captured and sketched insects and sea life. As a young man, it occurred to him, he did much the same. His father had allowed him to attend college at sixteen, had never disputed his choice of studies (wholly unsuited to the family shipbuilding business)—had loved him that much. And so these last nine months had forced burdens on Ezra that he'd never borne before: managing business affairs; running a household; fielding too many well-wishers with their marriageable daughters in tow; hearing the shallow phrase "poor Mr. Doyle" again and again without walloping someone; dressing the bedsores of the ivory-and-blue wraith that had once been his beautiful father; planning the funeral of his last relation on this earth.

And now there was an undefined mourning period to endure: too short, and the town would mistake him for callous; too long, and he'd go mad. He needed to study. He could not live without wonder. Someday soon, he'd sneak away from Plymouth—put off the housekeeper and the lawyer and the foreman in the shipyard, promise to come back but not mean it—and hop on the Old Colony Railroad back to school to finish his studies. In the meantime, he would escape for a moment to the shore.

It had been drizzling when he went into the shop, with a sky so thick and heavy his evening plans seemed to have been thwarted. Now as he left, the clouds were punctured with luminous holes, spilling rays of sun like solid beams. He looked up at those beams as he stepped off the boardwalk—captivated by how extraordinarily *straight* light was, and how easy it must have been for scientists to mistake it for particles rather than waves—and collided with Olaf Ontstaan. His parcel fell in the mud on the dirt road of Leyden Street, and Olaf's cotton sack crashed with the sound of breaking glass.

"Clumsy oaf!" Olaf barked, picking up the bag. Shards of a bottle slipped out and fell to the ground.

"I'm terribly sorry," Ezra said. "My head was in the clouds."

Olaf looked up then. "Mr. Doyle! Poor Mr. Doyle, how are you? Think nothing of this. A simple mishap. Eleanor reminds me time and again, there is no sense in weeping over shed milk."

Ezra bent to help him pick up the sharp pieces. The smell of something stronger than milk wafted around them.

"I would appreciate your not mentioning my purchase to Eleanor," Olaf murmured as they worked.

"Of course not."

"She will not tolerate liquor, and I respect her wishes in the house. But I work hard, Mr. Doyle, I am a good provider—and at the end of the day if I may not stretch out my legs with a drink and relax in my own home, I deserve to take it elsewhere, do I not?"

Ezra rescued his own parcel from the mud as they stood up. He quickly removed the wet paper wrapping before it could damage what was inside.

"Ah, a book," Olaf observed. "We have only the Bible at our house. I expect yours is for university?"

"It's a journal." Ezra flipped the empty pages for him to see.

"You are a writer, sir?"

"A researcher, a scientist in training: botany, zoology, marine life. But when I'm home I seem to be drawn to the history of legends and mythical beings. This will be a field journal in which I record observations and sketches of the ocean environment that might sustain such creatures."

"Mythical creatures." Olaf's face sagged, suddenly doughy. "You are not by chance speaking of sea folk?"

"That's right," Ezra said. "Although I don't tell many people. At best, it must seem to the outside observer a frivolous pursuit, and at worst, lunacy. I suppose now we must keep each other's secrets, Mr. Ontstaan." He smiled, but Olaf did not reciprocate.

"You ought stay away from that subject, Mr. Doyle."

"It's too late, I'm afraid. After all, I was weaned on such stories since before I could talk, from my father's customers—in the shipyard, around the dinner table, at the fireside. The fascinating thing, scientifically speaking, is how consistent the legends are, and how persistent. Think on it, Mr. Ontstaan: even the Indians have oral traditions of such creatures. How could they generate the same descriptions independently of the foreign merchants, the sailors, and the local fishermen?"

"Mr. Doyle, would you consider coming home with me for supper this evening?"

"That is kind of you, but I cannot. I want to tally the number of mollusks and crustaceans that are at or below the high-water mark on the rocky outcropping. I have a theory that the abundance of food sources there could account for the high number of sightings in the bay." He gave a helpless shrug. "I am a prisoner of the tides."

"If you would allow me to say my piece, sir, I would dissuade you from this dangerous obsession."

Ezra looked at Olaf more closely now—his leathery face and tired eyes. A man eroded by life, whose small-mindedness would extinguish Ezra's last pleasure, if he let him.

Ezra bowed his head and said, "I thank you for your invitation. Please give my regards to Mrs. Ontstaan." He turned and took quick, long strides toward the bay.

Chapter 3

Hester wound her way through dozens of flickering Japanese lanterns on the lawn near the beach. In the waning evening light they were lovely, she conceded—like randomly clustered honey stars in a night sky. It was cool for mid-June, and as tiny raindrops speckled her arms she harbored a small hope—unfair to the others, she knew—that the weather might provide an easy way out. She was there only because Peter had asked her to come and he was graduating soon. She would do what she did at every school party: chat with him—shout with him—over the music, have a soda with a few other wallflowers, avoid stumbling on couples sharing saliva in dark corners, and steer clear of Joey Grimani, who prowled school events for anything with two X chromosomes.

The band finished setting up in the gazebo and began tuning their guitars and testing the amplifiers. They started a slow ballad as a warm-up. She looked at her watch: five minutes early. In her eagerness to get the party over with, she was paradoxically the first one there. The misty rain hadn't extinguished the lanterns yet, but it had raised the hairs on her arms, so she made her way to a tree for shelter. How much moisture could speakers and amps tolerate? she wondered. How much rain would it take to decompose Japanese paper?

Her classmates began arriving by the carload—laughing and tumbling from vehicles whose booming, rumbling radios hammered over the relative calm of the band's song. She leaned against the trunk of the tree, her hair falling in curtains on either side of her face.

When she looked up, Peter was walking toward her with Jenn and Claire. He pushed up his glasses and smiled as he approached. She tucked her hair behind her ears.

Looking at Peter was like looking out her bedroom window: she knew every tree, every nest in every tree, each tile of the neighbors' roof, the lawn and the flowers, every splotch of color, in every season. She even knew the befores and afters: his teeth, before and after braces; his glasses, which she had joked were part Buddy Holly, part bio nerd when they were new, and which now had a scratch on the left lens from when he'd dropped them into the harbor and dove in to retrieve them. Whenever she saw him, he seemed glad to see her. Someday she'd figure out a way to tell him just how much comfort that had given her over the years.

"Hi, Jenn, hi, Claire," Hester said.

"Hey, Hester," Jenn said. "Aren't the lanterns incredibly romantic?"

"Sooo romantic," Claire agreed. "They make me wish the perfect guy were here to sweep me off my feet."

"The lanterns are very pretty," Hester managed to say.

"Don't forget to dance this time, you guys," Jenn said to Hester and Peter, tugging Claire away by her sweater sleeve.

"Yeah, have fun!" Claire wiggled her fingers goodbye.

Hester fixed on their bouncing ponytails as they merged effortlessly with the party. "Why do they always do that?"

"Do what?"

"Deposit you and run; try to make us a couple."

"Aw, relax. They don't understand the magic is gone once you've seen the guy projectile-vomit double-chocolate cake on his eighth birthday."

She laughed. "Or when you study for finals together and the girl is wearing a week-old sweatshirt and hasn't showered in three days."

Peter pushed his glasses up again. "Yeah—Hester—that's not actually gross when you're a guy." He pulled a narrow box out of his back pocket.

"I got you a present."

"Why?"

He shrugged. "No reason. Just something to keep that mop out of your face. You hide behind your hair, you know."

She lifted the top of the box. Inside, nested in white tissue paper, was a long silver barrette shaped like a seashell. It had smooth, plump whorls that formed a tightly wound cone, with ribs like a staircase traveling along the whorls.

"It's meant to be a wentletrap, I think," Peter said. "It's pretty accurate."

"I've never seen anything like it before." She hugged him and said into his ear, "I'm going to miss the crap out of you."

"Me, too," he replied, squeezing her and then letting go. "But I'll only be an hour away."

"You'll be studying." She handed him the empty box. He stuck it in his pocket again. "And making college friends." She put the barrette between her teeth and started to pull her hair back.

He took a breath, as if to say something, and then closed his mouth.

She watched him gaze at the ocean. In the waning light it was the same color as his eyes.

"What's up?" she said, clipping the barrette in place.

"I'm just thinking about how next year you'll go to college, too."

"Yeah."

"And eventually you'll become this famous historian who'll never need to set foot here again if you don't want to. Meanwhile after college I'll wind up in charge of Captain Dave Boats against my will and be the fifth generation in my family to die in Plymouth."

"Captain Dave Boats is more than just sunburned tourists. The naturalist program is really important."

"Forget about that." He shook his head. "That's not what I meant to talk about."

"What, then?"

"I want you to know—" He stopped. "I just feel like you're . . ."

"Two minutes till my departure from hell," she warned him.

He frowned at her and said in one breath, "There it is, exactly. Why do you always run away?"

"You know I hate parties."

"It's because you need to shut people out. Because you're afraid of something."

"I'm fine."

"I know you are. You're better than fine. You're smart, and funny." He smiled. "And now that I can see your face, you're not as hideous as I remembered."

She laughed, but she also took a step back.

He raised his eyebrows, as if to say "See?"

Maybe he was right: she did in fact have the urge to pull away from him whenever he got serious; she did always bolt from social situations.

She forced herself to stand still and listen to him.

His voice was quiet, direct. "I'm only saying this because I care about you. I want you to have a normal life—I mean, not that you're *ab*normal—just that you shouldn't miss out on a whole chunk of potential happiness. You have to let someone in at some point—let someone care about you."

The band's song had changed to a pounding mess of drums and guitar to welcome the crowd, and apparently roil them into a frenzy. It was working. Peter raised his voice over the noise. "So that came out horribly, but I had to say it—once." He clasped his hands on top of his head. "Honestly, I feel like an idiot right now, so I'm going to walk away. I'll see you later."

Hester watched him until he reached the parking lot, and then she turned around and smacked her back against the trunk of the tree. She felt the warning pricks of tears. She wiggled her nose to keep them at bay. She'd lose him soon, but that was the way it always had to be, wasn't it? She should be glad for him that he was going on to college, where he'd make new friends. Where he'd eventually, inevitably, find a girlfriend. She would be someone lovely, that girlfriend, for sure—lovely inside and out. How could she not be?

She turned toward the ocean and drew in a breath of evening sea air. It had the flavor of salt and moist sand tonight. And right on cue, there was the longing. An image of the shore below flashed in her mind as if it were calling to her. It was the antidote she needed to the party. She left the shade of the tree, crossed the lawn, and walked down the cool stone stairs to the water. The tide was out, leaving a broad swath of beach, so she opened the old iron gate at the bottom and stepped onto the sand.

The farther she walked, the more the music faded to a distant thump, the more she was able to retreat into herself. A little farther, and she could hear the nearly silent expanse of water at her side. There were no lapping waves, just the wonderfully dull sound of a wide sky meeting the horizon. She knew the stillness was an illusion. Below, there were dolphins, porpoises, whales, fish, crustaceans, anemones—a hidden world, consumed with the business of life.

She came to a section of the bluff that was reinforced with riprap: rough-quarried granite blocks jumbled together to protect the shore from erosion. A breakwater made of the same material, which everyone called the rocky outcropping, extended into the bay to her left. She looked ahead and realized that her escape was taking her to the hangout cave—a portion of riprap in which the stones happened to form an opening. The entrance was underwater when the tide was in, but at low tide like this it was rumored to be a den for lovers and potheads. If she was lucky, everyone was up at the party and the cave would be vacant.

The raindrops began to fall in earnest. Within a few paces the splatters on her head and shoulders quickened to a drumroll. She broke into a jog with her chin tucked to her chest, making it inside the entrance just as the sky opened, spilling its contents.

She had never been in the cave before. It was narrow, with a low ceiling, but it was deeper than she had imagined. She couldn't see all the way to the back.

"Anyone home?" she croaked. She heard only silence. She sighed with relief and slipped her sandal off to shake a pebble out. The fabric of her dress clung to her body, so she peeled it from her legs and shook it. The air against her damp skin made her shiver.

She heard the crunch of shifting rocks outside the cave, and turned just as Joey Grimani stepped inside. The dim light of dusk was behind him, his face was in shadows. He was soaked through, as if he had jumped in the ocean. He shook his head to get the water out of his hair and then ran his fingers through it to make it look tousled—expertly, and without a mirror.

Ick, she thought.

"Hester!" he said, as if it were a surprise to find her there. "It's raining buckets, huh?"

He stood between her and the cave opening. She calculated that she'd have to physically move him if she wanted to leave.

She crossed her arms in front of her chest. "What are you doing here?"

"Gettin' out of the rain, same as you," he said.

"All the way down the beach?"

He came toward her. "How about we hang out for a while . . . and then I'll walk you home when the rain quits?"

"I don't want to 'hang out,'" she said firmly. "Go back up to the party."

"There is no party; it broke up as soon as it started to pour."

She tried to squeeze past him to leave, but he caught her wrist and pulled her to him.

"Wait," he said. He pressed so close that she felt the contours of his chest through their wet clothes.

"I'm glad we're alone . . ." he started, sounding suave and practiced.

"Stop it, Joey," she interrupted. She pushed his upper body away, but he wrapped both arms around her waist and pressed his hips against her.

"You're not as cold as you want people to believe," he said in a low voice. "There's a lot of passion in the way you carry yourself."

Her voice came out in a growl. "Take your hands off me and get out."

"I know I can open you up—like a flower." He started swaying slightly, as if they were slow-dancing. "All you have to do is say yes."

She was actually considering angling her knee to jam him where it would hurt the most when a man's voice sighed from the darkness. "This cave is occupied, Lothario."

"Thank God," Hester said. "There's another couple in here!"

Joey stiffened, loosening his hold around her waist. He cocked his head and listened, squinting into the blackness at the back of the cave.

"What're you talking about?"

"Find your own spot to make love to her," the voice replied. It was husky and lethargic, as if awakened from sleep, with maybe a little edge of irritation. Hester wriggled out of Joey's arms.

"Hey!" Joey said.

"I told you. Get the hell out of here." She pushed hard against his chest; he staggered a step back.

And then she raised her voice to the stranger in the cave. "Do you seriously call that assault *making love*? Are you some kind of fucking misogynist? This jerk doesn't give a shit about me."

Joey fixed his hair as he said, "You're out of your mind, Hester, you know that? A total crackpot. I was trying to get close to you, to lighten you up a little—I forgot what an ice bitch you really are."

"Get out," she said.

"I've seen you lead Peter on. That wimp *does* give a shit, and a lotta good it's done him."

She moved toward him at full force and shoved him out of the cave. "Get out!" she screamed.

Joey stumbled before walking away, shouting insults she couldn't hear over the pounding of the rain. Hester's heartbeat was quick with adrenaline. A couple of wet strands of hair had come loose and were stuck on her cheek. She took a deep breath, slid the strands behind her ear, and then checked for the shell barrette, which was still snug.

She kept her back to the rear of the cave. She didn't want her eyes to get used to the dark, in case the stranger and his date were in some stage of undress.

"Don't mind me," she said over her shoulder. "I'll leave as soon as the rain lets up a bit. I promise."

"Whom are you speaking to?" the voice asked, cautiously.

Another weirdo. "Do you see any other cave dwellers in here?"

There was a long pause. She heard no kissing, no heavy breathing, no sounds of grappling or moaning. Just silence.

If only it would stop raining, Hester thought. She wanted to be home, in her pajamas, under her covers with a thick British novel, listening to the rain patter against her window.

"I am not a misogynist," the voice said after a minute.

"Hey, I don't give a damn what you are." Then she felt bad for being rude. He had helped her after all. She should probably apologize, but she didn't want to engage him in conversation.

She heard a quiet snort. "I've known drunken sailors from Liverpool who used fewer profanities."

She didn't know what to say to that. She had always honored her parents' request not to swear in front of her brother, Sam, but she had never held back in front of her peers. This voice sounded like it came from a young guy—young enough to take it—but . . . *different* somehow. It was slow and contemplative—out of the mainstream. Maybe he had been homeschooled as a kid.

He broke into her thoughts. "Though I do admit that the crassness of the word 'fucking' next to the erudite 'misogynist' seized my attention."

It was old-fashioned; that's what his voice was. She had to admit to herself that it was also appealing: rich, measured, and so expressive she could hear a warm timbre when he was smiling. Her curiosity took over, and she turned to peer into the darkness but saw nothing. And then she realized that his eyes would be used to the dark, and that she was standing near the faint light of the cave opening. He would see that she was searching for him. She turned away.

The rain began to slow. It would be weird to stay any longer, she knew. And by all rights a stranger in a cave ought to be giving her the creeps, intriguing voice notwithstanding.

Hester said, "I'd better go now."

"I'm sorry to hear it," the voice said, with an awkward sincerity that surprised her.

"Tell me," she said, "are you alone back there?"

"I never said I was with anyone."

"Huh." She tried to recall his exact words to Joey and wondered if that was true. "Well, anyway, thanks for helping me get rid of that idiot."

There was a small hesitation before he said, "Goodbye."

Chapter 4

1872

AT HIGH TIDE, the rocky outcropping was mostly underwater; at low tide, it was possible to clamber all the way to the end, but with difficulty. Ezra picked his way over the slick, algae-covered boulders and started the task of recording the variety and quantity of shellfish along the water's edge. He worked for several hours, until the light became gray and the color left the sea.

He was on his belly, his head hanging over the edge of a boulder, when something caught his eye. A giant turtle swam in place below him, lumbering from side to side as it swung its flippers, tearing a mussel off the granite block with beaklike jaws.

"A loggerhead so far north," he whispered. He hurried to sketch it.

He was drawing the eyes, black and heavy-lidded, when a figure swam up in a blur from below and snatched the loggerhead around its middle. It was a woman—as pale and luminescent as a ghost, with swirling white hair. Ezra startled, dropping his pencil into the water. Her face snapped toward him. Her eyes were too large, clear green, and had horizontal, slit-shaped pupils, reminiscent of an octopus.

The loggerhead desperately stretched its neck to bite her, but she twisted to swim down and away with it.

"Come back!" Ezra shouted, without hesitation.

He caught sight of her tail as her body was absorbed into the dark depths. It was longer and more slender than any written account had described—maybe five times her torso length. From the hips down she was covered not in scales, but in armored scutes, like a sturgeon. Her tail fin was shaped like that of a dolphin rather than a fish: muscular, with flukes that lay in a horizontal plane. His heart pounded, his mind tried desperately to memorize what he had just seen.

His hands shook as he searched his coat pocket for another pencil. Finding the stub of one, he took a deep breath to calm himself, hunched over his journal, and began to record his observations and sketch the vision he still had of her. Tears came to his eyes, distorting the image on the page, dripping down the bridge of his nose. He clumsily wiped them away.

He sat working for an hour, until the light was nearly gone. There was a sharp sliver of a moon and the night was clear, but it would still be difficult for him to get to shore. He didn't care. He would crawl over the boulders if he had to. He closed the journal.

"What were you doing just now?" A low voice came from the water.

He felt prickles along his scalp. For a few seconds he couldn't say a word, though he wanted to. Had she been next to him the whole time?

"You came back." His voice cracked.

"In a thousand years, only one other has called out to me," she said.

A thousand years. He turned his head in the direction of her voice and saw her faint aura. Her pale arms were crossed, resting on a block of granite, with her chin propped on top of one hand.

"Why was there water coming from your eyes?" she asked.

"They're tears. They mean either great sadness or great happiness." His eyes became moist again.

"Which is it for you now?"

He let out a laugh. "This moment is currently ranked first among the happiest of my life."

She was silent. He waited, containing himself, though his body felt electrified.

"What were you doing before, with such care?"

"I was writing in my journal—recording what I saw."

"Me?"

"Yes. And before that, mussels and crabs . . . and the logger-head, the turtle. What did you do with it when you took it away?"

"I ate it. What will you do with the journal?"

"I don't know," he said truthfully. "I intend to study the history of"—he could no longer say legends and mythical beings while she was within arm's reach, could he?—"the natural world. I want to record what I see so that I might remember it forever."

"You will not live forever."

He laughed again, twice in nine months, and all in the last minute. "That's right. But if I become good at my research, I might publish it so others may read it. Then it will be on earth for a long time—though not forever."

She said quietly, "I will live forever."

He could not imagine it to be possible.

"In truth I can be killed. Many of us have been killed. But left alone, I will not die."

Many of us, he repeated in his head. She was not the only one.

She was silent. The darkness had swallowed the outcropping so completely he could no longer see the ghost of her form. After a long minute he began to worry that she had slipped away. But then he heard the soft *splish* of her tail.

"There is no satisfaction in eternity," she said. "There is only loss."

He knew that the tide was rising and his time with her had to end.

"My name is Ezra," he said.

"I am Syrenka."

"Will you meet me here again, Syrenka?" He tried to sound calm; he mustn't rush her. "There is so much I want to know."

"I will meet you as often as you like, until you are no longer interested."

He smiled to himself in the darkness and thought, *As if I were not in danger of losing interest in everything else.*

Chapter 5

THE AFTERNOON OF PETER'S GRADUATION, with the windows rolled down and the music turned up in his truck, Hester felt it was truly the beginning of summer, and perhaps the end of an era. Peter and Sam wore suits and loosened ties, and Hester had on a filmy dress with a camisole slip. The weather was perfect: not too warm, not too cool. The rocks were in sharp focus along the shore and outlined by a crisp blue sky. Sam was wedged between her and Peter, singing along to the music, his voice a crackly blend of high and low despite his new six-foot frame.

"Letting the days go byyy; let the water hold me down!"

Hester's eyes were drawn to the ocean. It was speckled with gleaming reflections of sunlight, winking at her like thousands of stars. Thoughts of the shore, sand, riprap, and the cave looped through her mind without her willing them. When the truck approached the picnic area along Water Street, she shook away the trance. "Guys," she said impulsively, "let's walk on the beach."

"No way," Sam said as Peter pulled into a parking spot. "That's for old people. I'm getting fried clams with my droogs at Squant's Treasure."

"Peter?" Hester asked, getting out of the car, her heart already on its way.

"I can't stay long, I have to go to a reception for an exhibit of old toys at Pilgrim Hall. My dad is letting them use my great-great-great-great-"—he counted on his fingers—"aunt Adeline's doll."

"A half hour," Hester promised. "And you're already dressed for the reception."

"All right," Peter agreed. "There won't be much beach right now, but I'm with you."

"See you at home," Sam called, jogging toward the wharf.

Peter got out of the truck, tossing his suit jacket inside. He rolled up his shirtsleeves as he strolled across the grass. It was a relaxed, summery pace—the pace you might expect if aimless walking were the goal, if there weren't a pressing need to get to the beach. Hester tried to restrain herself but wound up a step ahead of him anyway.

"Hey, Hester? About the party," he said, mostly to her back. "I'm really sorry I said that stuff."

"You don't have to apologize," she said over her shoulder. *Hurry,* she thought.

"You're doing fine without my telling you how to run your life."

"I'm pretty sure I'm a mess."

"Then you pretend well." They were almost at the stone steps. She skipped ahead and looked down toward the beach.

"Oh," she said, disappointed. The rocks near the shore were completely submerged but for their slick green tips. The narrow spit of sand still showing along the bluff glistened black and spongy.

Peter caught up to her. "Listen to me," he said quietly, putting his hand on her shoulder until she turned to look at him. "What

I should have said the other night is that you can talk to me about anything."

"Thanks. I know." She could hardly concentrate on what he was saying. "Look—it's high tide. There goes our walk."

"Technically we're in flood tide. High tide will be at 5:05 today. And we can wade."

"You know when the tide comes in and out?"

He looked at her over his glasses. "I work on a boat, remember?"

"But you didn't today."

He shrugged, starting down the steps. "The chart is on our fridge."

At the bottom of the flight Peter took off his shoes and rolled up his pants while Hester unclasped her sandals. Peter opened the gate, and they waded into the cool water up to their knees. The wavelets lapped the shore, rhythmically but without urgency. The resistance of the water made Hester's steps sweeping and unhurried. She began to feel calm. Sandpipers followed the leading edge of the waves with staccato steps, probing the wet sand near the bluff with their beaks.

"The tides are roughly on a twelve-and-a-half-hour cycle," Peter said. "Which makes them move around the clock over a period of fourteen or fifteen days. It's pretty complicated—it depends on the earth's rotation, the gravity of the moon and the sun . . . even the shape of the bottom of the near shore. A tide calendar is the only way to get it right."

Hester looked ahead to where the riprap began. The cave should be a little ways beyond that, but everything looked the same when the water was high.

"Is the hangout cave submerged now?" she asked.

"Mm-hm."

"Have you ever gone inside?"

"Sure. I was sailing the pumpkinseed and the tide was going out, so I brought her ashore and poked around a little. How about you? Have you been?"

"Me? No." She shook her head.

"I'm not sure what the attraction is. It was pretty dark in there, and kind of slimy. A couple of kids were smoking weed—I could hardly breathe . . ."

Hester had stopped listening. She was taken aback by her own response to Peter. Why had she lied about going in the cave? The sound of the stranger's voice played back in her mind—expressive and intelligent. She remembered how irritated she was at first that he seemed so callous, but how quickly his manner had softened. By the time she left for home she had the distinct sensation that he didn't want their conversation to end. And more: if she hadn't been so rattled by the party and Joey's aggressive advances and the fact of the voice belonging to a stranger, she might have been oddly tempted to stay longer to talk to *him*.

She looked out over the water. It wasn't the first thing she had ever hidden from Peter. She had never been able to confide in him about her family history, and her private worry that she had a medical problem lurking in her genes. He knew that her mother had died after she was born, and that the doctors had never found a cause, but that was all.

Their families had been close, even before Susan's death. After she was gone, Peter's parents had been there—not only for Hester's father, Malcolm, but for Hester's late grandfather, who had lost his daughter in the same awful way that he had lost his wife. Grief had weakened him, allowing his leukemia to take over. The Angelns had helped care for them all, including Hester. Two years later Dave had been the best man when Malcolm married Nancy, Hester's stepmom. A year after that they had welcomed baby Sam into the world, and little Hester had stuck by Nancy's side for weeks, making sure she wouldn't die.

But it had taken until high school for Hester to worry for herself. It had taken the possibility of falling in love. *Love.* A new and different feeling—initially pleasing, full of hope and desire. But then, after rational thought—bleak and melancholy. And pointless. The more she had turned the problem over in her mind the last few years, the more her future dilemma unraveled backward, to the present. Why start a relationship when nothing could come of it? Birth control was not foolproof, unless it involved surgery— something she'd have to wait years to contemplate. And how would she convince a doctor it was necessary, when she was a seemingly healthy young woman?

Love. Sex. Loss. It was safest to avert the whole sequence.

Peter stooped to reach into the water. He came up with the shell of a large marine snail, but after turning it over and seeing the soft body retracted inside, he lowered it into the water again.

She knew he wouldn't judge her if she told him her worries. But he might debate, he might press. And she had solved the problem on her own; she had found a private path that required approval from no one but her. It was simple and logical: stay single. It left no opportunity for failure. She would be happy with a career. She'd be a doting aunt to Sam's kids someday. She didn't want to be talked out of it.

They paused to look out over the water. A gull hovered above them, cocked its eye at her, and laughed, "uk uk uk uk," before flying away. Peter looked up at it, and then Hester felt his eyes drift down to her. She had been quiet for too long.

"Did I ever tell you that my dad once saw a mermaid in the bay?" he said with a grin.

"Oh, God, I think so! Ages ago," she snorted, grateful for the offer of levity. "Tell me again."

"It was before I was born. She swam right alongside the boat, the way dolphins do. She was so white, the phosphorescent organisms in the water made her look like she was glowing green—you know, like the underside of a humpback? He thinks she was white because she lived at great depths and didn't need pigments to protect against the sun."

"It was probably a molting seal or something."

He shook his head. "He knows the animals in the bay like the back of his hand."

"I've read that the ancient mermaid legends all sprang up from manatee and dugong sightings. Mariners who were out to sea for years on end were lonely enough to imagine they saw women in the water. Dugongs have pale skin, and when you look down at them from a boat they look like they have a human head, because they have a sort of slender neck."

"Horny mariners? Hester Goodwin, you have no sense of magic."

"It's historical, scientific reality."

"So all those tales of men getting it on with mermaids . . ."

She nodded mischievously. ". . . Sailors trying to justify bestiality."

"Now you're just being gross."

She laughed. They turned back. And suddenly she recalled a story she had never told him. A genuine secret she could share.

"Do you remember when we were little and my dad took us swimming at White Horse beach?" she asked.

"He took us a million times."

"I mean the day I drowned."

A sober look flashed across his face. "I remember. You were diving for bocce balls. You were fanatical about that game, like a golden retriever."

"I made him throw the target ball . . ."

"It was light, so it flew way too far, and your dad yelled not to go after it, and you went under anyway, deep under, because you've always been ridiculously stubborn. And you never came up."

"What they say about drowning is true. It was peaceful."

He kicked gentle falls of water ahead of them.

"It was scary as hell."

"Not for me. I didn't feel any pain. I just forgot to hold my breath. I was still alive."

"You coughed out this huge spray of water when your dad pulled you from the bottom. He took us to the emergency room, and you kept saying the whole way there that you were fine."

Hester dragged her toes through the rippled sand. It was ice cold below the sun-warmed top layer.

"There was a woman down there with me."

"What?" He stopped walking and turned to face her.

"Yeah, and get this: she was really pale. Like white-blond." She raised her eyebrows. "Maybe it was one of Dave's mermaids."

"What did she do?"

"She put two fingers to her lips, as if she were telling me to be quiet. And then my dad was dragging me out of the water and she was gone."

"A hallucination."

Hester shoved his shoulder, laughing. "Why is it a hallucination for me and a scientific sighting for your dad?"

"Well, *you* were drowning . . ." He started walking again, and she joined him.

"I've never told anyone this," she said, thrilling at the revelation, "but I was sure I breathed water that day, like a fish."

"And I've never told anyone this," Peter said, putting his arm over her shoulder and tipping his head toward her ear. "I peed my trunks when you didn't come up for air."

Chapter 6
1872

EZRA MET SYRENKA EVERY EVENING at dusk, always in a different location, always far from shore. She never had any difficulty finding him. In the late afternoon he would row a boat out until his muscles were hot and sore, and then he would drift, working on his journal until she appeared. His arms became strong, his shoulders broad, and his skin slightly weathered from the wind, sun, and salt air. His clear blue eyes became intense with passion and purpose. Syrenka answered all of Ezra's questions and matched them with her own, eager to know about human life. At the end of their time together she would unerringly guide him back to the harbor and then disappear again.

On one of these evenings Ezra examined the sharp, bony-spined dorsal fin on her neck and upper back, the smaller, razor-sharp fins that followed the line of her thumb on the undersides of her wrists, and the webbing between her fingers. But he examined from a distance. He knew she had only one rule for their meetings: she would not allow Ezra to touch her. Even in cases where it would help his research, she was strict.

"I should dearly like to know the texture of your skin," he finally ventured.

"You shan't," she said, smiling—readily showing her sharp teeth.

She cocked her head to the side to look at him with one eye. It was a mannerism he adored.

"You do such a disservice to science," he grumbled cheerfully.

"In keeping you safe, I serve science. And myself."

"I don't understand why touching you would be unsafe. Are you electrified, like some rays?"

"I am not. But I have eaten such a thing."

He was quiet for several minutes, sketching in the dim light. She closed her eyes as he worked, and he saw something familiar pass across her face. She sighed, for the first time in his presence. He wondered if she had learned it from him.

"It's bittersweet, isn't it," he murmured.

"What does that mean?"

"Being together, but not being together."

"The word should be sweet-bitter, then, as you describe it," she said. He looked up from his page and smiled. She had the quickest mind he'd ever encountered.

They were quiet again.

"What are you protecting me from?" Ezra asked.

Syrenka said nothing. He put the journal aside. The light had become too dim to continue working.

"Please tell me."

"I am protecting you from me," she finally answered.

"You've been nothing but kind and gentle."

"As long as I am an immortal, tied to the sea, and you are a mortal who belongs on land, I am a risk to you."

"The only danger I see is that I may forgo food and sleep, so distracted am I by the distance between us."

"I want you to live to be a very old man. I want to be near you for as much of that time as you'll allow me."

"The rest of my life, then," he said.

She was stubbornly quiet.

"I am scientific enough in nature that I believe all difficult problems have a solution and yield to effort," Ezra said.

He thought she might not reply again, until she said softly, "There is a way for us to be together."

"Tell me."

"There are two parts: one would be simple for me, the other requires a price that no person should pay. I cannot even speak it. Please do not press me."

"For now," he agreed.

"In time, you may tire of me and find a woman, and I will welcome your happiness—"

He shook his head. "There is only you."

She looked at him with her enormous eyes.

"Can you, I wonder," he said quietly, "can you tell me the simple part?"

He heard the swish of her tail, which he knew meant she was thinking.

"If I carry a man's child, I will become mortal. I will acquire a soul."

Ezra's mind leaped through the implications. "You would choose mortality to be with me?"

"I cannot be truly human without it. If you had lived even half as long as I have you would understand, the exchange is fair."

He remembered his father at the end, how death had been a

mercy. Perhaps an eternity of loneliness would be equally unbearable.

Syrenka looked out toward the ocean and Ezra barely heard her whisper, "I am exhausted by wanting you."

"Syrenka." He leaned over the edge of the boat to see her profile in the darkness. Her mouth was set, and her eyes revealed ancient pain.

"Dear, kind, brilliant Syrenka, I—"

"No," she interrupted, turning to him. Her face was closer to his than it had ever been. "Do not say it."

"You already know how I feel, then. Why should I not say it?"

"Because it will only increase our agony. There is so much you still do not know."

He felt her breath—moist and cool. The space between them was almost nothing, and yet he was safe—as safe as on dry land. How could one kiss hurt?

"Mr. Doyle!" Ezra heard a man's voice. He startled.

"No! Mr. Doyle! Stay away from her!"

He looked behind him. It was a fisherman in a boat, with a lamp—he was almost upon them. They had been so caught up in their conversation they hadn't noticed his approach.

Syrenka slipped under the water.

"Who's there?" Ezra shouted.

"It's Olaf Ontstaan. Listen to me," he yelled. "She's a demon!"

"Leave me in peace, Olaf!"

Where had Syrenka gone?

"She's murdered dozens of sailors and fishermen—for hundreds of years—since before this land was colonized. One pitiful lad I knew myself, in my youth. Driven mad with love . . . Washed ashore a week later, he was. Bloated and stinking. She seduced you so she can kill you, Mr. Doyle!"

Suddenly, Syrenka's face was above water.

"Caught!" she said, before disappearing underwater again.

What did she say? Was she admitting guilt? Ezra's heart pounded.

She came up again. "My tail!" He could just see her eyes, wide and blazing with anger, and then she was gone. This time her arms clawed the water as she sank, and he saw that she was being pulled under.

She surfaced explosively and grabbed the side of Ezra's boat. Her tail was caught in the fisherman's gill net.

Ezra looked back at Olaf, and by the light of the lantern could see him pulling on the net, hand over hand. He was drawing Syrenka—and Ezra's boat—toward him. Syrenka thrashed to free her tail; water sprayed in every direction.

Ezra instinctively put his hands on Syrenka's hands. Her skin was slick, firm, and pliable, and cooler than his own.

He shouted in Olaf's direction. "You bastard! Stop!"

Her fingers were being pulled off the edge of the boat. He caught her forearms, but they slid through his hands until the fins on her wrists cut into his palms. He held on. He felt warm blood, and the sting of the salt water. He was being pulled so hard, the boat was tipping.

"Let go, Ezra," Syrenka said.

"No!"

"You're hurt!" she said, enraged.

And then she went under. Ezra—still holding her tightly—fell in after her.

The ocean was black and cold. Ezra's clothing and shoes instantly became leaden. Water rushed around his face as bubbles escaped his nose. And then he was no longer holding Syrenka's arms, she was holding him. He felt himself being dragged in the direction of Olaf's boat, but deeper. Syrenka held him around his waist, and the side of his body was pressed against hers. She was more powerful than he could have imagined. He was more fragile than he'd thought.

His empty lungs felt as if they had collapsed, as if a painful weight were crushing his chest. His diaphragm began to spasm, urging him to breathe against his better judgment. He swallowed, again and again, to stop his body from taking a breath. All at once, she turned him to her and her cool lips pressed against his. His mouth opened involuntarily, responsively. He was blacking out; he knew he would die kissing her.

And then a miracle happened: the pain in his chest disappeared. His muscles relaxed. He was conscious. It was as if he had taken an enormous, sustaining gulp of air. Her kiss seemed to allow him to live underwater. He was revived now, and a real kiss—so long denied—lingered between them.

He felt her body jerk, and he realized that Olaf's net still ensnared her. Syrenka gripped him around the waist again. She used her free hand to try to wrest her tail loose. She wrenched back and forth. She worked to untangle the netting with her hand, and then tried slashing it with her wrist fin. All the while she held tight to Ezra.

•

The kiss began to wear off. It was not permanent, as he had imagined. She had somehow oxygenated him temporarily. He thought he might be able to distract the fisherman, to reason with him, to save her, if she would only let him surface for air.

He pushed on the arm that was around his waist, but it held like a vise. He tried to pry her fingers loose. He became alarmed. He squirmed like a child. He shook her shoulder, but she took no notice of him. How could she forget about him? He began to panic. His air had run out. He looked up and saw the lantern on the fisherman's boat, the light quivering through the waves—he was dying, within sight of the surface!

He flailed and thrashed, and in utter desperation he screamed at her, expelling the last bit of air that was left in his lungs. This time he did lose consciousness, and Olaf Ontstaan's accusation flashed through his mind as his world went black: "She seduced you so she can kill you."

Chapter 7

THE DAY AFTER PETER'S GRADUATION, Hester was at work at Plimoth Plantation, her first full day of the summer season. She tossed a handful of cabbage into the pork pottage and stirred it with a wooden spoon. Rich broth vapors wafted out of the iron pot and escaped up the chimney. She leaned to breathe them in, the condensation beading on her nose.

"A mite more salt," she said, dabbing at her face with her sleeve. "But not so much as to be prodigal." She pulled her heavy woolen skirt away from the cinders of the open hearth and added a dash of salt from the salt box. The midday dinner was ready—and this time she could tell from the smell that it was downright edible. It would make their meal seem infinitely more authentic to tourists this year if her pretend-husband actually ate the stuff.

She looked over her shoulder. Her cottage was empty: there was no need to speak in character anymore. Most of the visitors, drawn by drumbeats, had gathered at the fort to watch the militia test their weapons. She was free to let her brain run loose as Hester for a moment, to stop thinking as a Pilgrim.

She straightened the blankets on her supposed marriage bed and sat with a sigh. The mattress was stuffed with lumpy cotton, the blanket was scratchy against her palms. Her training had taught her to say that the makeshift wool curtain around the bed was there to hold in body heat at night, but she had also assumed that in 1627 it provided the only pitiful privacy a young couple might find in a one-room home: send the children out to play; draw the curtain; hurry up.

In spite of the darkness of the hut, the heat was suffocating. The tiny, high windows let in little light and less breeze. Three layers of period clothing—all linen and wool and leather—were stifling on a warm day. She mopped her forehead with a handkerchief from her belt and tucked a few long hairs back into her linen coif. Any other interpreter might be tempted to remove her bodice jacket, but it didn't occur to Hester. She knew in her core that Elizabeth Tilley Howland would never unfasten even the top button.

She got up. There was always work to do in the cottage. She found a rag and began dusting. The packed-dirt floor made it nearly impossible to keep the room clean. She dusted the family's shelf—lifting bowls, trenchers, and spoons to clean under them—and then picked up the single book on it: a replica of the Geneva Bible of 1560, believably moldy, with crinkled pages. She flipped it open and a silverfish darted down the gutter. She dropped the book, her heart pounding. She felt light-headed, and suddenly queasy. She sat in the chair and covered her face, a memory washing over her.

She was dawdling on the way home from school, looking for her friend Linnie in the graveyard behind the church. She found her patiently building a fort near the old oak. Linnie always seemed to be waiting for her.

The air was too sweet, the sky too crisp to run and play. They lolled lazily in the young grass behind the church, listening to birds, watching just-born flies sun themselves on heated tombstones. Hester was seven, Linnie was eight and a half, and proud of being older. Hester lay on her back and tracked clouds, popping and expanding like heated corn kernels as they drifted slowly across the sky. Her eyelids closed, and she began drifting herself until she heard Linnie's voice.

"I dare you to go inside the church, Hester."

She opened her eyes and turned her head to see Linnie, propped on one elbow, facing her and fiercely focused, the way she sometimes was.

"That's not a dare," Hester mumbled. "I go there every Sunday."

"You never go without your family, when it's empty."

Hester yawned and looked at the back door of the stone building. It was slightly ajar, which she hadn't noticed when she'd arrived that afternoon. It was dark inside.

She sat up, groggy. "You want to play in there?"

Linnie shook her head. "I'm not allowed."

Hester lay back down. She sighed deeply. "No one is allowed, I bet."

"That's . . . that's exactly why I'm daring you," Linnie said.

Hester shrugged, and after a minute of silence Linnie blurted, "I happen to know that the real rule is . . . that you mayn't go inside a church—on a weekday—unless you're carrying a Bible."

"Where'd you hear that?"

"Please." Linnie shook her shoulder. "I dare you to go in the church carrying a Bible."

"I don't have a Bible here."

"I have."

Hester opened her eyes at this. "You do? Where?"

Linnie scrambled to her feet, grabbed Hester's hand to hoist her up, and dragged her over to the tombs facing School Street.

The tombs were in a long building made of granite blocks, nested into the hill and overgrown with bushes and weeds. There were four square iron doors on the front, and a marble tablet dating the building, A.D. 1833. Two of the doors had antique black padlocks on them, with keyholes for skeleton keys. Standing in the middle of the row, Linnie looked over both her shoulders, making sure they were alone. Hester looked around, too, and when she turned back, Linnie had pushed aside a curtain of ivy that dangled over the center portion of the building. Hester was surprised to see a fifth tomb that she'd never noticed before. It had the same black door and the same thick, round ring pull. There were two striped snails clinging motionless to the mortar above the door. Looking down the row of tombs, and at the spacing of the doors, she thought she might have guessed there was another tomb if someone had asked her.

"I hide my treasures here," Linnie said in a hushed voice. "No one goes inside the tombs anymore."

There was no padlock, just a large sliding bolt at the bottom of the door that was jammed deep into the ground. Hester tried to tug the bolt up, but it was tightly wedged in the packed, dry dirt.

"Hold the ivy so it won't catch my hair," Linnie said.

She lifted the bolt with little effort. She opened the door a crack and reached inside, bringing out a dusty, decrepit Bible, which she passed to Hester. The dank smell of mildew and earth wafted up from the book and pinched the back of Hester's nose.

"Now, I dare you to go in the church," Linnie said, forcing the iron door shut and pushing the bolt back into place. Hester let the ivy fall, and the tomb disappeared again, in full sight.

"Okay," Hester said, wondering if she had been tricked into the dare. "But if I get in trouble, you have to tell them it was your idea. Promise?"

Linnie's eyebrows furrowed with worry, and she shook her head. "I can't promise that."

Hester held the Bible out to her. "Then I won't do it."

Linnie's eyes darted toward the door of the church. Hester shifted on her feet.

"No, wait." Linnie looked back at her. "I promise."

"Cross your heart and hope to die? Stick a needle in your eye?"

"That's awful!"

"You have to *do* it."

"Stick a needle in my eye?"

"No." Hester laughed. She lifted Linnie's pale hand by the index finger and brought it to her chest. "Cross your heart, dummy."

With Linnie peeking from behind a tombstone, Hester tiptoed into the church. She went into the cool sanctuary and sat in one of the pews. There wasn't a sound other than the rustling of her own clothes as she moved—a noise that was amplified by the still air and stone walls, making her feel like she was the only person on earth. The Bibles in the racks on the pews had bright green fake-leather covers, with shiny gold lettering. Her own was black, with cracked leather peeling away from the corners, exposing damp, splayed layers of binder's board underneath. She opened the ruined Bible on her lap and then dropped it with a cry.

It was teeming with insects. Their segmented, fishlike bodies writhed in a silvery-blue mass. There were no pages left in the book: what was once paper was now a pile of silverfish, engaged in horrific stages of fighting—or mating. The mass rose and billowed and overflowed, an undulating ocean of squirming bodies and trembling antennae. Hester stood on the bench screaming as the silverfish fanned out from the floor upward in numbers impossible from one small book—hundreds of thousands of insects—swarming the pews and invading the newer Bibles. She leaped into the aisle and ran toward the back door of the church, her heart beating fast, her stomach feeling sick.

Just as she reached the exit, a pastor blocked her way.

"Don't go," he said huskily, putting his hands on the doorjamb.

Hester squeezed her eyes shut and ducked under his left arm, pushing his jacket flap aside and ramming past him to sunlight and freedom. When she reached the stairs she took them up and over the hill, two by two, toward the west exit of the cemetery, glancing back only once. From the darkened doorway she heard him shout, "Hester, please!" as she crested the hill and disappeared on the other side.

Linnie was nowhere in sight, even though she had crossed her heart.

Hester ran home, out of breath, brushing tickling phantom silverfish off her arms, swearing that she'd never be friends with Linnie again, not in a million years.

Hester uncovered her face and rubbed it. She hadn't thought of Linnie in ages. She had never seen her again after that day. She'd changed her walking route home from school to avoid Burial Hill, and her family had stopped going to church for a decade—until Nancy had recently declared it necessary to tame Sam before he entered high school.

Hester remembered that the Sunday after the silverfish incident Malcolm had marched the family home—with little Sam snoozing limp over his shoulder—muttering about last straws, and how any congregation that inflated an ordinary insect infestation into a haunting was not worth an hour and a half of his time each week. Hester had decided then and there, huffing as she skipped to catch up, that it was probably best not to tell anyone that Linnie's Bible had caused the whole ruckus.

Chapter 8
1872

Syrenka realized with horror that Ezra had become limp in her arms and was dying. She put her mouth on his, but it was only a fleeting kiss—not enough to save him—before he was jerked loose from her grasp by another massive tug on the net. Having almost no air in his lungs, he sank. She strained to reach him and summoned all her strength to push him to the surface. She held him from below, with his face out of the water, until a spasm of choking racked his body and gave her hope that he might fight to live.

Olaf pulled hard on the net again until the tip of Syrenka's bound tail was on his boat. Much of her long tail and all of her torso were still in the water, but she could no longer reach Ezra.

She curled on her tail like a snake and clawed her way up the netting, wild with rage. She was no longer focused on freeing herself, but on killing Olaf. He reacted quickly. He had hauled aboard many powerful bluefin tuna, as heavy and slick as her, with as much fight in them, and he had the skill and burly weight to pin her to the deck on her stomach. She screamed in desperate frustration. She tried to reach back to slash him, but he was ready for her. He used a strong rope to tie her elbows together, above the sharp wrist fins. She was at his mercy.

Olaf flipped her onto her back. He had a knife attached to his belt, and he unsheathed it. She did not stop fighting, even while bound. He had intended to stab her in the heart, but he instantly regretted that it meant facing her as he killed her: even in rage she was eerily beautiful.

Syrenka sensed his hesitation and took advantage of it. She stopped resisting.

"Please, let me go," she pleaded.

"You're a killer," he said. "And with God's help Mr. Doyle will be your last victim."

"I could never hurt Ezra. He's alive, I am sure of it," she said. "You must believe me . . . I love him."

"That's repulsive. It's a sin against God. You aim to damn Ezra's soul for eternity."

"If you release me I will stay away from humans forever. I swear to you."

"Oaths from a monster are worthless." He raised his knife.

"I'll consign myself to the deep! Please untie me, I beg you." Her eyes were imploring as she thought of this to say: "I only wanted a baby."

"You disgust me."

"You of all people can understand. You who longed for a son, who placed hope in his future, only to have him taken from you too young."

"How do you know that? That's none of your concern!"

"I hear you talking with your friends on the water. I have . . . I have wept with you," she lied. "I want to help."

He was beguiled by her voice. In the lamplight he could see that her white skin was firm and young. He devoured her nakedness with his eyes, but hastily and furtively, because it was wrong. No, more than that: it was savage and depraved. Yet it had been so long since he had seen his wife, Eleanor, unclothed. So long since she had barred him from their marital bed, declaring that her age had shut off hope of another child.

He used the knife to cut away some of the net entangling Syrenka's tail. The slickness of her body was sensual and inviting. He could see where he might enter her. He set down his knife with a trembling hand. He unbuttoned the fall front of his trousers, and then stroked her hip with his fingers splayed.

"Don't . . ." Syrenka said.

Then, suddenly, he was angered and embarrassed by his thoughts. What was he doing? She had tempted him with unholy magic. She had deliberately cast a fog around his conscience—he, a good man and a God-fearing Christian! She had made him want her— she, a beast, and a monstrosity of nature! She would not trick *him* the way she had tricked others for hundreds of years.

He kissed her violently, in punishment. She spat a viscous green mucus in his face and began to fight again. He threw himself on her to stop her writhing. Her movement beneath him electrified him. His hot, panting breath spilled onto her face.

"You're jealous of Ezra," she hissed, "because he has a lover who wants him."

"Stop talking!" he shouted, spraying her with spittle. His body felt a rush of power and hatred that he was sure now he could not control. He pushed inside her.

"No! Please!" she screamed.

"Stop talking!" he repeated, over and over again with each thrust, until he could no longer speak and his body shuddered.

He heard her cries too late. He pulled away from her and onto his knees, wheezing. His eyes were wide. He quickly buttoned the front of his trousers, hands shaking. As if he could erase what he had done by setting his clothing right.

"Kill me," Syrenka said. Her voice was gravelly and dry. She was motionless now, with her arms behind her back.

Olaf realized with shame that she had been bound the whole time. He wanted to erase that, too.

He rushed to cut away the netting from her tail.

"Kill me," she said again.

He cut the rope on her arms, intending to push her back in the bay. He would accept her oath to stay away from shore. She would disappear into the depths forever. He could forget what he had done. He could repent in his heart, for the rest of his days. Eleanor would never know. God would forgive him.

As soon as the rope snapped, Syrenka struck, seizing him around the neck with her left arm.

"You should have killed me," she said into his ear.

She forced his chin up and slashed his throat with the fin on her right wrist.

She laid him at the bottom of the boat, with a pool of dark blood growing beneath him. She had to make her decision now, while his heart still quivered in his chest and his life ebbed away. She peered out over the black ocean, hoping that Ezra was alive.

She would take the chance. She might never have another. To give herself human form, she ripped open the fisherman's chest, broke his rib cage, and ate his warm, moist lungs.

Chapter 9

IT WAS ONLY HER SECOND SUNDAY of church in ten years, and Hester could not concentrate on the service. The smell of the wood and the wax from the candles, the hushed echo of the sanctuary, and the rich red of the runner flooded her with the awful memory of the silverfish. She wondered if Linnie had known that the book was infested. Now that Hester was older and more mature it didn't seem likely: why would Linnie have set a friend up like that? And yet Linnie hadn't wanted to take equal responsibility if Hester got caught, and she had disappeared rather than stand up for her. Hester thought of the tombs—dank and dark, a perfect breeding ground for those insects; but Linnie couldn't have known that. And then she thought about the graveyard, which she hadn't visited in years. She struggled in this way through a hazy mental fog, transported by disjointed visions of her time with Linnie for the better part of an hour.

In the three months that they were friends, Hester and Linnie only ever played together on Burial Hill. Hester had loved the old churchyard: it was on her way home from school, it was loaded with spots for hide-and-seek, and she liked imagining that the graves held the deepest, forgotten memories of her town in safekeeping.

The hill overlooked Plymouth Harbor on one side and was dotted with several large trees for shade, thousands of chipped and mossy headstones, and a few benches for resting. No one had been buried there for more than half a century, so she and Linnie usually had the hill to themselves, giving them the freedom to climb trees, run races around the graves, and watch the fishing boats and cruise ships crisscross their own wakes.

Hester was in the spring of first grade, carrying her lunch bag and her favorite baby doll, Annabelle, when she met Linnie for the first time. Annabelle had a plastic head, plastic legs, and a soft stuffed body. When she was new she'd had real-looking blond hair in a wavy bob, but during a particularly hot summer Hester had given her a trim to make her feel cooler. Annabelle's hair was now a dirty stubble, and you could see the plugs planted like rows in a garden. Hester had long ago lost the hooded bunting Annabelle came with, but she had replaced it with one of baby Sam's graying snapped undershirts.

Linnie was building a twig fort by one of the graves on the hill when Hester walked by. Hester hadn't noticed her, but Linnie called down, "*That's* a sorry-looking doll!"

Hester looked up and squeezed Annabelle tight to her chest. She saw a little girl in a plum-colored dress with a white sash.

"Shut up, you!" Hester said, knitting her eyebrows together.

"Oh!" Linnie said. "I didn't think you would hear that!"

"I have ears, don't I?"

"Well, of course you have, but no one ever pays attention to what I say!" Linnie smiled—her front teeth were still growing in— and called out, "Do you want to see my fort?"

"Sure," Hester said, tossing her lunch bag and Annabelle on top of the retaining wall and shinnying up after them. The instant Annabelle fell to the ground, Linnie snatched her up.

"Hey! Give her back," Hester said, wiping the dirt from her hands onto the back of her pants.

"I just want to see her," Linnie said. She hugged Annabelle, as if trying her on. She closed her eyes and swung her torso gently from side to side.

Linnie opened her eyes and saw Hester staring. She looked down at Annabelle and finally held the doll out.

"Here," she said.

"Thanks," Hester said. "Her name's Annabelle."

"She's not properly dressed."

"What?"

"My doll Poppet has a violet dress with real lace, and a petticoat. And she has beautiful long hair and black satin ribbons."

"I don't care! Annabelle is comfy like this, and she loves me." Linnie looked wounded.

Hester said, "Where's your doll, anyway?"

Tears pooled in Linnie's lower lids. "I lost her. I brought her here with me, and I've searched everywhere."

"Oh, gosh. I'm sorry." Hester watched as the tears reached critical mass and spilled onto Linnie's pillowy cheeks. "I can help you look for her . . ."

Linnie shook her head, as if it were hopeless. Her blond ringlets thumped lightly on her cheeks.

"Is that your fort?" Hester asked, trying to distract her.

Linnie sniffed and nodded. "Do you want to help me build it?"

"I can only stay for a few minutes. My name's Hester."

"Pleased to make your acquaintance," Linnie said, like a grownup. "My name is Linnie."

"Cool, I never knew anyone named Linnie before."

"It's the diminutive form of my Christian name, which I detest."

Hester guessed that diminutive meant "short for." She already knew that detest meant "hate." She looked sideways at Linnie as they wandered together, collecting twigs and small branches.

Hester knelt to poke some of the stronger branches in the dirt, shoring up the fort's walls, as Linnie wove the thinner, flexible twigs together to form a flat roof.

"Whoa, you're good at that," Hester said.

"I make a lot of forts."

"I'll snap off the tops of the twigs to make the walls straight for your roof." Hester began whistling as she worked.

After a while Linnie said, "I can't whistle because my teeth are late growing in." She laid the roof on top of the walls of the fort. "But I have a scar. Do you want to see it?"

"I guess so," Hester said, trying to think if she had any scars of her own she could show off.

Linnie turned around, parting the golden curls on the back of her head. And there was the biggest scar Hester had ever seen: a thick white rope of skin about four inches long.

"Wow, does that hurt?"

"No, silly. It's all better."

"I mean, did it hurt when you got it?"

"I don't remember. It was a long time ago. I just like having something to feel on the back of my head."

"Cool," Hester agreed.

* * *

Sam nudged her. It was time for Communion. Hester slid out and got in line with her family behind her. As she shuffled in a slow march toward the pastor, she was vaguely aware of stirrings among the parishioners. The man ahead of her accepted the host and turned right, to file back to the pews. Just as Pastor Marks laid the bread in Hester's hand, she heard a cry and saw the man spit his partially chewed wad into a handkerchief. He looked over his shoulder at Hester and the pastor, shaking his head, with his eyes watering and his face contorted. Beyond him, several parishioners ran toward the vestibule in the direction of the water fountains. Pastor Marks lifted the chalice to his nose and winced.

Hester was curious, so she nibbled a tiny edge of the bread. Her stomach rose, and her throat spasmed in a stifled gag. The bread had the overwhelmingly musky, sour taste of rotten meat. Not *like* rotten meat, but actual, rancid flesh. She scraped the pasty crumbs off her tongue with her fingernails, but the taste lingered. The pastor held the chalice at arm's length and hurried behind the wooden screen to the chancel. A cloud of stench wafted after him and rolled in a wave to the pews. Hester could hear the congregation around her buzzing.

". . . a haunting!"

"It happens—remember the silverfish?"

"Ten years ago—"

"I saw it myself. Never been explained."

"But there's been worse, much worse," the most elderly parishioner, Sylvie Atwood, was saying. "Something terrible happened in the crypt . . ."

Hester felt Sam drape his bulky arm over her shoulder.

"I didn't get to taste it!" he complained in her ear.

"Believe me, you were lucky." She held up the bread on her hand for him to sniff. The smell made her feel sick again.

He recoiled and then instantly brightened. "Do you think everyone will get food poisoning? Maybe church will be canceled next week."

Hester's stepmom, Nancy, said in a low voice to Malcolm, "It's true that bread usually just stales—it doesn't go rancid."

Malcolm replied, "Maybe the host has a cooking oil in it, and the oil went bad. It's a manufacturing error. These people who are talking about ghosts are medieval idiots."

Nancy had another thought. "Then why wouldn't Pastor Marks have smelled it while he was consecrating it?"

Hester excused herself and ran to the ladies' room in the hall, where—along with a handful of other women—she rinsed the host out of her mouth and washed it off her hands. She splashed water on her face and headed back to the sanctuary, trying to recall if she had ever tasted rancid oil. The host just wasn't the same as any spoiled food she had ever eaten.

She ducked into the crowded vestibule to search for Sylvie Atwood. Mrs. Atwood knew more about the supposed hauntings in the church than anyone, and in her dotage was eager for receptive ears. She had started to lecture Hester many times before, back when the Goodwins were a churchgoing family. But Hester had been too little to care and had always slipped away to play with baby Sam in the nursery.

Hester found her with Nancy and Sam in the vestibule.

Mrs. Atwood had once been an important voice in the town, as the aggressive director of Pilgrim Hall Museum for nearly half a century. Now she had blue-white hair and crepe-paper skin, and she was hunched from bone loss. Time had robbed her of so much, Hester thought, leaving her with only this crooked body and the self-assurance to announce, "You'll be glad to know I told Pastor Marks to have an exorcism performed."

It was a good thing Malcolm wasn't there to hear that, or he'd blow his top, Hester thought. Nancy only smiled politely and nodded.

"Excuse me, Mrs. Atwood, isn't exorcism a Catholic rite?" Hester asked. "Would Pastor Marks know how to do that?"

Mrs. Atwood pointed a knobby finger at her and said, "They can borrow a priest from St. Peter's for all I care, because it needs doing. And it has needed doing for over a century, since that dreadful tragedy in the church."

"Yes," Hester said quickly, "what happened back then?"

"My grandmother told me all about it," Mrs. Atwood said, her eyes gleaming. "A few people from the town died, including a pastor."

Hester said, "The church burned down about a hundred years ago, didn't it? Did they die in the fire?"

"Oh, no. The big fire was later, in 1892. No, as I remember, these deaths were unexplained, and violent."

Sam's interest was finally piqued. "You mean they were *murdered*?"

"Or perhaps it was what we'd call a murder-suicide nowadays? My grandmother told me the story when I was a young girl. She no

64

doubt spared me the frightening aspects." She grinned, showing too-white dentures that were straight as piano keys. "Being a girl with an active imagination, I believe I supplied the details myself, and I convinced myself that a forbidden romance was involved."

A forbidden romance. A murder-suicide. In a church, of all places. Hester thought the story was just dramatic enough to have inspired over a century of haunting legends.

"Do you remember the names of the victims?" Hester asked. "I'd like to research it."

"It's fascinating, overlooked local history, isn't it?" Mrs. Atwood nodded. "But I'm afraid I never knew the names."

"What year did it occur, do you remember?"

"Oh, my feeble old brain," Mrs. Atwood said cheerfully. "I used to have such a knack for facts—names, dates, phone numbers. Now I'm lucky if I can remember my own grandchildren's names. But it was before the fire, dear. I'm sure of that."

Nancy offered Mrs. Atwood the crook of her arm and began walking her to the door.

"Isn't it awful?" Mrs. Atwood said. "I'm the last of my generation, and there's no one else to ask."

Chapter 10

1872

Ezra had long since kicked his shoes off, but he was losing the energy to tread water. He heard clappers strike a bell somewhere nearby, and he searched the horizon for the navigation buoy he knew caused the sound. He could just make out its black silhouette against the starlit sky, and he struggled to reach it. As he moved, the water circulated through his clothes, cooling his skin. When he reached the buoy, he realized that it was much larger than it appeared from the vantage of a boat. The iron base, studded with rivets, was rounded below the water. The circular platform, although large enough to hold a man fully stretched out, floated so high out of the water that he couldn't climb up it. He could only hook his hands onto the edge of the base, with his body dangling in the water.

Overcome with the urge to sleep, he let his chin dip toward his chest. His face dropped into the water, a few fingers slipped. If he took a breath, he thought hazily, it would be over. A hand came from somewhere below him and lifted his chin. Over the next few minutes, in this dreamlike state, he imagined he felt Syrenka's hands tentatively propping him up—his leg now, then his buttocks, his back, another leg. But it was many hands—too many hands—all of them cool and strong like Syrenka's. He was hallucinating, he knew. He would die if he didn't get his body out of the water.

He groped his way around the base of the buoy to a spot below one of the three upright supports that triangulated to form the cage of the bell. His muscles would hardly obey. His arms had been raised above his head for too long, and the blood had drained from his hands. He waited. The wind was light, but when the buoy tipped slightly in his direction he lunged with his right hand to grab the support, knowing he had only the energy to try once. His hand touched, slipped, and then tightened around the support, and as the buoy swayed slowly upright, he was lifted out of the water to his waist. He grabbed the support with his left hand now, too, and pushed the ball of his foot against the rounded base of the buoy underwater to try to climb aboard. Instantly he felt barnacles slit the bare skin of his sole. He heard himself scream. He hauled his body the rest of the way using just the strength of his arms, and collapsed on the base. He was far from shore—too far to swim—and his sodden clothes were ice cold in the breeze. He shook uncontrollably. The raw gashes that Syrenka's fins had cut on his hands were still bleeding, and his foot was now bleeding as well.

Meanwhile a lone fisherman in a dinghy lowered his nets south of the bay. Eventually he realized that he was drifting, despite being anchored. He was drifting *against* the current, into deeper water. He lifted his anchor and tried to row against the drift, but, burly as he was, he made no headway. He heard occasional thumps on the bottom of the dinghy that raised the hair on his scalp. He prayed out loud to the Virgin Mary for safety. His heartbeat quickened: it was possible that he could become lost at sea. He caught sight of a shadow of a vessel—a dark patch on the horizon. His dinghy was being carried toward it. Salvation! He turned and began to row again, this time working with the mysterious drift.

As he approached the boat, he saw to his dismay that it was no bigger than his own. Closer still, and it appeared to be empty. The force that was guiding him suddenly disappeared. He breathed deeply in relief. He rowed the rest of the way on his own power until he pulled up alongside the abandoned boat. There was nothing inside but a jacket, a book, and an extinguished lantern. He used a rope to attach the second boat to his own. He peered into the darkness of the water, wondering if there was a survivor.

"Hullooo," he called out. He listened for the sound of splashing, or a cry of distress.

Then he heard a bell in the distance—the bell of a buoy. The sea was calm, yet the bell rang urgently. He rowed in the direction of the sound and discovered a young man, no more than twenty, draped on the buoy, near death. How had the poor fellow rung the bell so vigorously before he fell unconscious? And how had he spied the dinghy at such a distance in the darkness?

The fisherman pushed his questions aside. He stood in his boat, moored it to the upright support of the buoy, and struggled to drag Ezra from the platform, easing his limp body onto the floor of the dinghy. He crossed Ezra's arms so that his hands were wedged under his armpits for warmth and reached into Ezra's boat for the jacket, tucking it around his torso. And then he examined him under the lamplight: the young man's lips were blue-purple, his breath was shallow, and his skin was cool to the touch. The fisherman took off his own coat and tucked it around Ezra's legs and bare feet. He reached in the pocket of the coat and took out a knitted cap, which he pulled over Ezra's head. He unfastened his dinghy from the buoy and rowed steadily toward land, towing the spare boat behind them.

Two hours later he reached the channel entrance to his marsh. He pulled both boats ashore, tucked the young man's book in his waistband, and carried him over his shoulder, up the bluff, to his cottage.

The fisherman's wife bathed Ezra in warm water, bandaged his wounds, and put him in dry clothes. With her husband's help, she settled him in a bed with several blankets and spooned hot tea into his mouth. There Ezra lay in a feverish state for days, before he was strong enough to return to his home.

Chapter 11

THE MURDER-SUICIDE prowled Hester's mind, teasing her in the quiet moments of the day. It was a history puzzle, and therefore irresistible. It had also likely set the stage for the haunting paranoia at the church, sucking in her own innocent silverfish incident with it. She spent the workweek puzzling over the paltry information Sylvie Atwood had given her whenever she had a private moment in the Howland cottage or garden. She had no doubt that details about the event existed somewhere, hidden, and it was only a matter of figuring out how to uncover them. The Internet had proved useless; this was an obscure piece of local history that had never made it into any sort of larger digital memory. She needed an old-fashioned lead—a single, solid lead.

On Saturday her cottage had emptied and a crowd had gathered outside William Bradford's house across the lane. It was a hot day, and the bolster under her skirt had soaked up so much sweat it weighed damp and heavy on her hips. With her back to the door, she put her foot on a chair and yanked up her stockings. She heard a low whistle behind her.

"What have we *here*?" a cocky teenage voice said.

A group of boys ducked under the short doorframe into the room. A particularly tall one stared through the open window with his mouth gaping, as if she were an animal in the zoo.

"Good day t' ye," Hester said. "I did not see ye at my door, or I should not have carried out such a graceless act. Would one of ye care to rest yourself?" She motioned to the chair near the door.

A boy with a Boston T-shirt who looked to be about her age pushed his way past the others. He pointed in the direction of the bed. "I'd like to rest myself there, with you." Machine-gun laughter burst from behind him.

She stared at him for a second, just short of a glare, and then she got out the napkins to set the table.

"She's the only Pilgrim I've seen today who looks cute without makeup," the dope in the window said.

Boston took a couple of steps toward her, "Yeah, how 'bout it, do you have a boyfriend?"

"I regret that I do not comprehend that word, sir."

"A dude. A steady. Some dick that every hour of the day you just want to f—"

"Ah, I am married, sir," she interrupted. "And God has blessed us with two children, Desire and little John, who are fetching water at the stream."

Boston rolled his eyes. "I mean, do you have a boyfriend in real life."

She was not allowed to address him with her contemporary voice. And she knew that he knew that. "My husband, John, is with the militia down past the redoubt, and returns presently. You'll know him easily because, unlike yourself, sir, he has an impressive rapier hanging from his waist." She glanced at his crotch meaningfully, but he was too dense to get the jibe.

The redhead behind him piped up, "Two parents and two kids in a one-room shack? Did you have to sleep in shifts?"

It was an honest question, at last. But it was not a use of the word "shift" that Elizabeth Howland would have understood, and with all those eyes running amok over her breasts and hips and waist, Hester's patience had dissolved.

"Just so," she said, mocking him. "Everyone wears a shift as sleeping clothes—men, women, and children. You are no doubt a scholar."

She put six eggs in a basket. Escape was the surest way to shake Pilgrim baiters.

"Will ye come with me to visit across the lane?" She walked purposefully past them and out the door.

"How now, Governor Bradford," she called over the heads of the tourists gathered in front of his cottage. "'Tis Elizabeth Howland, come with spare eggs for Alice." She waved sweetly at Boston and the redhead as the crowd of tourists parted and then closed their ranks behind her.

Bradford was seated at his desk, pontificating about a newspaper—a reproduction that the curators had printed on a Gutenberg-style press using aged cotton paper and authentic ink. The ornate typeset manuscript was always a hit because it looked so real.

"What have you, sir, that causes such a state in your visitors?"

"Ah, Elizabeth, welcome. I was showing my guests the pamphlet that Isaack de Rasieres sent to the colony as a gift from New Amsterdam these last days. The purpose is to descry the news of the week from France and the Low Countries." He laughed. "Though after such a long journey 'tis, I find, no longer news that concerns anyone."

"Good sir, I cannot agree," Hester countered. "I hear so little word from our old home, I should be enthralled to read even the chronicles of those long dead!"

Suddenly Hester realized how she might research the murders. "Oh!" she blurted, straightening her back.

The local newspaper! Every single back issue of the *Old Colony Memorial* since 1822 was archived at the Plymouth Public Library—Hester had used the records a handful of times for school projects. She was certain that a murder-suicide in such a small town would have been splashed all over the paper for months.

Bradford folded the paper and mused, "How curious that the ink is impressed on both sides of the folio."

"I beg your leave, sir," Hester blurted. "I have only just remembered the fire under my pottage. Pray tell Alice that I have called for her."

Bradford's mouth hung open as she deposited the basket on the desk in front of him and hurried out the door. If she washed the dishes and swept her cottage before the all clear, she calculated, she could make it to the library an hour before it closed.

Chapter 12
1872

SYRENKA TOOK OLAF'S SHIRT, trousers, socks, and shoes for herself, carefully washing the blood off the clothes and wringing them nearly dry before she put them on. She rowed Olaf's boat past midnight, searching for Ezra. Eventually, fearing the arrival of dawn and the earliest fishermen, she pulled in to a remote spot on the shore and staggered across the sand on her new legs, dragging the boat up and past the tide stain.

She wandered for days, hiding off small dirt roads, bewildered by the land beneath her feet, and by insect bites, hunger, cold, and her own unbearable weight. She stole food from open kitchen doors and a blanket from a barn. She ruminated for the first time in her long life over how she might kill herself.

Deep in a pretty wood by a pond she stumbled upon a cedar-shingled cottage, painted forest green and nearly camouflaged by tall pines, whose branches brushed as high as the chimney and left tufts of brown needles bunched in the eaves trough. There she was taken in by two spinster sisters, the Misses Floy, and nursed until she regained her strength. The sisters earned their living selling jams made from beach plums, blueberries, and wild strawberries, by making tea from rosehips, and by keeping sheep in a nearby meadow for milk and wool. Syrenka felt sheltered and safe in the company of only women. They called her Sarah, because Syrenka was not a biblical name. The anonymity suited her.

The older sister, Lydia, asked no questions. It was obvious to her that young Sarah was an immigrant with an abusive husband. Why else would she arrive wearing only his clothes? What other explanation was there for her lack of familiarity with the customs and manners of this country? Lydia imagined, in some detail, that Sarah had been held prisoner in her husband's locked bedroom, and that she had escaped while he slept.

Every urge in Syrenka's body told her to seek out Ezra—to see if he had lived or died that night in the bay. But she resisted: she was not ready yet. These women could teach her much. If she gained the skills of a human she might blend in well enough with the townspeople to avoid their prying questions. Time spent now would spare heartache later.

The Misses Floy were delighted when Sarah was well enough to join their daily routines. She was physically strong and exceptionally bright. Listening to them speak, she became fluent in the local dialect, so that there was nothing but her odd paleness and almost imperceptibly oval pupils to set her apart from them. More often than not, when the sisters brought their goods to sell in the town, Sarah stayed behind with domestic chores and the peacefulness of the pond.

It was two months later, when Sarah began to excuse herself from the sisters' constitutional sunrise swims, that Lydia followed her to her bedroom and heard the retching sound through the door. She waited quietly until Sarah emerged, her face shiny and freshly washed.

"How long have you been ill upon rising in the morning?" Lydia asked gently.

"I am not ill. I will feel well again after I eat."

"Forgive me, you are correct. It is not an illness to be with child. It is a blessing. It is a miracle."

Sarah's eyes opened wide. "With ch——?" She clamped her hand over her mouth. "No! Please. It can't be. It's rather the newness of this place. I'm still growing accustomed to the food and to the air—that is, the *fresh air*—which are so different from . . ."

"From where, my dear? Perhaps this is a sign from God that it is time to write to your husband and see if your differences can be worked out." She smiled and looked pointedly in the direction of Sarah's belly. "For the sake of the child."

Sarah conceded to herself with growing revulsion that there was a sensation of fullness low in her abdomen that she had ignored. Her breasts were tender. She fatigued easily of late.

So it was done, through violence rather than love: she was mortal.

Her mouth became a tight line. She stood up straight and put her shoulders back. "He is dead."

"Who . . . ?"

"The child's father is dead."

Lydia's mouth opened. "I'm so sorry."

"I am not."

Lydia was silent, with her mouth still open. Sarah sensed that more was needed. A sign of compassion, or hope; a lie.

"He was . . . from a wealthy family. His mother has longed for a grandchild. It will be beloved and cared for." She clasped Lydia's wrinkled hands. "Please, I could not bear to live with her now while she grieves for him; may I stay here until my confinement? I beg you."

"But this woman should know . . ."

"I'll send word. I shall write a letter today. She'll take comfort in knowing I am safe in your hands."

Lydia smiled. "You may stay until the baby is born. We will help you with the delivery and recovery, and take you to your mother-in-law when you and the baby are strong."

"You are all kindness," Sarah said. "It was fortun— It was a blessing that you found me."

Lydia took her to the secretary in the front hall and gave her a sheet of paper, an envelope, a wax seal, and pen and ink.

"I have no postage, but I will make a trip into town later today and take your letter with me."

Sarah said, "I should like to come with you, if it is not an inconvenience."

Sarah prepared the envelope as if it contained a letter. In town, she excused herself on the pretext of mailing it, threw the blank letter in a dustbin outside of a pub, and went inside. It was early in the day, so only a few drunkards lingered there. She inquired of them about a man named Ezra Doyle.

Mr. Doyle? Yes, he was alive, although he'd had a nasty brush with drowning down the coast and had been melancholic ever since. No, he had not married. How could he form an attachment? He spent all his days at the bay, brooding on the rocky outcropping or rowing his boat aimlessly offshore.

Sarah had scarcely allowed herself to hope that he was alive, let alone that he was still searching for her. She was unable to speak. A sober man might have seen that her lower lip trembled.

"And whom might we say is the ravishing lady who inquired after him?" the bar owner called across the counter, his eyebrows raised and his mouth half smiling.

She pinned him with her eyes and found her voice again. "An old friend. A very old friend. My name is Sarah."

She knew that her paleness would distinguish her in their memories. Eventually they would tell Ezra of her visit, and perhaps he might guess it was her, in human form. If he still wanted her, he might not give up his search. He might sustain his hope for the seven months it would take her to be free.

A part of her—the part that had learned compassion from him and from Lydia—was grieved to deceive him by hiding her pregnancy. But she could not stop herself from wanting him, and she could not bear to let him see her carry another man's child. If he still loved her seven months from now, she would find him. If he would have her, she would devote herself to him for the remainder of her mortal days.

Chapter 13

HESTER CHANGED into her street clothes and hurried to Nancy's car. The public library was just a five-minute drive from work.

As architecture went, the library looked like a high school in the suburbs: it was a large contemporary building with red brick walls and a domed skylight above an open staircase to the second and third floors. She was disappointed to discover that the strategy of looking up the murders in the *Old Colony Memorial* newspaper was fruitless. The archives were stored on microform—an antiquated set of film reels that were not indexed. She should have remembered this from her school assignments: the only way to look anything up on microform, other than educated guessing or browsing, was to know the exact date of the event you were searching for. She tried reading headlines starting from 1892, the date of the church fire, and working backward in time, but quickly gave up. There were too many films, the librarian had to retrieve each one for her, and the reader was a finicky machine, making winding and unwinding the film a slow process.

On the way home she passed Burial Hill and her mind returned to Linnie. She had never even asked Linnie what her last name was. If she had, she could search for her online. She might contact her, and find out what college she was going to, and what she looked like now that she was eighteen. They could reminisce about their creepy childhood playing in a graveyard, and Hester would apologize for dropping Linnie's friendship after the Bible incident.

On an impulse, Hester pulled into a space in front of the hill. She got out of the car and climbed the long steps, past headstones that were still familiar to her so many years later. It was a lovely place, she realized. She should come here more often, just to read or to think in a peaceful setting. She strolled for a while, and then she searched out a bench that she remembered under an ancient tree. The wood was parched and splintered, but she sat down carefully and leaned back. The evening breeze off the bay was damp and salty and wonderful.

The three headstones in front of her were made of blue slate. The first had one of her favorite decorations: a cherub's face with wings, chiseled in a charming folk-art style. She glanced at the inscription:

ISAAC ONTSTAAN

Dec. 6th 1866–Jan. 19th 1870

Stop traveller and shed a tear

Uppon the sod of a child dear

Hester sat up straight. Ontstaan was the last name of her great-great-great-grandmother. Surely she had read this headstone many times before, while playing on this very bench. She tried to remember if she had known Marijn Ontstaan's name when she was seven. If she had, it had not made an impression.

She quickly read the second headstone, which had a skull above crossed bones carved at the top:

Here lies Buried the Body of
MR OLAF ONTSTAAN
deceased by the hand of a Fiend Unknowen
and departed this Life July 8th 1872
O ye whose cheek the tear of pity stains
Draw near with pious reverence and attend
Here lie the loving Husbands dear remains
The tender Father and the courteous Friend
The dauntless heart yet touched by human woe
A Friend to man to vice alone a Foe

And next to that:

ELEANOR HANNAH ONTSTAAN,
the wife of MR OLAF ONTSTAAN
and daughter of MR THOMAS and MRS RUTH SMYTH
whose Life was cruelly taken from her
July 11th 1873 in the 48th Year of her Age
It belongs to God's Judgment to punish the Wicked

Hester searched her bag for a pen. There was no paper. She wrote this on her hand: Olaf 7/8/72, Eleanor Hannah 7/11/73. These were undoubtedly her *relatives*, and they had both been murdered, about a year apart. She laughed with excitement. Their deaths were sure to be in the newspaper archives, and she had exact dates. She looked at her watch. The library was still open, but only just. She ran to the car.

Her discovery was more intriguing than she could possibly have imagined. The *Old Colony* reported that Olaf's body had been recovered in his underclothes, lying in his boat—which had been carefully pulled ashore—with his throat slashed and his lungs savagely cut out. The murder had never been solved. It was like the plot of a thriller movie.

Hester quickly scanned through the headlines in the days after Eleanor's death date. Eleanor had drowned in the crypt of the First Church of Pilgrims, as part of a suspected triple murder. A drowning? In the crypt? It didn't make any sense, and it wasn't explained further. She read on: the other victims were a minister of the church, whose name would not be printed until his family had been located, and Eleanor's niece, Adeline Angeln. *Angeln*. It was Peter's last name. And it was undoubtedly the murder-suicide that Sylvie Atwood had told her about—the tragedy that had spawned all the haunting rumors at the church.

She searched for Eleanor's obituary and found it in the paper a week later. A rush something like a caffeine overload made her heart patter and her hands tremble as her eyes caught on the name Marijn.

Eleanor Ontstaan was the devoted adoptive mother of a foundling infant, surname unknown but given name Marijn, who has been sent to live with Eleanor's grieving brother-in-law and loving sister, Joseph and Eliza Angeln, in Carver.

Chapter 14

1873

WHEN THE TIME CAME for Sarah's confinement, she left a nosegay of wildflowers tied with twine for the Misses Floy on the kitchen table. She slipped out the back screen door and walked six miles to the town, stopping to rest through the contractions. She hid until nightfall, biting a stick to keep herself from crying out with pain, and when no one was near, she walked into the cold, soothing waters of the bay. She gave birth to a baby girl submerged in the water—where only she heard the first lusty cry. The infant had human legs but was covered in delicate scales. Sarah brought her to the surface, washed her, and carefully swaddled her in seaweed. She kissed her forehead, her cheek, her neck.

There was a boat in the distance—a lobster fisherman checking his traps—and Sarah acted swiftly now. She fastened the bundle underwater by wedging the trailing ends of the seaweed under a rock, giving her daughter to her companions, to be nurtured as one of their own. She slapped the water with her hands to draw their attention from the depths, until she feared the attention of the fisherman instead. Finally, with a lump in her throat that she could not identify, she retreated to land to begin her new life.

The wind picked up suddenly. Within minutes, a storm churned the bay. The lobster fisherman struggled to take his boat in through waves that battered the shore. He saw something in the foaming, churning surf—something that tumbled forward and then was clawed back by the retreating undertow, again and again—something pale. It was crying.

The baby was bruised and entangled in a mass of seaweed, but in the mind of the fisherman, who did not know her lineage, it was a miracle that she had not drowned. Many of the scales had been ripped off her body, showing raw pink patches of skin that he assumed were abrasions. A bachelor, he did the only thing he could think of: he wrapped her in his coat and took her to the widow of his longtime friend Olaf Ontstaan. He knew that Olaf and Eleanor had wanted a child after the death of their son. Who better than Eleanor to care for the infant until the parents came forward to claim it? *If* the parents came forward, he thought to himself. *If* they had not died in a boating accident.

Over the next couple of weeks, the remaining scales dried and flaked off the baby's skin. Eleanor was certain it was because she had applied burdock root oil mixed with chamomile—a remedy from the Old Country for stubborn cases of cradle cap. Soon, she forgot about the scales entirely. The baby was perfect in every possible way: strong, engaged, healthy, and pretty.

Meanwhile, no parents claimed her as their own, and no reports surfaced of a boating accident. Eleanor gave her the Dutch name Marijn, because it meant "of the sea." Recognizing that Marijn was the daughter she would never otherwise have, Eleanor unlocked her hope chest to retrieve a gift she had planned thirty years ago, as a new bride, to give to her own baby girl some-day.

She opened the clasp and carefully put the necklace around Marijn's neck, admiring the tiny gold heart against her fair skin. With tears in her eyes, she scooped the baby up in her arms and kissed her.

Chapter 15

JUST AS HESTER'S DAD OPENED the heavy door of the church on Sunday, Pastor Marks flew past him, his robe flapping, headed toward the church office.

"I'll be right back, Malcolm," the pastor barked over his shoulder. "I'm calling the elders for their advice."

"Uh . . ." Malcolm said.

"Please keep track of your youngsters," Pastor Marks called out to Nancy as an afterthought. "It's really not suitable for them to see."

Nancy and Malcolm stared at each other as Malcolm continued to hold the door.

"Who uses the word 'youngster' anymore?" Sam said, ducking under his dad's arm.

Hester followed him. "Only the interpreters at Plimoth Plantation."

The parishioners who had arrived earlier were in the vestibule— their faces close together, speaking in gossipy whispers with wide eyes. The doors to the sanctuary were shut, when they would normally have been propped wide open.

Hester skirted around the crowd and cracked open the door, slipping inside. Other than an assistant pastor and the director of education huddled in a private discussion, the room was empty.

The sanctuary looked completely normal to Hester. The carved wooden pews, the chandeliers nested between hammer beams, the organ, all seemed exactly the same as ever. There were two large bouquets of fresh white roses on either side of the altar, and white bows tied at the aisle-end of each pew—sure signs that there had been a wedding there the day before. She was about to slip back out, unnoticed, when she glanced up at the stained-glass windows.

The windows were a particular source of pride for the parish. They were crafted by the actual Tiffany Glass Studios in 1898, and depicted various important Pilgrim events: the arrival of the Mayflower at the rock, the signing of the Compact, and Governor Carver exchanging gifts with Massasoit before they signed their peace treaty.

Hester's mouth dropped open. All of the figures had massive clouds of pubic hair where their genitals would be. The hair appeared to be real—not painted on, sprayed on, or scribbled in with a streak pen. She couldn't help but snicker, which she knew wasn't quite right in a church.

The assistant pastor snapped his head in her direction.

"Is vandalism funny to you?" he asked humorlessly.

"I'm sorry," Hester said. "Is it . . . is that real hair?"

"Hester Goodwin," the director of education said, recognizing her, incredibly, from Sunday school a decade before, "go back to the vestibule, please. Pastor Marks is calling the elders, and we'd like to handle this with as little hoopla as possible." She smiled the way only Sunday school teachers can—like Sweet 'N Low, when you were expecting honey. "We'd appreciate it if you didn't gossip about this to the other children."

Hester was not a little girl anymore. "To be honest, Ms. Strickland, I'm completely incapable of not mentioning this to my brother, Sam, but I do promise that I'll ask him to be tactful with the information."

She left through the side door of the sanctuary, intending to return to the vestibule as she had been told. But there, to her left, was the door to the crypt—old and solid, with a plastic plaque nailed to it that said "Staff Only." And now she knew that the crypt was where Eleanor Ontstaan had mysteriously drowned. She tugged the door open and peered in. There was an antique light switch at the top of the stairs—the push-button kind where the second button pops out as the first is pushed in. Hester pushed, and nothing happened. Two more tries, and the lights flickered on, first uncertainly and then confidently. A string of bare, dusty bulbs snaked down the ceiling of the stone stairs, connected by ancient, fabric-covered electrical cord. They generated plenty of light: a stark, unsentimental light.

Nothing could have stopped her from going down.

As she entered the cool stairway she shivered. Rubbing her arms to calm herself, she turned over in her head the still-surprising news that Marijn Ontstaan, her great-great-great-grandmother, had a connection to the crypt murders. It was a brief connection, but it was there: she had been adopted as an infant by the woman who was murdered—whose death had likely triggered nearly one hundred forty years of haunting myths at the church. After that, little Marijn was cared for by a second family—one that was undoubtedly distantly related to Peter. It created a tie between her family and Peter's—not a blood relationship, but a sort of historical one. And it made her wonder who that little orphan, Marijn, really was. Not an Ontstaan, not an Angeln, but still Hester's direct ancestor.

The crypt had no windows. It smelled musty and earthen. The whitewashed walls were made of large stones of odd shapes, expertly fitted together like puzzle pieces. She imagined them being laid nearly three hundred years ago by husky masons—strenuous work by men who were in the prime of their lives at the time, each loved by a woman, perhaps starting their young families, and who were now most likely dry bones in unmarked graves, lost to time, their entire lives summed up in this one church foundation.

The joists of the floor above were supported by square brick posts, also whitewashed. The floor was made of hard-packed coastal earth. It would be nearly impossible for even the most torrential rain to flood a space like this with enough water to drown someone: the water would be absorbed by the ground.

There were tombs built along one wall, with blackened family name plaques on each. And there were a few discarded pieces of ancient furniture, a couple of organ pipes, and broken wooden file cabinets. But what caught Hester's attention were two stone sarcophagi, spaced between the brick posts. They were simple things, large limestone coffins with very little decoration: a carved angel's head on one, a bas-relief of drapery around the perimeter of the other. She walked up to the first one and bent to see the inscription:

REV. JOHN ROBINSON, M.A.

"Then I proclaimed a fast there,
at the river of Ahava,
that we might afflict ourselves before our God,
to seek of Him a right way for us,
and for our little ones,
and for all our substance." Ezra 8:21

She looked at the second sarcophagus: Elder William Brewster. It was fascinating to her—the two sarcophagi were like trick questions of history. From years of studying for her various Pilgrim roles, she knew that neither could ever have held the body that was intended for it.

She walked around the coffins, examining them. They must have weighed a couple of tons apiece. They both had heavy lids, but they were plenty large enough to hold a person, and they seemed to be watertight. It wasn't completely impossible that Eleanor could have been drowned in one if it were filled with water. Perhaps the lids had been off in 1873? She was running her hand over the inscription when she heard shuffling footsteps. She stood up straight and turned around, her cheeks heating up.

An elderly minister came down the hall from the direction of the stairs. He had a weathered face and wild white hair, and his arms were crossed, as if he were holding his fragile body together.

"Thar's a youth en the crrrypt!" he said joyfully, with a thick Scottish accent.

Damn, she was probably going to get ratted out to Ms. Strickland.

"I'm sorry, I didn't disturb anything, I promise. I was just exploring," she said.

His face dropped. He stopped where he was and put both hands to his chest. He stared at her. His eyes seemed to be building tears.

Hester said, "Are you all right? Do you need to sit down?" She retrieved a wooden chair from the corner, brushing cobwebs off the ladder back as she rushed over to him.

"Sit here for a minute and rest," she said. "I'll go up and get help."

"Na," he said. He gripped her arm with both hands and looked into her eyes as she eased him into the chair. "Na, lassie, truly, I feel well. En fact, I feel be'ter than well." He said the word "better" with the t's missing: beh-er.

"Are you one of the elders Pastor Marks called to investigate the"—the words "pubic hair" popped to mind, but struck her as improper—"the stained glass?"

He laughed, with a pleasing high crack in his voice. "The pubes waere a wee bit carlish, eh? Losh, I'm fond of a good joke, tho'." He shook his head and said, "But na, I wannae summoned here." He motioned vaguely to the tombs along the wall. "I'm re-saerchin' some o' the family names for the chaerch records."

"Well, then, maybe you know about these two sarcophagi."

He became serious. "I wonder why those in par-ticular would interest you?"

"No reason," she said defensively. "I mean, I'm curious, that's all. They were built for two bodies that couldn't possibly be using them. Reverend Robinson died in Leiden before he could join the Pilgrims in America, and William Brewster is thought to be buried somewhere on Burial Hill."

His lips curled into the impish smile again. "And she's as sharp as a needle. Such luck! These coffins waere carved en 1624 as a tribute to the leaders of the faerst congregation. I often wonder how Elder Brewster responded to the gesture, seein' as he was a vigorous man o' fifty-eigh' a' the time. Which is to say you're correct: they're empty. Empty as a bo'tle of scotch on my baerthday!" He burst out laughing again. Hester found both his laugh and his missing t's delightful. Her wariness evaporated as a bubble of laughter escaped her, too.

"I didn't think pastors drank," she said. "Or at least that they admitted it."

"Ah, bu' I'm retired, you see. And I'm also Sco'tish, so et's my baerth righ'." He stood up, with some signs of stiffness, and extended a bony, frail hand. "Michael Morangie McKee."

She shook his hand. It was cool and dry, with thin skin. "Hester. Hester Goodwin."

"Hester," he said, squeezing her hand. "Et's *awfully* good to speak with you, I cannae tell you."

"I have to say, you have the most charming accent."

"Losh, and she's kind t' boot! I grew up en the town of Tain, a' the edge of the Morangie Forest. Tha's the origin of my middle name. You may have heard tell tha' Morangie makes the bes' scotch en the world; well, the McKees made the bes' scotch en Morangie." He looked into the middle distance, and his eyes became glassy with tears. "Och, my darlen mother loved tha' forest."

"I'm sorry . . ."

"And she also loved haer scotch!" He guffawed with his eyebrows raised so high his forehead was a mass of lines.

Hester laughed, too. She was beginning to like this dotty old preacher with the rubbery face and a penchant for drinking.

"I wish you could taste the scotch from Tain," he said.

She shook her head. "I don't drink."

"I had a beau'iful li'tle flask once—hand-hammered selver, et was. A geft from my mum when I took orders." He patted his waistcoat pocket. "Used to keep et right here." He laughed. "Et fet enside there like a glove! Tha' flask was full o' McKee family scotch, the las' time I had et."

"Where is it now?"

"Och, I lost et—en the ocean, of all places. Years ago. But I'd dearly love to have et back."

There was a slight pause, and Hester wondered if her family might be looking for her.

Pastor McKee saw her eyes wander to the stone stairs.

"Tell me, Hester Goodwin, wha' were you saerchin' for en this forgo'ten place?"

Hester looked back at him. "To tell you the truth, I read that a woman drowned here, a long time ago. I was confused about how she could drown in a crypt, so I decided to look around."

"Who was she, this woman, do you know?" he pressed.

"Her name was Eleanor Ontstaan. I don't know much about her but . . ." Hester hesitated.

"But wha', lamb?"

"Well, there's a connection between her and my family. My great-great-great-grandmother was also named Ontstaan."

He nodded, listening intently, but didn't say anything.

"Pastor McKee, do you think we really have a ghost up there

in the sanctuary? I mean, does the church even believe in ghosts? Because—if there is a ghost—maybe it's related to this drowning?"

It sounded so ridiculous when she said it out loud.

"Tell me, lassie, have you paerchance heard any local tales o' sea folk?" he said out of the blue.

"Uh . . ." Hester wondered where he was going with this.

"I've haerd tell they live en the deepes' par' of our own bay."

"Why do you ask?"

He shrugged and shifted his feet, preparing to sit in the chair again. She held his arm while he lowered himself into it. "Jus' tha' tales o' ghosts and tales o' sea folk paersist en the world. Even an educated paerson mus' wonder ef thar's a reason for et."

Hester considered telling him about what Peter's dad had claimed to see in the bay, and her own childish underwater vision, but decided not to encourage him.

Pastor McKee was suddenly somber. "They're all women, so I've haerd. They've kelled feshermen and sailors. They're no' human. En fact, they're emmortal. They have no soul . . . unless they carry a human child."

Hester listened politely. Why was he telling her this? She could only assume the poor man had the beginnings of dementia.

She heard Sam's voice in the distance: "Hess? You down here?"

"It's my brother," she said. "I'd better go. Should I send someone for you?"

"Na, lassie. I'm as strong as I ever am. You may safely leave me to my work."

"It was nice to meet you," Hester said.

"I hope very much to speak with you again," he said, his voice cracking with emotion. It gave Hester a little pang in her chest to leave him like that.

"Me, too." She leaned down and patted his hand. "G'bye."

She ran to the stairs and took them two at a time.

When she emerged from the basement, Sam was in the hall outside of the sanctuary door, peeking through the crack. He turned when he heard her, and a smile peeled open on his face. He looked a bit like a gigantic, cuddly stuffed bear.

"There you are!" he said. "What were you doing?"

"Looking for clues to the original haunting."

"Well, you managed to miss all the action, Sherlock." He pulled the sanctuary door open as if it were the night before Christmas and gifts were hidden inside. "C'mere."

She stuck her head through the opening. The room was empty. The stained-glass windows were . . . perfectly hairless.

"The pubic hair spontaneously shriveled," Sam whispered over her shoulder. "It smelled like real burned hair, and it blew away before Pastor Marks had even finished phoning the elders. I saw it with my own eyes. It vanished without a trace!"

"Nancy is going to freak out that you saw it." Hester grinned, standing up straight.

Sam smiled back and carefully closed the door behind her. "It was so worth it."

95

Chapter 16

THE NEXT DAY after work Hester drove to Burial Hill. Her plan was to walk methodically through the graveyard, studying the inscriptions and looking for something else she might have missed in addition to the Ontstaan graves. As she strolled, the blanket of dreary clouds and misty pinpricks of rain reminded her of the end-of-year party at the picnic area. At the top of the hill she looked out over the bay. The water was a murky gray: choppy, unreflective, out of sorts. She couldn't see the beach, but she could imagine it. Her mind took her down the stone steps, as clearly as if she were there, and set her feet on the sand. The tide was low in this vision, the cave exposed and captivating. She stood there in a distracted sort of trance for a few minutes, and then willed herself back to the moment, shook her head clear, and focused on the task at hand.

It took some time to find the grave of Bartholomew Crotty and his two wives, facing away from the path, nestled near a chain-link fence. It was a single, bleached headstone with a simple cluster of carved flowers as an embellishment at the top. She squatted to push down the weeds that blocked the lowest lines.

BARTHOLOMEW CROTTY

1863–1955

Short is our longest

day of Life

MARIJN HIS WIFE

1873–1892

Called by God

from the side of her

infant Daughter Nellie

LUCY HIS WIFE

1870–1942

Farewell dear Wife untill that day more blest

When if deserving I with thee shall rest,

With thee shall rise with thee shall live above

In worlds of endless bliss and boundless love

Marijn Crotty *must* be her great-great-great-grandmother, Marijn Ontstaan. Really, how many women named Marijn could have been born in 1873 and died in her town?

Hester quickly did the arithmetic. Marijn was nineteen when she died. Her husband, Bartholomew, was only twenty-nine when Marijn died—too young to remain a widower—and so he married Lucy. Lucy lived to be seventy-two, dying when Bartholomew was seventy-nine. He lived until he was ninety-two.

She stood, staring at the inscription. A story bloomed in her mind's eye. When Marijn met Bartholomew, she was fresh and young, and likely innocent. He must have seemed to her to be mature, experienced, and worldly. At the time, a man would not propose marriage unless he had earned money to buy a home and was settled in his profession. Marijn had to have been beautiful or brilliant or bitingly witty—in some way completely irresistible—for him to scoop her up at such a tender age. Hester imagined a whirlwind romance, and the Angeln parents expressing nervousness at her leaving their home so young, but also relief at Bartholomew's good prospects. *What were the Angeln names again?* Hester asked herself. They were printed in the *Old Colony* article about the deaths in the church.

"Joseph and Eliza," she said out loud, remembering.

Joseph and Eliza. She imagined how they felt when their adopted daughter got married, nearly two decades after the horrific deaths of their birth daughter and Eliza's sister. What joy a wedding would have brought them. A wedding, followed by a pregnancy, and the happy birth of a baby girl. But then, because of the sheer caprice of nature, or the will of God, Marijn had suffered a delivery complication that the doctor failed to identify or cure.

Hester started for home, still unfolding the past in her mind. Marijn's daughter, Nellie, never knew her. Her husband undoubtedly grieved—swallowed up for a time in sorrow. He raised Nellie alone. He got on his feet again. Soon, he realized that Nellie needed a mother. Later, he admitted to himself that he was lonely. He longed for a lover—not the memory of a lover, but a person of flesh and blood to greet him with warm arms when he arrived home every night. He needed someone to laugh with, someone to pursue his dreams with, someone to wake up in bed with, and to grow old with.

Lucy's epitaph was extensive and adoring because Lucy was the one who had lived a long life with him. Lucy was the one Nellie grew up loving as her mother, and running to when she skinned her knee or had her feelings crushed. Lucy was the person at Bartholomew's side for business functions, at church, at dinners and dances. Lucy was the woman who grew old and respected, and was mourned by friends and family and townsfolk when she died. Marijn's epitaph, by contrast, was perfunctory and already distant. She was almost no one: a blip in Eleanor's life, a mystery to her daughter, Nellie, and a fleeting blaze of fire early in Bartholomew's plodding ninety-two years.

Hester reached the stairs leading down to School Street, with the old church looming at her side. She held on tightly to the iron railing, teetering at the top. She felt mentally buffeted, as if the secrets of that headstone, locked up and neglected for so long, were finally liberated and hurling themselves at her. Marijn had been practically her age when she had died. So young, with her entire life ahead of her. Everything she might have done or become was lost to the world. Because of Marijn's death, Bartholomew's passion never had a chance to evolve into a deeply comforting love—like the bond Hester saw between Malcolm and Nancy after their fifteen years together. Nellie had never been held by Marijn as a little girl, had never grown irritated by her as a teen, had never returned to her for guidance as a young woman.

Hester's own biological mother, Susan, was the same mystery to her: she was merely stories from other people's memories. She was the same handful of photographs that never moved or laughed. She was wistful looks in other people's eyes.

Hester sat down on the top step. Susan had died knowing this—knowing that she would be only a phantom limb in Hester's life; knowing that Hester would run to another woman's arms when she stumbled. In the most recent generation of her family's mysterious series of deaths, Nancy had played the role of Lucy. Nancy had been by Malcolm's side as he worked his way up from a postdoctoral researcher at Woods Hole, to staff scientist, to the head of the Ocean Life Institute. Nancy had taken Hester to ballet class, and then soccer practice, and then fencing lessons, until finally Hester had discovered her real hobby—and her passion for history—as an interpreter at Plimoth Plantation, where Nancy drove her every weekend during the school year and every day of the summer until she got her driver's license. Nancy had comforted her and buoyed her when she got her period at age ten, too young to understand, while *Susan*—lovely, pitiful Susan—was ashes, scattered from a Captain Dave boat in a private ceremony, indistinguishable from the sand and the algae at the bottom of the ocean.

Hester began to cry. She cried for Nellie, because she never knew Marijn. She cried for Marijn, because she never knew Nellie. She cried for Malcolm and her grandfather for losing Susan, for Susan for losing her entire future, and for Nancy, who filled another woman's shoes with such grace. And finally she cried for herself— for all that she had missed with her mother, and for all that she would miss in her own future.

She could no longer deny that she wanted a deep love of her own, with marriage someday, and children, and a lifetime together—like what Malcolm and Nancy had right now, and what Bartholomew and Lucy had over a hundred years ago. But in her world, Hester could never play the role of a Nancy or a Lucy. She was doomed to be Susan. She was Marijn.

Chapter 17
1873

Ezra propped himself on his elbow in bed, facing his wife. The early-morning light filtered through the billowing curtains, and the sheets and duvet nested white and clean against her pale skin. She sighed deeply.

"Syrenka," he whispered.

"You never told me how magnificent sleep is," she murmured. Her breathing became regular and slow again.

"Syrenka."

Her lips formed a tiny smile, but her eyes were still closed. "Sarah," she corrected sleepily.

He moved a strand of near-white hair off her bare shoulder and kissed her cool skin.

"Forgive me," he said, grinning, "for calling my lover's name while in my wife's bed."

She laughed quietly and opened her eyes. After knowing her more than a year, he was still elated by their shade of green, and by their liveliness. He leaned in and kissed her neck.

He murmured, "It *is* rather a convenience that my lover and my wife are one and the same woman."

She ran her fingers through his hair. ". . . a woman named *Sarah*. It's not safe to reveal anything from my past."

"How can you bear to lose such a beautiful name, in exchange for something so ordinary?" He kissed the palm of her hand.

"It means nothing to me. Noo'kas renames us whenever she pleases, as frivolously as a man might change his necktie."

He kissed her lips. Her breath was cool and lightly sweet—not unlike a newly cut cucumber.

"Where did you learn the word 'frivolous,' you brilliant creature?"

"From the books you've given me," she said. "Have I thanked you for them?"

"Not today," he said, kissing her again.

"Today has only just begun," she said. Then she lowered her voice. "Would you like to know what I find most useful about having legs?"

"More than anyth—"

Before he had finished his sentence, she pushed him onto his back and climbed on top of him. She was still strong. She pinned him with her body and wrapped her legs around him. With her hands holding his arms to his sides and her hair streaming onto his face, she kissed his eyelids to make him shut his eyes, then the hollow of his cheek, and behind his ear.

"Your legs are . . . useful," Ezra conceded with a silly smile on his face. She kissed the space between his collarbones. She released his arms and he wrapped them tightly around her, pulling her close, free to participate.

On Sundays the housekeeper had the day off, and Sarah enjoyed cooking breakfast. She was happiest this way—completely at home, in Ezra's home—in a featherweight negligee, with loosely braided hair and bare feet.

She glanced over her shoulder. Ezra was watching her, leaning in the doorway with his journal under his arm. He smiled, and for the thousandth time she admired to herself the creases next to his eyes and the single tooth that was slightly awry.

He said, "I've been thinking about what we discussed this morning in bed."

"Did we speak?"

"Yes, well . . ." He blushed. "The few words between us stuck with me. When we talked about your name, you said it wasn't safe to reveal anything from your past."

She put eggs and toast on a plate for him.

He sat down and tossed the journal on the table. "By the same token, I think I should destroy this."

She scooped the book up. "But this holds months of work."

She leafed through it as he ate and came upon a page full of sketches of her tail. "The drawings are perfect in their detail, and yet rendered with such beauty. You have so many talents." She put it down on the table, open. "We could keep it for ourselves, at the very least."

"If anyone happened to come across it, it would put you in danger."

"No one will connect me with the creatures in that book. Only a few drunken sailors even believe they exist. Humans see only what feels familiar to them. I'm Sarah now."

He had taken a large bite of toast, so rather than speak he shook his head and dragged the book toward him. He turned to the next page, where there was a portrait of her face. He handed the journal back to her. In the image her eyes were larger, her teeth were sharp, and her pupils were horizontal slits, but the resemblance was unmistakable.

"I see. Perhaps we could tear this page out," she suggested.

"When I say it's a matter of safety, I believe I am selfishly thinking only of you. But there is also cause to be concerned for the others of your kind, including your sister. I am confident that people would try to profit from them in some awful way that we cannot conceive. If you will not think of yourself, think of them."

She closed the journal and held it to her chest. "I understand."

He stood and kissed her cheek. "Put your astoundingly clever mind to work on how we might keep it without risk. I've tried, and I can't see another way. If you agree it's necessary to destroy it, we shall burn it in tonight's fire.

"I must be off to church, to show my face." And then with a twinkle of amusement he added, "Although I'd gladly drown myself again if it meant I might stay here with you."

She straightened his collar and pulled him close to her. "Don't even give life to such words. You are sometimes quite maddening, do you know that?"

"Ah, but you love it," he whispered into her lips before he left.

The hour and a half of Sunday services was the only time Ezra and Sarah spent apart. He did it solely to preempt any intrusion into their home life. She was a newcomer—a foreigner, according to local gossip—and the spiritual standards were lower for her, but Ezra's family had a long pedigree in town, with certain expectations.

Sarah used her time alone in the same way every week. Carrying a bag containing a towel and a petticoat, she walked to Leyden Street and down to the bay. The entire town was at church; the streets were silent and the shops she passed were closed. A dog wandered unattended, knocking over dustbins and scavenging for scraps. The boats in the bay were moored, waves lightly slapping their hulls in the gentle breeze.

In a stand of trees, she took off her dress. She wore a bathing costume under it: an absurd outfit of a long blue serge blouse bound with white worsted braid, with cap sleeves and a sailor collar, plus three-quarter-length trousers. A person could hardly be expected to swim any distance at all wearing such a thing, but propriety demanded it and there was always the chance that someone might see her in the water.

She looked about her, making sure she was alone, and stepped into the waves. She waded in until she was completely underwater and out of sight, with her hair blooming up and around her, and the salt water refreshing her hot, dry skin. She stayed completely submerged as she removed the leaden swimsuit and anchored the two pieces under a rock. And then she swam free. She was clumsier than she liked with her human legs, but efficient enough that swimming reminded her of how lithe she used to be.

Before the hour was up, her sister Needa had joined her, with another called Weeku. They swam to the rocky outcropping together to catch lobsters and dig for clams, being careful to stay on the side away from the beach.

"Let me open the shell, Syrenka." Weeku took a clam from her. "You have such soft fingers now—I wonder how you can eat at all."

"Needa," Sarah said in a hushed voice. "Is there any news of the child?"

"No, dearest. I am sorry. We've traveled far, but we still find no trace of her. I heard your hands drum the water that night," Needa assured her. "I heard the baby cry. When I arrived, she was gone. You know we would have taken her—all of us—and cared for her as our own."

Syrenka touched her sister's shoulder. "It is my fault. When I think that I exposed her, that I assumed she would be safe, without thinking through the possibilities—" She broke off. "Why did it not occur to me that a shark could be near, or that a storm might take her out to sea? How can I be a thousand years old and still understand so little? What if she suffered? I am tortured by the thought."

Weeku scolded, "That is the human in you speaking. You followed a sensible plan, no more, no less. We will continue to search."

"We will never give up," Needa agreed.

Their time together was drawing to an end. They swam to the spot where Syrenka's bathing costume was anchored and helped her dress underwater. Needa and Weeku followed Syrenka until her feet touched, and then into the shallows, where their bellies nearly grazed the sandy bottom.

There they remained partially submerged, inspecting her legs—such amazing things they were!—and tracing the contours of her ankles and toes with their fingers.

Syrenka sensed someone's presence and spun around. The shore was empty.

"Go, now!" she said. "You are not safe here."

They wished her farewell and slipped under the surface.

But it was too late. They had been seen.

Eleanor Ontstaan had suffered a migraine in church. Leaving baby Marijn in the care of her sister, Eliza, at the service, she had started home, and had caught sight of Sarah entering the water. Hiding her body behind a thick tree, she had waited patiently for Sarah to emerge, the pain on the top of her head and the shimmering visual aura apparently cured by a growing, invasive curiosity. Within the hour she had seen everything, and she knew what her observations implied: that Sarah Doyle—the supposed foreigner who had suddenly appeared in town with no explanation, no history, and no family—was a monster, like the ones that cavorted in the water with her.

But how does a sea monster become human?

Eleanor was not a stupid woman. She knew the answer was through a monstrous act, through the taking of a human life. She had heard tales from her earliest childhood of sailors and fishermen found dead in the sea, their corpses mangled as Olaf's had been.

It became a cancer in her thoughts. Sarah Doyle was the demon who had viciously murdered Olaf and mutilated his body, in service of her evil magic.

Chapter 18

ON THURSDAY Peter was waiting in the break room when Hester finished work.

"Your mom called and said you were car-less today," Peter said, "so I told her I'd drive you home."

"Great, because I'm falling down with exhaustion." She pulled the coif off her head and stuffed it in her bag. "Let's get out of here."

"I hope it's okay that I have to stop at the wharf on the way. I left my paycheck in the kiosk."

"No problem. I'm ready."

Peter raised his eyebrows. "Aren't you going to change?"

"Nah." She lifted the hem of her skirt. "I burned a hole in my costume that I need to sew tonight. I've been really spacey lately, like I can't concentrate on anything. I might have gone up in flames." She hoisted her bag onto her shoulder. "I'm way too tired to change. I'll just be a dork for another fifteen minutes."

He patted her head. "You're not a dork, you're adorkable."

When they pulled up to the wharf, Hester saw that the tide was low. As Peter let himself into the kiosk, Hester's eyes were drawn south, in the direction of the grassy picnic area near the beach. The cave suddenly filled her mind and crowded out every other thought. It would be fully exposed now, and there was plenty of daylight left to venture inside.

Peter got back in the truck and fastened his seat belt. As he reached for the gearshift Hester said, "Wait. I'm going to get out here."

"What?"

She grabbed her bag. "It's a pretty evening, I feel like walking the rest of the way home."

"I thought you were tired," he protested as she shut the door.

She leaned her arms on the open passenger-side window. "I am. I mean, I was. I'll be fine!" She realized that she was being evasive again. He seemed to notice it, too. He was just about to say something, so she preempted him with a baffled smile.

"Am I acting weird?"

"Now that you mention it . . ."

"I'm sorry, we had a million tourists today, so I had to be on my toes nonstop. I think a walk alone is just what I need to decompress, and it's not far."

"You sure you don't want to change first?"

Hester looked down at her period clothing again. "Ha! I might as well make a spectacle of myself." She smiled. "Thanks for the ride."

She watched him pull away before she walked briskly down Water Street, brimming with excitement, not really knowing why. A flock of cormorants flew along the shore and skimmed the bay in a quick succession of landings. The hazy distraction of the last week—the preoccupation with nothing apparent—was distinctly lifting with each step. It was the oddest sense of purposefulness she'd ever had.

When she got to the stone steps she looked down the beach in the direction of the cave. She could just make out the shadowed smudge of the opening in the riprap. It looked desolate. But curiosity nibbled at her and demanded satisfaction. She had to go inside again. She held up her skirt to walk down the steps, opened the gate, and picked her way around the stones on the beach.

She passed a couple with a little boy. The dad was kneeling in front of his son with a hermit crab cupped in his hands. He did a double take when he saw her clothes. The parents both smiled broadly at her, like she was a celebrity. She waved a special goodbye to the little boy.

Several minutes later when she got to the mouth of the cave she glanced back at the family. They had lost interest in her; the boy had gotten his sneakers wet and was crying. She ducked inside the cave.

The back of the cave was as dark as night. The front, where she was standing, was bright. She moved a few steps in and waited, wondering if her eyes would adjust enough to see the back wall. She stayed still, listening for rustling, or shifting, or breathing . . . anything. She held her own breath. She waited. There was nothing. She exhaled.

She cleared her throat deliberately. Then she listened again. Silence.

"Hello?" she said timidly.

Nothing.

"Helloo," she said, louder. "Are you . . . are you there?"

She waited a moment, and then she huffed her air out. What had she come here for? Who was she calling to? If she was thinking about the stranger from two weeks ago, she was being ridiculous. She was more likely to bump into him in Squant's Treasure than in a cave on the beach.

And then she had a horrible thought: what if he had fallen asleep that night and drowned when the tide had come in?

She dropped her bag. "That's it. I've lost my marbles."

A quiet voice responded, "You're a bit old for that game, I believe, but if they're here I promise you I'll find them."

It was him. She was secretly elated, although she couldn't fathom why. And then a prickly irritation welled up inside, because he was using her own wordplay tricks against her. Was she that annoying to the tourists at the village when she did it?

"Very funny," she said.

"Then why is there sarcasm in your voice, I wonder," he said. Now she heard shifting, as if he were sitting up from a reclined position.

"Let's see, maybe because you were poking fun at me and my nerdy idiom?"

"I wasn't poking fun. I'm . . . not actually familiar with that particular idiom. I meant it literally: I know this cave rather intimately."

His voice was slow and deliberate, even though his thoughts were quick and articulate. Somehow, their conversation was out of synch.

"I'm sorry, I guess I misunderstood, too." She changed the subject. "Hey, why are you here?"

"I'm much more interested in why you're here." His voice was beautiful: husky, deep, and quiet—with that little edge of amusement that she was beginning to find maddening. Or perhaps endearing.

"I came to . . . to check on you," she said.

"How did you know you would find me here?"

"I didn't know. I was . . ." She told him the truth. ". . . Sort of drawn here."

She kicked herself mentally. She sounded like a stalker, when she was really just concerned for his safety. She was the last person who would chase a man, but how could he know that?

He was quiet. Very quiet.

"So you're okay then?" she said.

"I'm well, thank you. Actually, I'm touched, which I find a bit bewildering."

"Damn, but you talk in riddles," Hester said.

"I'll try to speak more plainly, if you'll control your language." He sounded more entertained than upset.

"Agreed. You first," Hester said.

"What I meant was, it has been a long time since anyone asked after my health."

"Step into the light," Hester said all at once. She surprised herself with her nerve.

He didn't move for a moment, and in that span of time Hester imagined with a little rise of panic that he might be damaged somehow—that there might be something shocking in his appearance. She swallowed and resolved to herself that if he came forward she would not show any reaction. She would treat him normally, as he deserved—as any human being deserved—no matter what was different about him.

"Very well," he said.

As he approached the center of the cave, he held his right hand in front of his eyes, palm out, to shield them from the glare. He was tall, thin, and wiry. He looked rumpled, as if he had just awakened. His clothes were unusual: a white blousy shirt with the sleeves rolled to his elbows, and black linen pants, also rolled once or twice. He was barefoot. He had scruffy black hair, unkempt but clean, and fair skin. He lowered his hand and squinted at her through one eye. He had the clearest blue eyes she had ever seen. His features were delicate, almost pretty, but also weary and worn. He was gorgeous.

Hester burst out laughing.

He tilted his head and raised one eyebrow, as if to say "What's so funny?"

"I'm so sorry," Hester said. "Y'see . . ." She couldn't stop laughing. She held up her finger. "Wait . . ."

She took a deep breath and held it. She looked away from him, at the wall. She exhaled.

"It's just that while you were in the shadows, I imagined, you know, more like Phantom of the Opera."

"No, I'm afraid . . . I don't know what you mean."

She made the mistake of looking at him again. His eyes were quizzical and penetrating. He had a hint of stubble and thin, expressive lips. He crossed his arms in front of his chest. Laughter bubbled up again and escaped explosively.

Inappropriate, she scolded herself. *You sound like a hyena. So . . . so schoolgirlish. He'll think you're a silly flirt.* That last thought was all she needed to gain control.

"I'm sorry." She cleared her throat. "It's just not every day you find a male model hiding in a cave."

He looked at her but didn't say anything. It seemed as if he hadn't understood her explanation, or perhaps had disregarded it. He couldn't possibly be humble with looks like that, could he?

Then she noticed he was studying her.

"What's wrong?" Hester said.

He shook his head. "This doesn't make sense to me."

"Remember our deal? The fucking *riddles*?" she said, swearing on purpose to tease him.

He smiled and showed beautiful teeth, with one lateral incisor irresistibly crooked. She noticed that the skin next to his eyes creased adorably. She resolved to ignore it.

"Plain English, then: I'm marveling at us standing here, in a cave, talking together like two ordinary people."

She looked around her, nodding. "Yeah, the setting is unusual." She looked back at him, but he hadn't taken his eyes off her.

She said the first thing that popped into her head. "Your clothes look handmade."

"I suppose they are," he said.

"They're almost period-looking . . ."

"If you're implying they're in an outdated style, I would have to say the same of yours."

"These are my work clothes," she said defensively. But seeing the blank look on his face, she wondered if he even knew about Plimoth Plantation. "They're a costume. They represent clothing from 1627."

"I see."

"I role-play at the historic village. I interpret Elizabeth Tilley."

"Elizabeth Tilley," he said, pensively. "John Howland's wife."

"That's right," she said. Not many people her age would have known that fact, or given a damn for that matter, yet he looked to be only a couple of years older than she was. She wondered about his exact age.

"John did remarkably well for himself, no?" He raised his eyebrows meaningfully.

"What's that supposed to mean?" Was he coming on to her?

"He started his journey as an indentured servant, I believe, and finished it by marrying the governor's daughter. Half of the other Mayflower emigrants were dead by then."

"Ah," she said with relief. He was a history buff, not a lecherous bastard. "Pretty good. Except that Elizabeth was Carver's ward, not his daughter. And Carver was the governor for barely a few months before he died and William Bradford took over."

They were standing face to face. He smiled at her again—so warmly for someone who didn't know her yet—and Hester wanted to look away, but she couldn't.

"You're an excellent sparring partner," he said.

"And you're enigmatic as hell. I mean, heck."

She felt unnerved by him—off balance somehow, when she was usually so in control. It had something to do with the way she had his undivided attention, the way she couldn't look away from him, the way he seemed to be soaking up the details of her face and her words, and the way she felt drawn to him despite every brain cell fighting to extinguish the attraction. He was eroding years of her carefully crafted emotional wall in the span of minutes.

"Why do you spend time in here, anyway?" she asked, more aggressively than she intended. "It could actually be dangerous, with the tides, you know."

"I am aware of the tides." His face hardened.

"But what are you doing in here?" The pitch of her voice was rising; she hated how shrill she sounded.

"What concern is it of yours?"

"It's just weird that I found you in here twice." She motioned toward his legs. "I mean, where are your shoes?"

"I didn't ask you to come," he said crisply. A cloud passed outside the cave and dimmed the light. His face became darker, almost foreboding.

"Of course you didn't!" She stamped her foot. "You're being maddening."

"And you're being quarrelsome for reasons I can't understand. We were enjoying each other's company until—"

"Now you're speaking for me!" She put her hand up. "Listen, I just came to make sure you hadn't drowned that night. I didn't come for the scintillating conversation."

A wind whipped up, and wisps of water blew off the tips of the whitecaps, misting Hester's back.

He said, "And yet if you had no conversation in your life, you'd long for nothing more."

It was another cryptic riddle, which Hester decided smacked of arrogance.

"I can find plenty of people I'd rather talk to than you," she lied. Why was she being spiteful?

His lips were tight. The clouds over the ocean matched his

mood. Droplets of rain landed outside the cave and a few blew inside. "If you came to satisfy your curiosity regarding my well-being, I think you have your answer. Hadn't you better leave before another of your overzealous lovers corners you in a cave? I won't intervene this time."

"I haven't got any lovers, smart aleck." She startled herself with the thumping emptiness she felt in her chest as she added, "I can only ever be alone."

She couldn't think of anything else to do but pick up her bag and leave. He grabbed her elbow through the woolen bodice. His grip was sure, but gentle. Her arm tingled lightly.

"Wait." His face had softened. "Please explain what you mean by that."

"Let me go," she murmured, knowing she could pull away if she wanted.

The wind weakened. The rain ended. She felt her bag slip to the ground.

He persisted. "The way you phrased that, 'I can only ever be alone.' It implies that it's not a choice, it has been forced on you. But why?"

The familiarity and intensity of his question pulled words from deep inside her before she could stop to edit them. She felt her lips moving, but the product—faint and disconsolate—was a surprise.

"I'm afraid of dying."

It was the first time she had said it out loud. And it was too personal to have been uttered to a stranger.

"Why do you believe that love and death are intertwined?"

He let her elbow go now, and she found herself disappointed that he was no longer touching her.

"Because for me they are." She brushed the hair off her brow with the palm of her hand. "No, that's not true. Technically love is not the problem, it's what comes after. I can never have children, because the women in my family die within days of giving birth. It's some sort of undiagnosed medical condition, and the older I get the more it scares the hell out of me." She looked at the ceiling of the cave to suspend the tears that had built up. "This is ridiculous. Why am I telling you this?"

"Forgive me for being thoughtless and ill-mannered just now." She shook her head dismissively and wiped her eyes.

"What do you know about the deaths in your family?" he said.

"My mom died four days after having me. My grandmother died after having her. And my great-great-great-grandmother also died after having a little girl."

What was wrong with her? How was he making her spill her guts so easily? She had never discussed this with anyone before—not her parents, not Sam, not Peter. She needed to leave; to run away before he cracked her wide open.

"I'm late for supper."

He looked at her, seeming to weigh what he was about to say next. Hester picked up the strap of her bag.

"I would like to help you think through this problem," he said.

"Thanks, but I've thought about it for years."

"Please, I have a hypothesis that I'm confident you've not yet considered."

"That's okay, really." She lifted the strap of the bag over her head and across her shoulder.

"I understand," he said, but he seemed genuinely disappointed. "I shall be on the beach tomorrow evening. Join me, if you change your mind."

"I . . . I don't know," she said, shaking her head. She gathered the bottom of her heavy skirt into a bundle to keep it off the damp sand and left without saying goodbye. When she glanced back, he had stepped out of the cave. He was standing on the beach, with the tide just beginning to lick his feet. The setting sun was shining again, lighting his face from the side so that he seemed to glow.

She broke into a run, her bag bumping against her hip.

Chapter 19

1873

ELEANOR WAS A GOOD CHRISTIAN WOMAN, but that didn't prevent her from wanting to hurt Sarah Doyle. She found excuses to leave church the following three Sundays in order to spy on Sarah. Over the weeks it became as clear to her as anything she had ever known: her God would not want Olaf's murder to go unpunished. The sea creatures were unholy—the spawn of the Devil. Sarah's false human life must somehow be destroyed. As the mother of little Marijn, Eleanor felt the imperative of a safe, wholesome world more acutely than ever before; she would do everything in her power to protect this fragile soul.

On Saturday afternoon she put Marijn in her carriage, tucked a blanket around her, and hurried to the church rectory. The jostling of the dirt road put the baby to sleep. Eleanor applied the brakes to the carriage, lifted the baby out, and knocked on the door of the retired pastor's house.

The old man answered wearing slippers. His shirt was open at the throat, and he was missing the white linen neckband.

"Pastor!" she said breathlessly.

"Mrs. Ontstaan, es et no'? You see, they may've retired me, but I'm no' senile yet! Please, come en while I make myself presen'able for you."

"I'm sorry to disturb you, Pastor." She stepped inside. "But it's of the utmost importance."

It was warm in the room, which was heated by a small coal fireplace. Eleanor waited by a wooden chair while the pastor shuffled through the tiny receiving area to his bedroom and closed the door. He reemerged wearing his collar and waistcoat, with the slippers still on his feet.

"Now, may I offer you some tea—or somethen' more potent, perhaps? A nep of scotch?" His eyebrows twitched like caterpillars. "You look as ef you could use a nep."

"No, I should say not," she said disapprovingly, hugging Marijn to her chest. "I've come for your help—I have an urgent request, this is not a social call."

"Of course, madam." He motioned for her to sit down in the living room and became politely serious.

"If you don't mind, I'm a simple woman, with no airs, and I can only speak frankly. This conversation must rest between you and me and God alone." Eleanor jiggled the baby continuously in her arms as she spoke.

He nodded. "You may be assured tha' I—"

"You must perform an exorcism, Pastor."

He raised his eyebrows and laughed lightly. "An exorcesm, Mrs. Ontstaan?"

"An exorcism of the demonic possession of Sarah Doyle."

The pastor's face fell, and he sat dumbfounded.

Irritated by his silence, Eleanor enunciated: "*Mrs. Ezra Doyle?* Surely you know her husband, who is a member of our congregation."

"Yes," he said, coming to. "Yes, yes, I am well acquain'ed with Mr. and Mrs. Doyle. I blessed their marriage caeremony no' two months ago. She es a lovely woman, Mrs. Ontstaan—I am obliged to defend haer. A spirited filly, to be sure." He winked. "Bu' I daresay tha' shouldnae warrant an *exorcesm*."

"You performed the wedding ceremony? Tell me then, have you met her family?"

He thought for a moment. "I cannae recall tha' she had family en attendance."

"Because she has no family, Pastor. No *human* family. She appeared from nowhere and married Mr. Doyle without so much as a day's courtship. She is a monster."

The pastor rose from his chair. "I willnae listen any far-ther, Mrs. Ontstaan." He walked the few steps to the front door and opened it.

Eleanor stood up, and Marijn began to stir in her arms.

"Listening is your job, Pastor; and now that you have been relieved of the weekly sermons, it is the only function you perform here to earn your board from the parish. I am quite certain you would not want the elders to hear that you refused to counsel a member of the congregation."

He sighed, but he left his hand on the doorknob and kept the door open a crack.

Marijn began to squirm. Eleanor jiggled her.

"I am a useless ol' man, Mrs. Ontstaan. Why do you no' ask the new pastor for hes counsel?"

"I considered that, but I know that an exorcism requires proof, and you and I can only furnish it on Sunday morning. During that time Pastor Davis *must* give his sermon, to ensure that all the parishioners—including Ezra Doyle—are in attendance at the church. That will give you the opportunity to observe Sarah's possession."

Marijn began to cry.

"Mrs. Ontstaan, en all my years—an' I daresay I'm on the cusp of having more than my share (some would say I've even passed tha' mark)—I have never seen a true possession. Wha' I *have* seen are men tormented by an illness o' the mind; but those poor souls are lef' more properly to the care of doctors an' institutions than to the claergy."

Marijn was wailing now—red in the face, with sweat droplets on her forehead from the warm room and too much bundling.

Eleanor raised her voice over the noise. "Sarah Doyle speaks in tongues, Pastor. She cavorts with demons. And she breathes underwater. I can prove these things if you meet me at the bay this Sunday, at one quarter past eight."

Marijn was screaming now, piercing wails with long, painful silences at the end of each scream when she had run out of air. Eleanor's frenetic jiggling gave the baby's cry an unbearable vibrato.

"Fine. I'll mee' you, Mrs. Ontstaan. Bu' only to show tha' your theory es unjust and unfair—nay, et's slander." He opened the door all the way. "I'll expect an apology from you on Sunday mornin', whech I'll accept on Mrs. Doyle's behalf, after whech we shall never mention this to anyone, or betwixt ourselves, again."

Eleanor left with Marijn, and the pastor shut the door, wondering pityingly whether the cool air would relieve the child's discomfort.

Chapter 20

AT THE END OF THE NEXT DAY the curator swept up the hill through Plimoth Plantation, corralling any straggling visitors and ushering them to the parking lot.

"All clear, Pilgrims," she shouted to the rows of houses down the hill.

Hester scraped her pottage into a bucket to take to the pigs and climbed up a ladder to retrieve the twenty-first-century broom that was stashed in the loft. She swept the dirt floor hurriedly, hoping to make a quick escape. Nearly every thought she'd had that day had been about the stranger in the cave, until she finally stopped pretending to herself that she wasn't simply marking time until evening, when he had told her he would be waiting on the beach. She thought of his smile, with that wonky little tooth. She thought of his bemused eyes and his deep, quiet voice. She thought about how puzzling some of his comments were, and how proper his manners seemed. And she thought, although she tried not to, about how his shirt had been unbuttoned just enough for her to see the top of his chest.

She turned to sweep her pile outside and saw Peter in the doorway.

"Hey there!" he said.

"Oh, hey," Hester replied.

"Such enthusiasm," he joked. "Are you okay?"

"I'm fine. What are you doing here?" She could hear the irritation in her own voice.

"I thought we could stop for an ice cream on the way home."

"No!" she said. Of all days for him to stop by! "I mean, I've got a car today, thanks."

"I know. I thought we could caravan over there."

"Why didn't you call? I could have saved you the trip."

He pointed to the leather pouch hanging from her belt. "Your phone is off until the all clear, and it's, what, a grueling seven-minute drive for me from the wharf?"

He hopped aside as Hester pushed the debris past his feet. Straw and mouse droppings landed on his sneakers.

"Sorry," she said, surprising herself with how little she meant it.

"Wow, I can take a hint. See you, Hester." He turned and started up the hill.

Hester swept the ashes into a hasty pile near the fireplace, froze for a moment, and dropped the broom. She went to the doorway. Peter was almost at the fort.

"Another time, I promise," she yelled.

He lifted his hand and waved backward but didn't turn around.

She finished her chores, punched out, and rushed to the break room to change. Ten minutes later, she was running down Water Street toward the picnic area.

Eleven minutes later, it began to drizzle.

Twelve minutes later, she was breathless, teetering at the top of the stone steps.

Part of her didn't expect him to be there, even though he had invited her. Or maybe he had come earlier and left already. Maybe he knew it was going to rain and wouldn't show.

And then her heart tumbled in her chest, because he was there. He was sitting closer to the steps than to the cave, plunked in the sand, his legs stretched out and crossed at the ankles, leaning on his elbow, reading a book that was resting in the sand. He was passing the time; he was waiting for her. Just what was she getting into? She sighed deeply to calm herself.

Hester watched a couple walk past him, holding hands and laughing. The guy was huge, with a crew cut. A classic football-playing, fraternity-brother type—long on physical strength and party skills. The girl was petite and bottle-blond, gazing up at him with shining eyes. She opened an umbrella, and laughed when he took it from her and held it over her head. The stranger glanced up at them briefly and then down at his book again. *Silly girl*, Hester thought, *your hulk is nothing compared with my stranger. Just look to your left!*

Hester needed time for her heartbeat to slow. She straightened her T-shirt. She felt to see if the fly on her jeans was all the way up. She ran her fingers through her hair, which was getting damp. She wondered for the hundredth time how she could go through an entire day and forget to check herself even once in a mirror. She glided her tongue over her teeth searching for food particles; she'd had a spinach salad for lunch, for God's sake, what was she thinking? And all the while she stared hard at him, at this lanky, rumpled, puzzling guy who was at once intelligent and yet so out of touch—and whom she had to admit was simply, breathtakingly beautiful.

He looked up at her then as if she had reached over and nudged him.

She waved, as casually as she could, and walked down the steps hoping she wouldn't trip, watching each stair instead of him. The frat boy and his girl went single file to pass her as they walked up.

"Thanks," Hester said.

"Lousy beach weather," the girl said to her cheerily.

"Yeah," Hester smiled. "I'm just going to meet my friend over there."

The frat boy must have been a little slow, because he looked over his shoulder down the beach and responded with a confused "Sure."

The stranger smiled at her as she approached, and it was alarmingly like the first hit of a drug she had been craving all day. Something rushed through her arteries like liquid joy, and even as she reveled in it, she knew she had to have more. It must be endorphins, she decided. What an ephemeral thing human will is, to be manipulated by a couple of drops of hormone!

He stood up to greet her.

"Hello," she said, aiming for an ordinary cheerfulness.

"You came back." His eyebrows were raised with something like delight.

"I guess I did sort of bolt last night. We hit on a sore topic."

"I gathered." He wiped his hands and lightly smacked his backside, as if to get sand off, but Hester couldn't see a grain on him.

"Your book is going to get wet," Hester said.

"It's not mine. Someone forgot it on the beach this afternoon." She peered around him to see it. "*Jane Eyre*. I loved that."

"Did you?" He looked at her, dwelling a little too long on what she'd thought was just a conversation opener. "Well," he said after a moment, "I wish they had lost a book I hadn't already read. Shall we walk for a bit?"

Was he trying to politely tell her that he had been sitting there, bored, for a long time?

"I'm sorry if you were waiting. I was at work all day; this is the soonest I could be here. We didn't set a time to meet yesterday, you just said 'evening'—I wondered about that all day . . ." She was blathering.

"You're not wearing your work clothing," he observed, as they strolled up the beach. He didn't seem to notice the misty drizzle. Hester couldn't have cared less about it.

"I changed." She looked at him and recognized his white shirt and black pants as the same outfit from the day before. "I gotta tell you, I'm a little worried that you might be homeless."

"I have a home," he said.

Still, his clothes were clean, if becoming damp. His feet were bare, but he had no trouble walking on the rocky beach. Hester kept her shoes on.

"Where?" she challenged him. "Where is your home?"

"I live north of here, by the Cordage Company."

"You mean the Cordage Museum?"

"Mmm," he said vaguely. He stole a look at her. Their eyes met. What was he hiding?

She stopped in her tracks. "Wait," she said, touching his elbow to slow him. His sleeve was rolled up and her fingers met his skin, which was cool and inexplicably lovely. A tingle shot up her arm and exploded somewhere in her brain, like an electric shock, but immensely pleasant. She recoiled. He took a breath, as if he felt it, too.

"I . . . haven't had the pleasure of learning your name," he said. "My name is Ezra."

Ezra, she thought. *How absolutely perfect.*

"Hester," she said. "Hester Goodwin."

"Hester." He nodded slowly, looking at every inch of her face, which was now flushed and covered in mist. He seemed to be looking for something. "Goodwin is an old name in this area, isn't it?"

"Yes, embarrassingly old."

"Hester Goodwin," he said, drawing her name out under his breath, dissecting it, his eyes locked on hers now.

She had to snap him out of it. She couldn't bear to have him look at her that way—as if he were searching her soul. Not to mention the fact that she was becoming drenched by the relentless drizzle, and he had promised he could advise her about her problem.

"Yesterday?" she started, realizing at once that it was an incomplete sentence. "You mentioned an idea. About my family's medical history?"

He blinked. "Yes, your history. The women who have died. That could be important."

Could be important? It was only the most important thing in her life, she thought, suddenly irritated. How did he manage it? How could he annoy her and make her heart race all in the same minute?

"Tell me exactly what you know."

She took a breath to calm herself. "The women in my family seem to die within a week of delivering their first baby. It happened to my mother, Susan, and her mother, for sure. And my dad says my mom may have mentioned her grandmother dying young, too—my great-grandmother." She pointed toward Leyden Street. "And my great-great-great-grandmother is up there in Burial Hill, at age nineteen, dust and bones, after having given birth to a baby named Nellie."

He nodded, taking in the information. "And you believe there is a scientific explanation—childbirth fever, or an irregularity of anatomy—that compromised each woman at delivery?"

"There's no evidence that anything was medically wrong. But it can't be coincidence. It must be genetic."

"The infants were all girls?"

"As far as I know. Could that be important?"

"Tell me about your mother's delivery of you."

"My mom was healthy beforehand, with all the proper prenatal care, and my birth was uncomplicated. She had no fever, no excessive bleeding. The doctors tried everything to save her, but she just faded away."

Hester remembered something. "My dad said that I was the one who appeared weak at first. I didn't cry, and I wouldn't nurse for days. He said that he'd always felt guilty that he worried so much about me, not knowing that Susan was the one who was really in danger.

"We live in a civilized country, Ezra, where the field of medicine is at its peak, and yet her autopsy"—Hester's throat caught on the word—"failed to find a cause of death. How is that possible?"

His eyes didn't waver from hers. "I'm so sorry."

"It's okay, really." She looked away.

He crossed one arm in front of his chest and propped his chin on his knuckles, staring at the ground. Then he started to pace, absentmindedly rubbing his lips with his forefinger—those lips that Hester had imagined kissing as she beat her rugs and aired her mattress in the village. She let him think, and she took that minute to compose herself.

"Your mother," Ezra eventually said, repeating her list, "your grandmother, and your great-great-great-grandmother."

"And most likely my great-grandmother."

"Mmm," he said. "But we need certainty, not likelihood." He stopped pacing and looked at her. "I'm afraid you'll have to do a more exhaustive search."

"What?"

"You are keenly analytic, Hester, and I hope that trait will allow you to think broadly rather than dismiss what I have to say as impossible, or even absurd. What you've told me is consistent with the hypothesis that this may be a curse, and not a medical condition."

Hester snorted, but he looked at her evenly.

"You're serious?" she asked.

He nodded. "I've studied many myths and legends."

"Right. So," she said sarcastically, "curses are your hobby."

"I may have an insight, yes."

Peter's words rang in her head. *Hester Goodwin, you have no sense of magic.*

"I'm skeptical, naturally, but I'm willing to listen."

"I'm glad." He smiled. "There is an important criterion that you can confirm or disprove: curses never skip generations. If your great-grandmother or your great-great-grandmother didn't die after giving birth to their first children, or if any first child happened not to be a girl—or if they had documented puerperal fever or uncontrolled bleeding, or any genuine medical difficulty—then it's not a curse, and you will no doubt have a good laugh at my suggesting it. But you will need to check *all* the birth and death records."

"I'm pretty sure we have five data points already."

"We have at best three so far."

Hester cocked her head to the side to look at him with one stubborn eye. "Three and a half."

He smiled broadly—even affectionately, she thought—as if he actually found her hardheadedness charming.

Hester suddenly realized that even if it wasn't a curse, the death records of each of the women in her family were important for whatever medical information they could provide. There were so many holes in her grasp of her mother's family history.

"Hey, thanks, Ezra," she said. "You're absolutely right; I've been relying on word of mouth in my family, but I need to find the documentation and the missing pieces."

He nodded. His eyes were still trained on hers, with a trace of a smile left on his lips.

She shivered, and Ezra lifted his face to the sky, noticing the drizzle for the first time.

"I've been insensitive," he said. "You're soaked."

"So are you." She laughed. "Only somehow it makes you look

dashing and outdoorsy, while I probably look like a wet puppy with spinach in her teeth."

"You're just as lovely when you're wet as when you're dry," he said. And then a cloud passed over his face and he was suddenly serious, almost wounded. His chest caved just a bit, and he withdrew a step, as if she had punched him. What had she said?

"I'm sorry that I snapped at you yesterday," she offered, hoping an apology would help. "Oh, shoot. I did it the first time we met, in the cave, too, didn't I? You must think I'm a raving . . ." She caught herself. "But I'm so glad to know you. Really, I am."

He was quiet for a moment, and she wondered if he'd accept her apology. Finally he shook his head lightly as if to clear it, and that glint of amusement reappeared. "I never did enjoy complaisant companions, Miss Hester Goodwin. I believe I would be your friend even if you heaped abuse on me every moment of our acquaintance."

She grinned and put her hand out. "Bygones, then."

"No need for bygones," he said, taking her hand. This time Hester's body must have anticipated his touch, because the strange electric zap came like a welcome surge. There was something about the most innocent skin-to-skin contact with him that took away her breath and made her heart leap as if it had been defibrillated. But it was different this time. This was not a grazing touch, and the longer she held his hand the more there was a sensation of streaming, of flowing—she couldn't put words to it. It was as if passion itself were coursing from him through her core, filling her up, and bursting into the cool, damp air around her. It was unbearably pleasurable, and also frightening.

"Ezra," she said, trying to pull her hand away.

But he looked into her eyes, stricken.

"Stop," she said weakly.

"Syrenka," he whispered.

"No," Hester said, shaking her head, dizzy with confusion. "You have to let me go." She tugged her hand harder, and he released her.

He rubbed his forehead as if he had a massive headache. "Hester . . ." he started.

"What the *hell*, Ezra," she blurted, trying to hurt him with words, not knowing how to respond to what had just happened.

"I don't . . . I don't understand it. There's something about you that . . ."

"*I'm* perfectly normal. There's something about *you*—" She started to back away, toward the stone steps.

And then he said something that she instantly recognized as a truth she had been denying:

"There's something about *us*."

She turned and took the steps two at a time. She looked back once to see if he was following her, but he was rooted in the sand, with something she could only describe as grief on his face.

Chapter 21
1873

THE OLD PASTOR ARRIVED at exactly the appointed time, but he was still too late.

"She's in the water already, Pastor," Eleanor said, scowling. She had Marijn in her arms. "If only you had walked faster."

McKee scanned the horizon. "There es naught en the water, Mrs. Ontstaan."

"Well of course there isn't; she has gone *under* the water."

A look of concern flashed across the pastor's face; concern for Eleanor.

"Come to the trees with me," she said.

She marched him into the woods near the beach, where they picked their way for several yards. Eleanor stopped him near a fallen tree and lifted a branch to reveal a canvas bag. The old pastor opened the bag to see a towel and a dress neatly folded inside. He set it down again gently when he caught sight of undergarments.

"You're sayin' tha' this is haer clothing and she es now bathin' nearby en the water?"

"Yes, but 'bathing' is a human activity. Sarah does not come up for air."

"Now Mrs. Ontstaan . . ."

"There is still hope that we might catch her with her monstrous companions, if we are patient and stay out of view. I have seen her with them. Once she sat on the rocky outcropping fully clothed, once she was in the water wearing a bathing costume, and once"—she whispered the rest of the sentence—"she was in the water obscenely *nude*. The monsters devour urchins and other bottom-feeders that they pick from the rocks—they eat some of the creatures shell and all." She shuddered. "They think I can't see them, even though they loom bright white below the surface, like beacons from hell."

"The outcropping looks defficult to navigate, even for a nemble paerson, Mrs. Ontstaan."

"She is nothing if she's not nimble, Pastor."

"I'll have a look myself then," he said, walking out of the woods toward the shore.

"No!" Eleanor hissed. "She'll see you, and she won't show herself!"

But it was too late. The old pastor had climbed up and was gingerly picking his way over the slippery rocks.

"The damned fool!" she swore near Marijn's ear. "He'll fail to see Sarah, and then he'll *kill* himself, and where will that leave me?"

The rocks were much larger up close than they appeared at a distance, and they had a slimy algae growing on them, along with limp clumps of what the pastor had called green fingers when he was a child in Scotland—a branching seaweed with dark, velvety fronds and a spongy holdfast that anchored them. He smiled. The last time he had done anything like this was more than sixty years ago, on holiday at the seashore. He always did delight in giving his mother palpitations.

Each step required him to brace both his hands and his feet against the rocks, causing him to travel at a slow pace. After several minutes he had gone only a dozen yards. He stopped to rest and assess his progress by sitting down on a flat stone. He waved perfunctorily to Eleanor, ignoring her importuning gesticulations to return to shore. He looked out toward the ocean and breathed in deeply, filling himself with the cool, damp air.

He was still for a minute, until something caught his eye in the water—something deep under the surface, on the side of the outcropping away from the beach. He braced himself again in a nearly crawling position and crept across two large boulders to be closer to that edge. He leaned over to peer into the water and could hardly believe his eyes.

Beneath the water in the shadows was a pale woman, with flowing white hair and bare skin. She was intent on picking something from the outcropping. The pastor's arms, which were supporting his torso, trembled fiercely, and the woman looked up at him through the water with enormous clear green eyes. He cried out, and his hands slipped. He began to fall into the water headfirst, grappling to hold on to the slimy rocks, and a silver flask slipped silently out of his waistcoat pocket. He caught himself just as he might have tumbled in after it. The nude woman snatched the sinking flask and was gone.

His arms and right shoulder were soaked, and he had badly torn a fingernail. He sucked his throbbing finger, scanning the water for her, and in so doing, his eyes caught on another woman, waist deep, moving toward shore. She was wearing a blue bathing costume and walking quickly, head down, in the direction of the woods. It might have been Mrs. Doyle, but he couldn't be sure.

"Mrs. Ontstaan!" he called, looking over his shoulder. She didn't hear him.

He stood himself up as best he could, waved his arms over his head, and then pointed in the direction of the woods. Eleanor stood on the shore, on the other side of the outcropping. She looked toward the woods, but she was not in a position to see the woman in blue.

It took him a long time to make his way back to the shore. He got there out of breath.

"I saw a woman leavin' the wa'er on the other side of the outcropping," he said, neglecting for a reason he couldn't identify to mention the more fantastical woman under the water.

"It was Mrs. Doyle," she said emphatically. "You saw her."

"I cannae say wi' caertainty et was her."

"We've been here for three-quarters of an hour and haven't seen anyone swimming about on the surface for refreshment, do you not agree? You were on the outcropping for fully thirty of those minutes and did not see her. The only conclusion is that she was *underwater* that entire time!"

"Her emaergence es suspicious, but no' the proof I need. I mus' be sure of the charge, you understand. But ef I can establish et as truth—ef she's capable of breathin' underwa'er—you're correc' that there may endeed be cause to save haer soul."

Eleanor rocked Marijn with satisfaction.

"I'll find a way to prove it without a doubt, Pastor. And we'll take care of her soul. I'm certain of that."

Chapter 22

THE NIGHT SHE SPOKE WITH EZRA, Hester drew a table of information that she had gathered from the Ontstaan and Crotty gravestones and from her family history, leaving question marks for the gaps that she needed to fill.

MAIDEN NAME	MARRIED NAME	BIRTH YEAR	DEATH YEAR	AGE AT DEATH	CAUSE OF DEATH
Marijn Ontstaan	Marijn Crotty	1873	1892	19	"languishment"?
Nellie Crotty	?	?	?	?	?
?	?	?	?	?	?
Carolyn (Keep?)	Carolyn Crowell	?	1966	?	undetermined?
Susan Crowell	Susan Crowell Goodwin	1966	1993	27	undetermined

The next day she requested a two-hour lunch break and took herself to the public library. The genealogy room was a historian's delight: bright and sunny with a long research table, and filled with hundreds of books. A woman with salt and pepper hair sat at the information desk in front of a plaque that read "Sandra Cook,

History/Genealogy." She was looking at her computer over glasses that were leashed to her neck.

As Hester approached the desk, Ms. Cook swiveled her chair with a smile and said, "May I help you?"

"Yes, please. I need to fill in the missing pieces of this chart."

Ms. Cook studied it for only a moment before she said, "What a clever way to present the data. Did all the generations die in Plymouth?"

"I think so."

"Very doable then. This could be just a few hours of work if you're lucky. And most of it in this very room."

She pointed to the bottom row of Hester's chart. "In genealogy the correct way to begin researching one's family is with oneself, or in this case the most recent generation on your table—Susan Crowell Goodwin—and work backward. It's more efficient, and you're more likely to link correctly to the next generation. Working backward also applies to the individual: you begin to research a person starting with their death. The death record, obituary, or gravestone information provides loads of clues about where to look for marriage and birth records."

"Okay," Hester said.

"So in the case of Susan, here . . ." Ms. Cook got up and walked to the shelves at the opposite end of the room, with Hester following. "You can look up the record of her death in the *Annual Reports of the Town of Plymouth 1993*." She pulled the volume from the shelf. "This has all births, marriages, and deaths for 1993. The whole series runs from 1856 until the present."

Hester watched as she flipped quickly to deaths and scrolled her finger down the list of names.

"Here she is." She tapped the page, showing Hester the entry.

Apr. 25., Plymouth, Susan F. (Crowell) Goodwin, female,
27 y 5 m 16 d; wife of Malcolm E. Goodwin;
child of Christopher and Carolyn (Keep).

Hester took the book from her. It was only three lines: the skeletal demographic remains of an entire life. And it was so final. She slid her fingers over the typeface.

"Is Susan a relative?" Ms. Cook asked quietly.

Hester nodded. "My mom."

Ms. Cook did the perfect thing, which was to wait—for just a moment—and then move on to the next step. "Now, you see? You have her maiden name here, her parents' names, including her mother's maiden name, and if you needed to you could figure her exact birth date from her age at death—although you probably know it already because she's your mom, but for earlier generations you'll need that calculation. And then you'd go to the annual report of the year of her birth to check out her birth record, which will in turn give her parents' ages—which are very useful. You can also hunt for the marriage records of Christopher and Carolyn in the years preceding the birth of Susan. Do you see? It's easy as pie—but only because they're all from Plymouth."

"Great," Hester said. "This actually sounds fun."

"Oh, there's one thing, though. Only the oldest annual reports have the cause of death listed. Once you find the date of death, in many cases you'll have to either look up an obituary in the *Old Colony Memorial* newspaper, which you can access through our microform archives, or get copies of the death certificates from the clerk at Town Hall."

"Got it."

Ms. Cook smiled. "You're a quick study."

Within an hour and a half Hester had the entire chart filled and had jotted this note to bring to Ezra:

> *Marijn Crotty, age 19, 1892, lethargy*
> *Nellie Burroughs, age 24, 1916, enervation*
> *Grace Keep, age 25, 1941, exhaustion*
> *Carolyn Crowell, age 25, 1966, undetermined*
> *Susan Crowell Goodwin, age 27, 1993, undetermined*

The score was five for five.

Chapter 23

As Hester was packing up, Ms. Cook brought a book over to her and put it on the table.

"You might find this fun, since you have so many ancestors in Plymouth." It was a reserve-only volume called *Burial Hill in the 1990s—Plymouth, Massachusetts: A six-year cemetery mapping project with descriptions, conditions, and some photographs.* Hester smiled to herself. Her nerdiness must have been showing.

There was an index of names in the back. She looked up Nellie Burroughs and Grace Keep and discovered that they had both been laid to rest in Burial Hill. She drew a crude map for herself on a scrap of paper so she could visit the graves and clapped the volume shut.

On an inspiration she said to Ms. Cook, "Do you know if the library has any books about tales of sea folk in Plymouth Bay?" If she was going to go to the graveyard anyway, she thought, she'd like to pop into the church and see if that kooky old pastor was there.

"There are mermaid books in the children's section, of course."

"Mm . . . not fairy tales, but something historical, like a non-fiction account of sea creatures that local fishermen have claimed to see over the years. Is there anything like that?"

Ms. Cook searched the computer for a minute and shook her head no. Then she said, "Wait," and started typing again. "It's a long shot, but I'll check the locked cabinet. We have some handwritten manuscripts there that are not cross-listed with our public catalog. Lots of diaries, an ancient guest register from the Pilgrim Inn, merchant logs, that sort of thing . . ." Her voice trailed off.

The locked cabinet. It sounded mysterious and wonderful to Hester.

The librarian raised her eyebrows. "Well, I'll be."

"What?"

"We own the journal of a local naturalist by the name of E. A. Doyle, from 1872. It seems to be about myths and legends of the bay."

Hester had to see it.

"Am I allowed to read books in the locked cabinet?"

Ms. Cook smiled at her enthusiasm. "I'll take you there."

The so-called locked cabinet was in the drably modern Rare Manuscripts Room on the third floor, but the cabinet itself was just as lovely as it sounded: an antique armoire, with wood that had been darkened by age and sunlight. It had an iron skeleton lock with a tiny, sliding dustcover over the keyhole. Hester had to smile at the charming juxtaposition of the sturdy hardware with the glass doors, which a mere tap would probably shatter, exposing the contents of the armoire to any book-loving thief.

The librarian in charge of the locked cabinet was a small, sturdy woman named Ms. Lopes. She had black curly hair, stylish reading glasses perched on the top of her head, and the same contented demeanor that Ms. Cook had—born, Hester decided, of the satisfaction of doing what they loved to do every day.

"What's your name, dear?"

"Hester."

"First things first, Esther: go to the restroom and wash your hands. Lots of lather, lots of rinsing, *warm* water, not cold. Turn the doorknobs with a paper towel. You can leave your bag over here by your chair."

When Hester returned, Ms. Lopes took a skeleton key out of her desk drawer and opened the cabinet. Hester looked at the shelves inside. Every book was unusual in some way: there were leather-bound volumes with gilded decorations on their spines, cloth-covered books, books covered with handmade marbleized paper, and one small child's diary bound again and again with twine, undoubtedly as a crude privacy device.

Ms. Lopes pulled out a white box the size and shape of a book, tied like a gift with a white ribbon. She locked the cabinet again, put the key in her drawer, and took the box over to a table facing her desk. When she tugged on the ribbon, all four sides of the box unfolded to reveal a weathered book with a cracked leather cover and no markings. She gently took the book out and set it on the table for Hester.

"Ah, this one is a work of art," Ms. Lopes said lovingly. "It's the quirkiest manuscript we own. The person who wrote it was passionate about fantasy." She opened randomly to the middle of the book. The page was crammed with old-fashioned handwriting and sketches of what looked to be porpoise or dolphin tails, but with rough scales.

"See how this page is worked corner to corner, edge to edge, almost obsessively?" She turned the page. "And then, for no apparent reason the very next page is entirely empty. The author actually trails off in mid-sentence. Look . . ." She chose another section of the book. "Inexplicably blank pages, followed by overfilled pages! He had an unusual mind, this one."

"How do you know that E. A. Doyle wasn't a woman?"

"I was just assuming, because it's from 1872. We're understaffed here, and our handwritten manuscripts haven't all been fully cataloged yet, but I can look to see what further information we have about it while you're reading, if you'd like."

"That's not necessary, thanks." Hester sat in the chair and reached for the book, but then stopped. "Don't I need to put on white gloves or something?"

"Only in the movies," Ms. Lopes clucked. "Cotton gloves actually damage rare manuscripts more, because they make your fingers clumsy and dull while you're turning the brittle pages. A good hand-washing is all we require."

And with that, Ms. Lopes left the room.

Hester turned the pages slowly, straining to read the old penmanship, marveling at the drawings. There were pages and pages of the most beautiful sketches she had ever seen. Most were of fantastic sea creatures—all women, all drawn with pale hair and clear eyes. There was tightly spaced scientific text about the structure of the fins, the color and thickness of the scales—which E. A. Doyle called "scutes"—and the shape of the teeth. There were lists of food sources and diagrams of their varieties and locations. There were complicated historical accounts of tribal wars that had killed the males of the species. The journal was unique and wonderful—and irresistibly passionate.

She came upon the page with the tail sketches that Ms. Lopes had initially opened to and turned the page. There was a magnificent portrait of the face of one of the sea creatures. Hester looked into her eyes as if the creature were staring back. She was lovely, and intense. Hester examined every facet of her face, and then she snapped to.

"Wait," she said out loud. The page after the tail sketches had been blank before, hadn't it? There had been no portrait.

She turned back to the tail page, to make sure that she hadn't mistakenly turned two pages together. She looked carefully at the edge, saw and felt that it was a single page, and turned the page back. This time she thought she saw the drawing of the face materialize, like reappearing ink. She pulled her hands away from the book in surprise, as if it had given her a shock. The portrait page went blank.

Her heart pounded. She was imagining it; she had to be. She held her breath and swallowed, trying to get a grip. She lifted the pages of the book in her right hand and gently let them fall into her left hand. The book was filled, cover to cover, with information and illustrations. *There were no blank pages.* At least not while she was touching it. It was as if some parts were only there for her to see. That is, unless she was hallucinating—which might be a more plausible explanation than "the journal is magic."

She tried to regain her composure.

This journal was special. It was meant for her.

Even as she made the decision to steal the book, she couldn't believe it. She glanced at her watch; her lunch break was running out, and Ms. Lopes would be back soon. An urgency built inside her, trampling the last bits of her conscience.

She leaned over and rifled through her messenger bag. Not

finding what she needed, she looked around the room. She scooted out of her chair and went to the open shelves behind Ms. Lopes's desk, which appeared to contain the librarian's personal books. She tried to quash the panic that was rising in her chest. The door to the Rare Manuscripts Room was mostly glass. If anyone walked by, they would see her.

She slid her hand down the row of spines until she found a book that was about the same size, shape, and weight as the journal—a hardcover version of Strunk and White's *The Elements of Style*. She plucked it off the shelf and adjusted the books next to it so that there was no gap to indicate it was missing. Then she went back to her seat, carefully put the Doyle journal in her bag, and placed *The Elements of Style* in the archival folding box. Ms. Lopes appeared beyond the glass door, chatting with another librarian. Hester's hands shook as she tied the white ribbon around the box to close it, trying to mimic the original bow as well as she could so the librarian wouldn't see a need to fix it.

Hester took a deep, cleansing breath as Ms. Lopes opened the door. She bent down to pick up her bag. She put it on her lap and clipped the buckles closed.

"Done so soon?" Ms. Lopes asked.

"Yes, thank you. It wasn't quite what I needed. For my research I need to find something that documents the history of these sorts of sea-creature legends." She picked up the manuscript box, hoping that if she referred to it as if the book were inside, Ms. Lopes would subliminally believe that it was. "This is more of a fantasy diary, I'd say."

Ms. Lopes took it from her. "I agree, it's not historical, other than being old." She began to straighten the bow.

Hester slung her bag over her shoulder and said, "I've got to run. Thank you so much for helping me today."

"You're welcome . . ." Ms. Lopes said. "It's Esther, isn't it?"

"That's right," Hester lied. "Esther . . ." She reached for the first name that popped into her head, ". . . Angeln." She clenched her jaw. Why couldn't she have said Brown, or Davis, or some other completely ubiquitous name?

She forced a cheerful smile. "Well, thanks again!" She opened the door, clutching the bag and its treasure against her hip, walking too quickly, but being too frightened to slow down or turn to see if she was being followed.

Chapter 24
1873

THE OLD PASTOR NEEDED absolute proof that Sarah was possessed before he would speak of performing an exorcism.

Eleanor Ontstaan had already devised a plan.

"Sarah and Ezra are inseparable," she pointed out. "We must remove Ezra from the scene, or he will interfere."

"He's en church alone on Sunday . . ."

"That's a week from now, Pastor. Here is what I propose for a more immediate solution: you must think of a project that requires Ezra's help—he is bookish, it should be simple—and take him to the White Horse Pub to discuss it with him tomorrow night."

"I *am* workin' on a translation of a par-ticularly arduous La'in text . . ."

"Fine. Perfect. I only ask that you make it believable. While you and Ezra are at the White Horse, my sister's child Adeline will tell Sarah that he has suddenly taken ill. She'll take Sarah to the church by the back door."

"Ah, bu' Ezra may already have told Sarah tha' we're a' the pub . . ."

"Very astute," Eleanor said. "Which is why you must ask Ezra to meet you at the church, but divert him to the pub when he arrives. That should be effortless for you," she said pointedly.

He pinched his lips together.

She went on. "Do you know the two large sarcophagi that are in the crypt?"

"Reverend Robinson's an' Elder Brewster's, aye."

"The lid is off Reverend Robinson's sarcophagus. I shall fill it with water, so that you may see Sarah breathe underwater."

The pastor was silent.

"You will bid goodbye to Ezra at an appointed time and hurry back to the crypt for the test of water."

He shook his head solemnly. "Ef wha' you say es no' the truth—ef she cannae breathe underwater—this test es too dangerous."

"Not at all. We shall have complete control. The moment she appears to be in distress, we shall let her up, and a burden will be lifted from our conscience—she will be exonerated. That is the happiest of outcomes."

"She'll be destressed from the instan' she feels trapped with us en the crypt . . ."

"Come now, you understand my meaning, Pastor." She smiled patiently. "We will safeguard her life, of course. Our goal is to *save* her soul, remember."

The next evening, little Adeline dutifully knocked on the Doyles' door, wearing her best Sunday dress—plum-colored, with a square collar, a drop waist, and a wide white sash tied in a large bow in the back. Her fair hair was curled into corkscrew ringlets. The housekeeper answered.

"My name is Adeline Angeln," she said, clutching her doll. "May I speak with Mrs. Doyle?"

"Mrs. Doyle is reading in the study and not receiving visitors," the housekeeper said. "May I give her a message?"

Adeline shook her head, confused. "I'm supposed to ask for Mrs. Doyle."

"Step inside, please, miss."

The housekeeper disappeared down the corridor.

Sarah came into the foyer a minute later carrying a book in one hand with her index finger holding her place, wearing a lightweight dressing gown over a layered dress. Adeline took a breath when she saw her: she was the palest, most graceful woman she had ever seen.

"Mrs. Doyle?"

"Yes?"

"I'm Adeline Angeln, Mrs. Doyle."

"How do you do, Adeline?"

"Very well, I thank you." She paused, mesmerized.

"May I help you with something?" Sarah prompted gently.

Adeline blinked. "Yes," she said. "That is, she sent me to tell you . . ." she began to recite, "that *Mr.* Doyle has taken ill, and I'm to take you to the *church*. By the *back* way. Because . . . because it's *closer* to him."

Sarah had already set down her book and was quickly removing her dressing gown. Adeline stared at the dress that was beneath it: a simple off-white gown, with a diaphanous cape from her shoulders to her feet and an overskirt embroidered with faint flowers.

"Mrs. Banks!" Sarah cried. "Will you bring me my summer jacket?" She turned back to the little girl. "How ill is he, Adeline? What's wrong?"

"I don't know; she said to say he was ill."

"Who is *she*, Adeline? Who sent you?" Sarah slipped into the jacket but pushed a delicate bonnet with feathers and silk ties back at Mrs. Banks, refusing it.

"My auntie," Adeline said in a low voice.

Sarah bent down to look her in the eyes. "Mrs. Banks has some lovely cake and fresh milk. Stay here with her, and I'll send your auntie for you as soon as I get there."

"Please, Mrs. Doyle, *I'm* supposed to take you. She made me memorize her instructions, and my auntie is . . ." She hesitated, her brow furrowed. "She's awfully particular."

Sarah stood up again, hesitating. "It's more than a mile and a half down Court Street."

"My father says I'm a strong walker," Adeline said.

"Very well." She turned Adeline toward the door and marched her out. "But as quickly as you can, do you understand? I want to ring Dr. Stephens's bell on the way."

"Oh, no!" Adeline said, as they hustled down the street. "I'm not supposed to bring the doctor, just you."

"What do you mean?"

Adeline was flustered. "He's . . . Mr. Doyle is only a *little* ill. He'll be well soon, I promise! He needs you, that's all."

"You said you did not know how ill he is," Sarah reminded her, several steps ahead of her.

"I meant . . . I didn't know *what* was wrong with him, but he's not terribly ill, not ill enough for a doctor."

"I think it's safest if we pass by Dr. Stephens's home."

They turned the corner and Sarah ran the last block, leaving Adeline behind.

"Please, Mrs. Doyle, please don't bring the doctor," Adeline called out to her. She dropped her doll as she hustled along out of breath and went back to retrieve it. She dusted the doll off and straightened her satin bows.

When she turned around again, she saw that Mrs. Doyle was knocking on the doctor's front door. To Adeline's great relief, after several knocks there was no response. She wedged the doll securely under her arm and ran to catch up.

There was a slip of paper tacked to the Stephenses' door. Sarah turned to Adeline with her brow furrowed.

"He's delivering Becca Howe's baby down at the Howes' cranberry bog. He's miles away. How fast can you run, Adeline? Let's run to the church. Quick as you can."

When they arrived at the back door of the church, the old pastor was waiting for them. He beckoned to Sarah to enter. Adeline waited outside.

"Where is he?" Sarah said. "Where is Ezra?"

"Everything es fine, Mrs. Doyle, have no fear," the old man said, taking her hand in his and patting it.

"The little girl—Adeline—she said he was ill. Where *is* he, Pastor?"

"Come with me, I have somethen' to show you."

Outside in the graveyard, Eleanor emerged from her hiding place behind the row of tombs as soon as she saw Sarah enter the church. She was carrying Marijn.

Adeline blurted, out of breath, "There you are, Aunt Ellie!"

"Shhh," Eleanor hissed. She approached Adeline, walking softly and cradling the baby against her breast.

"Now take baby Marijn, Adeline," she whispered, "and tend to her until I return. I won't be long. Be very careful with her." She held the baby out.

Adeline looked down at the doll in her arms. "But what shall I do with Poppet?"

Eleanor's eyes pierced the girl like darts. "Put Poppet down and give your full attention to this child, do you understand? I haven't the time for argument, I must . . ." She clenched her jaw. "Help the old pastor."

"But I can't put Poppet on the ground, Aunt Ellie, she'll get dirty."

"Set her on a headstone, then, *right now*. And hurry," she warned. "I'm losing patience."

"Yes, Aunt Ellie," Adeline said, avoiding Eleanor's eyes.

Adeline went to the nearest tombstone and brushed dirt and dust off the top. She tried to balance Poppet in a seated position, but every time she released her, the doll would begin to tip backward or forward.

Before Adeline knew what was happening, Eleanor was upon her.

"Stupid girl!" she said, grabbing Poppet from the headstone and throwing her to the ground several feet away. Adeline gasped and moved to retrieve the doll.

"Leave it," Eleanor said through her teeth. Adeline froze in place and looked at her aunt. One small shoe had come off in Eleanor's hand, and she pitched it after the doll, with her eyes locked on Adeline. She held Marijn out, and Adeline accepted her with tears welling in her lower lids.

"This is a living, breathing child, not a worthless doll, do you understand?"

"Yes, Aunt Ellie." Adeline's voice quavered. The baby was heavy.

"Nothing will happen to this baby while I am in the church."

"No, Aunt Ellie."

"You will protect her with your life, is that clear?"

"I will, Aunt Ellie, I promise."

"If I return to find that your precious Poppet has moved even so much as a hair from that spot, I'll *tear her apart*."

Adeline looked at the doll, facedown in the dust, her curls spilling everywhere and a leg twisted under her body, and nodded, because her throat was suddenly too hot and swollen to speak.

Eleanor stormed into the church to set the world right again after Olaf's death.

Chapter 25

HESTER HURRIED through the library parking lot with her entire body trembling. She had never stolen anything before, or told such a bald-faced lie. What had come over her? She rummaged through her pocket for the car keys, and a slip of paper fell out. She picked it up and quickly let herself into the car. She put her head on the steering wheel and took a deep breath. No librarians were coming out of the building searching for her, no police cars were swooping into the lot. She unfolded the slip of paper in her hand. It was her hand-drawn map of the locations of the graves of Nellie Burroughs and Grace Keep. She wanted to see the graves, which she had probably passed a hundred times as a child playing with Linnie. And after that, she needed to see Ezra.

She went back to Plimoth Plantation and finished her shift halfheartedly. She was in the parking lot six minutes after the all clear.

On the way to the cemetery, she bought three small potted violets at a florist shop. She parked in the lot on the west side of the hill. She walked up the concrete steps and headed toward the obelisk commemorating William Bradford. Nellie's grave was southwest of it. The headstone was made of limestone, a material that was cheaper to engrave and install than blue slate, but weathered more quickly. It was difficult to read.

NELLIE BURROUGHS

1892–1916

Come view the scene twill fill you with surprise

Behold the loveliest form in nature dies

At noon she flourish'd blooming fair and gay

At evening an extended corpse she lay

Hester kissed her fingers and pressed them to Nellie's name. She bent down and pulled the grass and weeds away from the base of the stone and left a pot of violets. She stood up and looked around, trying to be the eyes and ears of the woman in the grave who was long gone. She took a deep breath of ocean air, for Nellie. Then she went off in the direction of John Howland's grave, to find Grace's grave east of it.

GRACE KEEP (NEE Burroughs)

Mar. 31, 1916–Oct. 6, 1941

Green as the bay tree, ever green,

With its new foliage on.

The young, the healthful have I seen,

I passed, and they were gone

Her throat tightened with the beginning of tears, but she swallowed the feeling away. Again she tended to the weeds at the base of the stone and left the second pot of violets. Then she took her last pot of violets up the hill to the Crotty headstone—Bartholomew and his two wives. She stood looking at Marijn's short epitaph and involuntarily reached up to touch her necklace—the necklace that Marijn had worn around her own warm neck more than a hundred years ago. How strange the world was, that a necklace should exist virtually forever, and a human life, worth so much more, should be short.

As she sat on the bench under the tree to rest, she lifted the messenger bag off her shoulder. She looked carefully around her. No one was in the cemetery, so she opened the buckles on her bag and slipped the journal out to read it. She was gentle—the least she could do after stealing the book was to take good care of it.

She admired the leather cover, opened the pages, and put her nose carefully inside to take a deep breath of the rag paper. Honestly, it felt like it was her book, like she had owned it her whole life. *What is wrong with me lately?* she wondered. She let the pages fall to a random spot and began reading. It was a passage about Squauanit—the oldest of the surviving sea folk and, after tens of thousands of years, a hideous sea monster. Despite her appearance, Squauanit was vain. She was also overbearingly selfish and possessive. The illustration of her was vague and shadowy, with smudges for eyes and only her thinning, stringy long hair drawn in detail, trailing the length of a hazy, doughy body.

"What's that you have there?" a high voice asked behind her.

Hester twisted in her seat to see a little girl looking at the journal over her shoulder. She had blond curls and was wearing a plum-colored dress with a white sash.

"I haven't seen a *single* book since you left," the girl said, frowning. "And that one has pictures. May I borrow it?"

Hester's mouth hung open. A strangled moan escaped her involuntarily and then, suddenly, she felt sick. The girl had not aged a single day after ten years.

"Linnie . . ." Hester stood up, knocking her bag onto the ground but still clutching the journal.

And then she did throw up. Or rather she heaved, right on the grass to her side, and nothing came out but a thick strand of saliva. She coughed and spit the saliva onto the ground.

"Linnie," she said, wiping her mouth on her sleeve. "*Linnie!*" she choked.

"Are you okay?"

Hester shook her head emphatically no. And with her second heave, she vomited the sparse remains of her lunch. "I'm sorry," she gasped when she was finished. "That was gross." And then she wondered why she was apologizing, and said more accusingly, "Why . . . *how* . . ."

"What's wrong, Hester? Are you ill?"

"How are you . . ." She paused, suppressing another heave.

"Very well, I thank you," Linnie said politely.

"No! I mean, how are you . . . just standing there? Look at you!"

Linnie looked down at herself and bent to pick a speck of non-existent lint off her sagging cotton stockings.

"You . . . you haven't changed a bit, Lin. Now look at *me*," Hester said.

Linnie looked straight at her, or rather into her if that were possible. "You look the same as ever, Hester." She cocked her head to the side. "It's been awfully dull here without you. Why haven't you visited me?"

"I *grew up*," Hester said. She held her forehead. "What's going on?"

"You're the only child who's ever heard me. I wish you'd come visit me again." Linnie frowned, and her eyes grew dark. "Why do you want to be with Ezra more than with me?"

Hester was too shocked to reply. Her mouth fell open again.

Linnie pointed past her at the church down the hill and stamped her foot. "And now Pastor McKee is calling for you, and I *still* won't get my turn."

Hester spun around to look at the church, but it was shadowed and quiet.

She turned back. The little girl was gone.

Chapter 26
1873

As THEY DESCENDED THE STAIRS to the crypt, Sarah became increasingly alarmed.

"Is Ezra down here, or is he not, Pastor? I demand to know!"

"I'm so sorry, Mrs. Doyle. Everything well be clear when we've had a chance to talk. Hurry now, thar's no time t' lose."

When she got to the bottom of the stairs, she looked quickly around and said, "I don't see him. He's not here. You've lied to me!" She grabbed the old pastor by the arms; she was strong for a woman. He felt her fingers press painfully into his shoulders. "I don't know what your motives are, but I am leaving to find Ezra, and if I discover that he is ill or injured . . ."

"Please, you're haerting me," the pastor said. "I mus' speak with you priva'ely."

Sarah dropped her hands. "Why should I listen, when you tricked me here?"

"Do you know about the sarcophagi?" He was speaking quickly, rushing, for reasons Sarah couldn't guess.

It was a word Sarah had never heard. "No, I . . ."

"The stone coffins, jus' there. They're empty, the two of them. Well, usually they're empty. A' the moment, the one on the righ' contains a fair amount of wa'er. Now dinnae be alarmed, because

I know et sounds daft, an' I'll be happy to explain la'er, bu' if I could ask you to get enside tha' one . . . ef you please." He tried to lead her over by the elbow.

"I will not! What has come over you, Pastor? I beg you, release my arm. You have no idea how strong I am—please, I don't want to hurt you."

"Thar's been an accusation against you," he said, still rushing, still tugging. "Ef I can please get you wet, Mrs. Doyle, before she arrives, I shall paersuade your accuser tha' I've tested you, and you're not possessed by a sea daemon. And then she'll stop petitioning for an exorcesm, and we shall all return to our quiet lives . . ."

Sarah wrenched her arm away. The poor man had pink-edged eyelids, and such a drawn face.

"Exorcism? Get me wet? *Test* me? You're speaking like a madman, Pastor. You're not well. I shall send someone down to help you, but I'm leaving."

"I assure you, I'm paerfectly well. Please trust me, Sarah." He looked into her eyes, and she saw that he was earnest, almost desperate. He lowered his voice and strained to speak coherently. "Thar es a parishioner who believes tha' you cavort with sea folk— tha' you breathe underwa'er, an' speak en tongues. She *willnae* be dissuaded, Mrs. Doyle. I've though' long an' hard about et, an' this es the only way. Ef I can make haer believe I have tested you and proved tha' you cannae breathe en wa'er, she shall leave you be, I shall continue to live at the rectory in peaceful retirement, an' the ma'ter shall be closed."

"The matter shall be closed before it opens."

"Ef I donnae make haer believe I've done et, she'll report me to the elders."

"I'm sorry for you, Pastor, I truly am. But I must find Ezra." She turned toward the stairs.

He caught her arm and said gravely, "Sarah, I have seen you emaerging from the bay."

She stopped and searched his eyes, trying to read his meaning.

"An' I have seen a siren in the same hour, under the wa'er, near the rocky outcropping—a most mestifying, engrossing creature." His eyes welled. "Ef your accuser goes to the elders, and ef the elders ask me, I shall have t' tell them what I saw. I am an old man, Sarah. I have no family here, and none left en Tain. Where would I live?"

Sarah stood frozen, unable to decide what to do. She felt a tingle of warning all through her body. She needed to think clearly, to stay safe, but her mind could not retreat from her protective worry: where was Ezra?

"Please," he said. "Submaerge yourself en the wa'er. Jus' give yourself a good soaking, leave puddles on the floor, an' I shall tell haer she was wrong. She'll be on haer way now; thar's so li'tle time. We could be done already."

"Who," Sarah asked firmly, "*who* is on her way?"

"Please, ge' in the wa'er. I beg you t' trust me. Let me end this nonsense."

Sarah looked at the sarcophagus. What he was asking was simple enough: for her to step in, submerge herself, and get out, and he would conceal what he suspected. She walked over to it warily and looked at the water.

"Where is Ezra?"

"He's no doubt home by now. He's well, I promise you. We shared a pint together a' the White Horse. I ded trick you here, an' for tha' I offer my profound apology." He glanced at the stairs, anticipating something, and looked imploringly back at her.

In and out. She could go home to Ezra, and keep her secret.

She took her jacket and shoes off.

"Yes, hurry," he said. He checked over his shoulder again.

She lifted her leg, put her foot in the water, and then paused.

"Who is my accuser?"

"Thar's no time. After! *Please.*"

She climbed up and in. She sat down, sank backward, and went completely under. She kept her eyes open and warily fixed on him the entire time, even through the water. She arched her back and came up face-first. She repeated, "Who is my accuser?"

"Et's the widow, Eleanor Ontstaan," he said, putting his arms out to help her. "Come quickly."

But he needn't have said it, because she could see past his shoulder that a woman was behind him, walking purposefully toward the sarcophagus. Her graying blond hair was coming loose from a bun, fanning out in strawlike wisps. She held her right arm behind her back. Her eyes were trained on Sarah. Something about her name was familiar.

The pastor turned. "Mrs. Ontstaan! I have paerformed the test . . ."

"You have not, Pastor. You're weak and cowardly, and you've failed us all. You're deliberately protecting a monster—a killer!—which goes against God. She cannot live among us."

A primal sense of danger swelled in Sarah's core as Eleanor dropped her right arm and rushed the coffin. There was a knife in her hand.

The widow, Eleanor Ontstaan. The *widow*. There was almost no time for Sarah to process what she knew must be true: it was the wife of the fisherman she had killed. She tried to leap out of the sarcophagus, but the layers of her dress along with her petticoat were unexpectedly heavy and slowed her. The pastor had only time to lift his hands in surprise before Eleanor was upon Sarah, slashing the knife at her, hitting mostly air as Sarah pulled away again and again with quick reflexes.

Eleanor caught the dress with the knife on one pass, barely missing Sarah's skin and entangling the knife in the sleeve. Sarah seized her wrist, and the pastor heard the crackle of bones as the knife fell from Eleanor's hand, clattering on the floor at his feet. Eleanor released a guttural, horrifying scream of pain. Sarah pulled Eleanor into the sarcophagus with her, falling backward, with Eleanor on top.

"You monster!" Eleanor screamed, pushing Sarah's face down with her uninjured left hand, trying to slam her head against the stone bottom. "You murdered Olaf!"

The two women grappled as the waves sloshed back and forth, spilling water out of the sarcophagus. Sarah grabbed Eleanor in a bear hug, and half rolled, half flipped her so that Eleanor was suddenly on the bottom, completely submerged, with wide eyes and puffed cheeks. Eleanor reached her left hand up, groping for Sarah's face.

The pastor tried to pull Sarah off Eleanor, but he was frail and old, and she was enraged and powerful. How long could Eleanor hold her breath? he wondered. He beat on Sarah's back—useless, flailing blows. "God, help me!" he shouted, anguished by his own impotence.

Eleanor's left index finger found Sarah's right eye and hooked itself in the socket. Sarah roared with pain and pushed her down so violently that Eleanor's hand was wrenched away. Eleanor writhed to push Sarah off her. The longer she was under, the more her thrashing became panicked and inefficient.

Eleanor's struggles weakened, and the bubbles no longer escaped her mouth and nose, but Sarah continued to hold her under, her arm muscles pulsating with effort.

"Le' her up, Sarah!" the pastor shouted. "Faith, you're kellin' her!"

He looked frantically around for some way to save Eleanor. He bent to the floor, picked up the knife, and did something that went against everything he believed in. He lifted the knife, clamped his eyes shut, and stabbed at Sarah.

Chapter 27

L INNIE?" HESTER SAID, her voice cracking. She scanned the graveyard, but there was no sign of the little girl. She picked up her bag and carefully put the journal inside. When she glanced up at the church, Pastor McKee was at the door, gesturing eagerly for her to come to him.

She looked back at the tombstones uncertainly, one more time, for her childhood friend. The evening sun bathed them in a pink light. The wind was calm. Linnie had said the old minister was looking for her. How had she known?

"I've been waitin' for you," he called impatiently as she finally approached him.

"Did you see that little gi—?"

"Please, come enside. Come enside!" he interrupted, scooping his hand toward himself again and again as if he could draw her in with the breeze he was generating.

The air was cool and damp as they descended the stairs to the crypt. There were two chairs facing each other this time. The old man must have brought out another for her. He eased himself into one and motioned to the other.

"Set, set!" He was out of breath.

"You'd better rest a minute, Pastor." Hester put her bag on

the earthen floor. She brushed dust off the caned seat as best she could. "You need to catch your breath."

"Na, et makes no defference, I'm always exactly the same. Tha's my problem."

She sat down. "The little girl—did you see her?"

Pastor McKee stared at her, considering his answer.

"Either you saw her or not." Hester laughed nervously.

"I ded. Haer name es Adeline."

"Adeline?" Hester repeated. "Her name is Linnie."

"I believe Linnie es the familiar form of Adeline."

"Did you notice anything unusual about her? Because . . . because she's not what she seems! I knew her ten years ago."

"Aye."

"And in ten years she hasn't aged a day!" She rubbed her eyes with the heels of both hands. "I know it sounds crazy, but she can't be a little girl. She can't be human. She's . . . she's an alien . . . or a . . ."

"An apparition."

Hester dropped her hands. He was nodding slowly.

"You don't think I'm crazy, then?" Her eyes opened wide. "Holy sh— you mean, *she* could be the ghost that's haunting the church? But no, she can't be a ghost . . ." Her mind raced.

"Listen, Pastor." She crossed her arms, suddenly feeling a chill. "She's *real*. I've played with her, I've touched her skin, and her dress. I've made her laugh." She thought of Linnie's lost doll that first day. "And cry."

He edged forward on his seat, intent on the conversation. "I've seen Adeline on the hill for ages. Far longer than you've known haer. Poor li'tle thing. She's harmless. No' an angry spirit, but en such pain."

"Pain?"

"Och! She was wee and innocen' when she died. I'm deeply troubled about the child tha' haer ghost represents. The u'ter loneliness and confusion of bein' a spirit is no' somethen' a youngster should have to endure. Et's a tragedy." He looked into her eyes. "I've long prayed someone would finally come along who could help haer."

Hester was silent for a moment, at a loss. She couldn't believe they were talking so matter-of-factly about a ghost. She warmed her hands by rubbing them together and then folded them on her lap.

"Why doesn't anyone else know about her? I mean, not just about the silverfish and the host and the stained glass. Why doesn't anyone know *her*? Why isn't she . . . famous?"

"Do you truly want to know?"

"Of course."

"Et may come as a shock."

"Tell me."

"No one else can see haer, Hester. Or hear haer. Or touch haer. Tha's wha' I meant about the loneliness and confusion she's been forced to endure."

"What are you talking about? Are you saying that you and I share a gift or something—the ability to see ghosts?"

He reached for her. His cool fingers touched her cheek affectionately, briefly.

"I'd say et was more of a caerse tha' we share, lass."

A curse. She narrowed her eyes at him.

"What made you use the word 'curse'?" It was eerie to hear the word twice in two days.

He smiled and tipped his head down, looking up eagerly through his bushy eyebrows. "Seeing ghosts is unusual—do you no' agree et must happen for a reason?" He lifted his crooked index finger. "Caerses can be lefted. Nothing es empossible. I can help you. The fact tha' you can see Adeline means you can help haer. And help *yerself.*" He sat back in the chair.

Hester bit her lip. Help herself? What was that supposed to mean?

He was studying her, letting her process what he had said. It occurred to her that his patience smacked of knowing more than he let on. She frowned.

"What are you getting at?" she said.

"I know I can help you. Bu', Hester." He paused. He looked at the floor and raised his fist to his lips, thinking. He muttered to himself: "I dinnae know how to say this withou' riskin' everything."

He sat up as straight as his bent back would allow and took a deep breath. "An' so I'll just say et outright, an' pray I'll not bollix et.

"Hester, you mus' trust *me alone,* an' stay away from the beach."

Hester's eyes widened.

"Et's no' good for you to go there, although I know the force drawin' you es powerfully hard to resest, truly I do. Och, you mus' trust me—he well no' further your efforts to left the caerse, he well disastrously *emperil* them."

Hester stood up. "I don't know what you're talking about."

"Aye, lass, y'do."

There was a deep rumble of thunder. She picked up her bag.

"I have to go."

He struggled to stand. She couldn't bring herself to help him, though she knew she should.

When he was upright he said, "D'ye hear tha'? The sea es angry, an' storming. She's restless. She senses change. Bu' I willnae stop. I cannae. You're our hope. At long last. You're here."

"Honestly, you're just babbling."

"Stay away from him, Hester. Promise me."

"I won't promise that."

"Please." He was pleading now. "Dinnae go to the beach. Rely on *me*. Et's no' just you who well be haert. Adeline well be haert—forever. Thenk of Linnie."

A crack of thunder.

"This is ridiculous." She raised her voice, surprising herself with her sudden rage. "You're . . . you're a nutty old man who believes in ghosts! You can't tell me what to do—I'll go where I please. The beach has nothing to do with Linnie. It has nothing to do with anything!"

He touched her arm with affection, apparently impervious to her insults.

"Everything es entertwined, lamb."

She ripped her arm away and ran up the stairs, out of the crypt. Heavy raindrops were already spattering the windows of the first floor.

Chapter 28

1873

Ezra returned home from the pub after a puzzlingly hasty departure on the part of the retired pastor. Poor old man, he was certainly suffering the beginnings of dementia in his advanced age. The house was quiet and smelled like roasting chicken and potato spice cake. Ezra took a deep breath. He hung up his jacket and his hat on the stand by the door.

"Sarah?" he called. He went into the library to find her. The fire had died to orange embers. His journal was on the table by the upholstered chair, stacked on top of Sarah's most recent conquest, *Jane Eyre*. He picked the journal up and flipped through it. Many of the pages were blank. He smiled. Weeks ago his wife had solved the problem of how to hide the book in plain sight, and her sea companions had helped effect the plan with their unfathomable powers: Sarah was able to enjoy the book in its entirety, which she often did, but no one else could.

He went to the base of the stairs and called up, "Sarah?"

Mrs. Banks appeared at the top of the flight with sheets folded over her forearm. "Mr. Doyle, sir! Bless my soul, you're well, thank heaven."

"Of course I'm well, Annie. Where is Sarah?"

"Why, she's gone to the church, at least half an hour ago, maybe more—to look for you."

He frowned. "We moved on to the pub."

He bolted out of sight as Mrs. Banks called out, "Someone sent a little girl saying you'd taken ill at the church—" She heard the door slam shut on the word "church."

Ezra took loping strides with his long legs and reached Town Square in sixteen minutes. As he approached the church, a reflexive cry escaped from deep within him. He could hear a man screaming—desperate, bursting screams, like a confused, trapped animal.

He pulled the left handle of the front door of the church, but it was locked. As he tugged uselessly on the right handle, he heard a woman scream.

He ran around to the back, his heart hammering in his chest, his breath rapid, his hair clinging to the sweat on his scalp. From the corner of his eye he glimpsed a little girl huddled in the dark, among the gravestones, clutching a wad of blanket and sobbing at the sounds coming from inside the church.

"Oh, sir!" he heard her say.

Mrs. Banks's words rang in the background of his mind: "A little girl said you were ill."

He ignored the girl and flung the door open. The light flooded out, and he heard the man scream again, muffled but with discernible words this time. "You're kellin' her!" It was coming from the crypt.

He leaped down the stairs three at a time, and the situation unfolded before him as he did. Sarah was on her knees in a sarcophagus, drenched in water and blood, and Michael McKee—the very man whose health he had toasted one hour ago—had a bloody knife in his hand.

Ezra ran at full speed, grabbed the pastor's collar, and wrenched him away from his wife. The old man toppled backward to the floor. Sarah looked at Ezra, and in the span of only a second her eyes showed concern—for herself, for him—and then a primal resignation before she collapsed into the water, face-first. Ezra reached for her. Now the sarcophagus appeared to be filled solely with blood—so thick and opaque that he couldn't identify the body beneath his wife—and he instantly saw why. One of the old man's blows had pierced Sarah's neck. Her carotid artery was gushing. It was a catastrophic injury.

"No!" he shouted, pushing his fingers into the wound, trying to stanch the flow of blood. The blood continued to gush, covering his hand and trickling down his wrist to his elbow. He struggled to turn her on her side. Her skin was no longer pale, it was gray. She was not breathing. The flood of crimson pulsing from her neck slowed as her blood volume dropped and her heart failed. He put his mouth on hers. He blew air into her lungs.

The old man climbed to his feet and reeled toward the sarcophagus, weeping uncontrollably.

"She drowned Mrs. Ontstaan," he said, gasping between sobs.

Ezra blew into Sarah's mouth frantically, knowing it was hopeless, but unwilling to admit it to himself. If he stopped breathing for her, he would have to begin life without her.

"I tried to stop haer . . . I didnae wan' to haert haer!" The pastor looked at the weapon in his hand.

"This is no' my knife! Wha' have I done?"

Ezra pulled away from Sarah. Her lids were closed and her face was composed. She looked peaceful in death.

In death.

He turned on McKee then. His eyes were wild.

He grabbed the pastor around the neck and shook his head forward and back, squeezing as he did. The old man's face turned deep pink. A gurgling sound escaped his mouth. His eyes bulged. Ezra's hands fit around the pastor's throat with fingertips overlapping, his neck was so thin. That frail body—all bones and skin and cloth—seemed to melt beneath him, and he found he was holding up the old man's full weight of what could not be more than one hundred thirty pounds. It was grotesque that this wispy nothing of a being had taken Sarah off this earth; McKee was pitiful. Now Ezra's eyes were shadowed with torment. He must loosen his grip before the old man lost consciousness. He must do it now, or there would be no turning back.

But it was too late for mercy. The knife that was in the pastor's hand sank deep into the left side of Ezra's chest.

It was pressure Ezra felt first, not pain. He looked down at the bizarre sight of the handle sticking out of his body.

His thumbs were over the pastor's Adam's apple. He pressed hard and felt it dislocate and then fracture. He crushed the windpipe against the vertebrae. And then he dropped him. McKee fell to the ground, purple-faced, with a high-pitched noise coming from his throat as he tried in vain to breathe. He was suffocating.

Ezra bellowed with grief. Sarah was dead.

The old man was dying.

And now he was dying, too.

The knife burned in him, and he felt an ominous weight on his chest, but very little blood escaped from the wound. He wanted to pull the knife out, but his instinct told him it was sealing the wound and holding him in a fleeting stasis.

There wasn't much time.

He thought quickly. He would not be able to carry Sarah in front of him without disturbing the knife, perhaps hastening his death. He turned his back to the coffin and lifted her right arm over his left shoulder, leaving her left arm dangling. He looped his right arm between her legs and lifted her so that her torso draped across his shoulders. Her body was still warm. Her face rested heavily against his left upper arm, as if she were asleep.

His heart ached at the sight.

He carried her up the stairs and out the back door, with tears and sweat blinding him.

"Oh! Poor Mrs. Doyle! Whatever is happening?" It was the voice of the little girl, somewhere at his feet. As he passed her, she followed after him and the toe of her boot stepped on the back of his shoe. His foot levered out of the shoe and he stumbled, nearly falling forward from the precious weight on his shoulders. A searing pain shot through his chest. He felt dizzy. His eyesight went black for a moment.

"Please help me, sir," the little girl said. "I want to go home. I want my mum."

He righted himself and took the time to slide out of his other shoe to even his gait. He was becoming alarmingly short of breath. This delay might cost him what little hope he had.

The little girl had circled around him and stood in front of him. Her eyes were puffed and red from crying. He saw that a baby was wrapped in the blanket in her arms.

"Out of my way!" he sputtered.

"But, sir, she's so *heavy*."

He was light-headed. His legs were trembling. He tried to skirt around her, but she sidestepped in front of him.

"*Get out of my way!*"

"I won't," Adeline said, stamping a foot, summoning disobedience from her fear. "I don't know what to do with the baby!"

"I can't help you!" he shouted, and he let Sarah's right arm loose for a second as he shoved the little girl aside. He gasped with the pain of it, and began his march down Leyden Street to the ocean.

But Adeline was small for her age, and the baby was heavy. The shove sent her flying. She staggered sideways, with each step missing its foothold, picking up momentum until she knew that she'd fall against a tombstone, with the baby's fragile head to hit first. Instinctively, she twisted her torso in mid-fall and squeezed the child against her. As a result, the back of her own head slammed onto the sharp edge of a new granite gravestone. Her scalp split, her skull cracked. Her body crumpled, limp. As she slid to the ground, her head left a streak of blood down the epitaph on the front of the stone:

> Remember me as you pass by,
> As you are now so once was I;
> As I am now so you must be,
> Prepare for death to follow me

The baby had landed safely on her stomach and began to wail.

Chapter 29

HESTER LEFT FOR WORK the next morning with a confusing, crushing urge to drop everything and run to the beach. She almost couldn't bear it when she remembered that it was the Fourth of July—one of the busiest tourist days at the village—and truancy was not an option.

She soon found that the only way she could concentrate on her job was to overburden herself. In a single day she did the chores that the curator had told her to nurse over the course of the week: she weeded the Howland vegetable garden, she picked medicinal herbs and tied them with twine for drying, she made a root stew for dinner, she mended the canopy of the bed, she beat the rugs, and then, having no assigned tasks remaining, she borrowed a hammer and nails from the men who were thatching Governor Bradford's house to repair a broken footstool.

She was pounding a nail into the hard wood when her co-worker Betsy walked up, carrying a bucket of water from the stream. A young family had gathered, watching Hester, but they were too shy to ask questions, which suited her mood fine. It violated her training not to volunteer conversation in that circumstance, but she didn't care—the rhythmic thumping of the hammer soothed her.

"How now, Elizabeth," Betsy called over the noise.

"What cheer, Priscilla." She set down the hammer reluctantly.

"Excuse me," the father said, emboldened now that they were speaking. "Would a woman be doing this sort of work?—I mean, during that time. Your time, that is, in 1627?"

"I do all that is required to keep my house and my family, sir, all that God gives me the strength to complete," Hester said. She motioned to the fire pit. "My husband's pottage is well boiling, is it not? The house is goodly swept. The children are fed and weeding in the fields. Have I not completed the duties of a wife? Shall I squander the remaining daylight dreaming and sighing? For t'would be a sin against God if that be what you suggest."

"I . . . no, I . . ."

Betsy laughed to interrupt. "Pay her no mind, sir. 'Tis true that a woman's labor honors God, however t'day I daresay Goodwife Howland's industry exceeds even Divine expectation." And then she said in a hushed voice to Hester, "Methinks the fire from that industry has caused a surplus of yellow bile and made you somewhat choleric, Eliza."

"Thank 'ee for your concern, dear Priscilla. I shall endeavor to find something cold and moist to eat, so that my temperament may please you better."

Betsy said to the family, "If ye care to follow me, I am off to water and feed the goats—mayhap the children would like to help?"

"They'd love to," the mother said, glancing sideways at Hester as they left.

When their backs were turned Hester rolled her eyes and continued pounding on the nail, until with great satisfaction she tested the stool and found it to be as steady as a rock.

* * *

At the end of the day, Hester peeled off her costume, rinsed her face, and pulled on a short skirt, a long-sleeve T-shirt, and flip-flops. Peter and Sam arrived to pick her up, with Sam smiling broadly.

"Ready?" he said, getting straight to business. "We've got to get to Squant's Treasure before the fireworks crowd arrives."

On the way to the wharf, Hester felt the sensation she'd had since the night of the party, only stronger—that something was tugging at her, drawing her to the beach. The only logical explanation was that she was feeling rebellious about Pastor McKee's request for her to stay away from it. But if that were true why would the pull feel so external, not internal? Why was it so nagging, so demanding, even when she wanted to forget it?

She looked over at Peter, who was silent and seemed to be concentrating on the road. He hadn't contacted her at all in the two days since she'd sent him packing at the Plantation. This was the first time they'd seen each other since then, and the outing had been organized by Sam weeks ago.

"Mom and Dad won't let me go to the fireworks with my friends," he had said on their way home from school. "They think we'll be an unruly mob, without supervision."

"That sounds about right," Peter had said.

"Yeah, I guess so," Sam agreed, laughing. "So you and Hester have to take me."

At the time, with the three of them squashed together in the front seat of Peter's truck and the liberating thought of an impending summer break, it had seemed to Hester like a fun idea. But now all she wanted was to be alone, on the beach.

The parking lot at the wharf was already packed. Hundreds of people had set up blankets on the shore, and some of the townies had jealously marked off their territory with police-style yellow tape. Peter pulled into the only empty space in the lot, reserved for Captain Dave Boats.

Sam sighed. "It's good to know people in high places."

Hester got out of the car, stretched, and looked down the beach. The water level was high, with almost no sand showing.

"Where are we in the tide cycle, Peter?" Hester asked as nonchalantly as she could.

"This is pretty much high tide. Maybe in the next fifteen minutes it'll peak."

"So low tide will be . . ."

"A little after midnight. I think I know what you're getting at, and it's not a bad idea."

"What?" Hester said. "What am I getting at?"

"The tide will have ebbed to halfway by nine o'clock, when the fireworks start. The lawn will be full, but maybe we'll still be able to find a good spot on the beach."

"Sounds like a plan," Sam said

Hester nodded. "Yes, the beach." Her mind was clouded with that incessant calling—the distracting tugging. An image of the cave flashed in her mind. That was where she needed to go.

She suggested, "How about after supper we walk down to the picnic area past the Rock, where we had the party? We can enter the beach there."

Hester ate only a couple of her steamers and gave the rest to Sam. It was too soon to go to the beach, so they wandered over to Scooper Dooper for ice cream, where they bumped into Sam's buddies. The ice cream parlor was a zoo, with Sam's booming voice the loudest.

Hester couldn't focus on anything but the pull she felt inside. The real world had become a foggy waiting area. They were at a tiny table near the window, and all around them was standing room only. Peter sipped a soda and laughed at some of Sam's antics, but otherwise he was quiet. Hester stared out the window, vaguely aware whenever Peter was watching her. She summoned the will to smile at him a couple of times—she should make up for being so horrible at the Plantation, shouldn't she?—but each time it was an empty smile, she had nothing to say, and her eyes were drawn out the window again.

Finally she said, "Let's stroll down to the picnic area now, huh, guys?" She got up without waiting for a response and pushed her way out of the crowded shop.

Walking there was effortless, as if she had a steady wind at her back. It was the direction her body was supposed to go. It was the path of no resistance. Sam and Peter trailed behind her, even with their longer strides.

When she got to the picnic area, she threaded her way through the crowds to the top of the stone steps, where her heart sank. The sun had set and there was not yet a moon, but she could see in the remains of twilight that the beach was full of people.

"Shoot," Sam said as he caught up with her. "Everyone had the same idea."

They walked down to the beach and found a rocky, damp spot to stand. Hester crossed her arms against the chill and looked longingly in the direction of the cave. She felt a crushing sense of disappointment not to be able to just walk over there.

In the next few minutes the sky became black, with pinpricks of stars, and the crowd buzzed with anticipation. The first firework went off and lit up the sky. The crowd cheered. A little boy next to her squealed. After the second firework, Hester felt Peter's hand on her shoulder. She recoiled from his touch and nearly glared at him before she caught herself; he was only trying to get her attention.

"Some stairs are still free, let's go up there," he said over the boom of the third burst. In the next pulse of light, Hester saw he was right: many steps were empty.

She nodded in agreement. It was a better view, and what did it matter if they left the beach? She was trapped tonight anyway, playing big sister to Sam, making amends to Peter, and pretending to be a part of . . . all this.

She looked over at Sam and felt a surge of guilt. Why couldn't she just enjoy herself? Why had she allowed that nagging feeling to consume her, to the point of snapping at the people she cared about? If she was honest with herself, she knew she was aching to see Ezra again. If she was brutally honest, she knew the desire was becoming obsessive. Maybe McKee was right after all, and it would be healthier for her to avoid Ezra. She touched Sam's elbow and motioned to the steps.

The second and third stairs from the top were wide open. She and Sam sat down, and Peter stood on the stair behind them. The tugging feeling resumed in her core, and she resolved to ignore it. She wrapped her arms around her bare legs to keep warm. Peter's jacket slid onto her shoulders. She tried to concentrate on the reflection of the fireworks on the water, but the calling became painfully insistent. She closed her eyes and miserably allowed it entry. She couldn't push it away, she could only endure it. The oohs and aahs of the people began to grate on her—they were mindless cattle, standing between her and . . . and what?

She opened her eyes. "I hate tourists!" she said, too loudly.

"Tourists pay your salary." Peter laughed from above.

With the next explosion of twinkling light, something forced Hester's attention on the crowd. The biggest fireworks threw strobes of neon, nearly as bright as day. She saw upturned faces one moment. She saw men with baseball caps the next. She saw women holding toddlers pointing to the sky. Something drew her eyes to one spot. On the next burst of light she saw that it was Ezra, in the middle of the crowd.

And then it was as if everyone around him had melted away. He stood tall and lanky—so extraordinary, so singular. He had his hands in the pockets of his black pants. He was staring at her. She slowly stood up. Peter's jacket slipped off her shoulders. Through three explosions of fireworks their eyes met, down the length of an entire beach. He took his right hand out of his pocket and raised it in a simple, discouraged greeting. There was so much standing between them: Peter, Sam, and about a thousand strangers. She raised her left hand, mirroring his.

"Who do you see?" Peter asked.

She startled. She turned to look at him.

"Was it someone from school?" He picked up his jacket and held it out to her.

"No, I was mistaken." She gently pushed the jacket back at him. "I'm warm now, thanks."

The finale started. Crackling, popping, and deafening booms took the place of all other sounds in the world. There was a powerful smell of sulfur and smoke in the air. So many fireworks exploded at once that the audience was bathed in nearly constant fluorescent light. But he was gone.

Chapter 30

ON THE WAY HOME from the fireworks display, Hester's thoughts returned obstinately to the beach. The urge to go back to the cave was not just nagging now, it was consuming. As Peter's truck took her farther away from it, her insides ached with the effort of resisting. The water had significantly receded by the time they'd left the fireworks show, but there were also hundreds of lingering tourists and partying teenagers. She didn't want to share the beach and the cave with any of them.

She calculated that if the tides were on roughly a twelve-hour cycle, the next low would be around noon tomorrow—while she was at work. She had already taken a long lunch the day before. She couldn't ask again, not in the high season. She shook her head and exhaled and then caught herself; she was sitting next to Peter, and even though his eyes were on the road she could feel him reading her mood.

Peter dropped them off, refusing Sam's invitation to come inside for a late-night snack. Hester forced a cheerful goodbye and ran straight to her room. She closed the door, opened her laptop, and found the South Shore tide calendar. The next low tide would be halfway through her lunch break tomorrow, as she had predicted. She had only forty-five minutes for lunch, and if she changed clothes and drove to the beach and back, she'd end up with less than twenty minutes of free time. She ran her finger along the computer screen: the low tide after that was at 1:09 in the morning.

She slapped the computer shut and slumped back in her chair. There was no way on earth that Nancy and Malcolm would let her go out alone after midnight.

By the end of the next agonizing day at work, she knew she had no choice: she had to sneak out of her house that night. She couldn't stay away from the beach any longer. Peter drove her home and Hester said goodbye, but this time she waited for him to pull away before she went inside the house. She had a sudden inspiration: she would get her bike out of the garage and hide it in the backyard, to be as quiet as possible later that night. Peter paused, and since Hester had no apparent reason for standing rooted to the spot, she waved with a silly shrug, realizing instantly how uncharacteristically attentive her behavior toward him must seem at that moment. As he left, his smile was half confusion, with a bewildered shake of the head.

After stashing her bike, she let herself inside the house through the front door. She picked at her supper, which held no interest for her, and tried to follow the conversation but couldn't. She helped clear the table and wash the dishes, and then excused herself to read. Upstairs, she showered, brushed her teeth, put on clean clothes, climbed into bed, and read the only thing that could keep her attention—the Doyle journal.

The book always felt warm in her hands, as if someone had been reading it before her and had just set it down. She read a section on how the males of the species had gradually killed each other in warfare and the last baby had grown to adulthood a thousand years ago. Because of this their world was childless, save for the occasional human foundling transformed into a water breather. There was a beautiful image of a pale female submerged deep in the ocean, with sharp fins and wide eyes, protectively cradling an apparently living human infant, with a fantastic architectural rendering of a shipwreck behind her on the ocean floor.

Hester touched the ink of the illustration. Doyle was long dead, yet still speaking to her and engaging her imagination. It made her think about how recording information, ideas, and stories can collapse the time and space between the writer and the reader. It was one of the reasons she was drawn to history in school: there was such romance in listening to voices of the past. She closed the book and took a deep sniff of the cover. What an intriguing person the author must have been in real life.

It was ten o'clock. She set her alarm for one o'clock on its softest setting. Somehow, miraculously, she fell into an exhausted sleep, with the journal nested beside her.

Her eyes opened at 12:52, before her alarm went off. She got up, tucked the journal inconspicuously on her bookshelf, pulled her hair into a ponytail, and grabbed the sweatshirt she had laid out on the bed. She walked down the stairs carrying her running shoes, heady with anticipation. She tried to reason the feeling away, to prepare herself for disappointment: it was one o'clock in the morning; she had no prior arrangement with him; he wouldn't be there; he *shouldn't* be there.

But the tugging in her chest told her differently.

She put on her shoes in the living room, tying the laces in the dark, and tiptoed toward the back door, through the kitchen. She froze when she saw Sam. He was bent at the waist, his entire front half illuminated by the light inside the refrigerator. Before she could think to turn around, he saw her.

He stood up and stared, with his hand still resting on the gaping fridge door.

Damn, Hester thought.

"You going out?" he said simply.

"Uh-huh." She started quickly for the back door, avoiding his eyes.

"I won't tell, but someone should know where. In case."

She stopped walking. She realized she was hunching, like a criminal, and stood up straight. Sam had long ago proved himself to be an unfailingly sensible and sensitive accomplice. Why was she worried? It had been years since he had been the snitching little brother.

She said in a low voice, "I'm going to the beach by the picnic area. I'll be back before Dad gets up. I have my phone."

"'Kay." He reached in and pulled out the chicken cutlets that were left over from dinner. Before she closed the door she turned back to look at him. "Hey, Sam?" she whispered. "I love you."

He shook his head, but he was smiling. "Where did that come from? You're such a goof lately."

The night was clear and cool, with calm winds. The streets were nearly empty. The picnic area was dim, with just the tired light of a few vintage wrought-iron lamps. She leaned her bike against a no-parking sign. Like a beacon, the familiar tugging homed its way inside her. If she allowed herself to think it, she imagined Ezra was calling her. With shaking hands, she hastily locked her bike. *That's crazy,* she thought.

Why was she here? How had this happened? How had she given up so easily on her resolve to be alone after she met Ezra? And what about McKee's warning? How did he know that she wouldn't be able to resist the beach?

She made her way to the top of the stone steps, away from the lamps. She closed her eyes and took a deep breath, engulfed by the call. She opened her eyes, waiting for them to adjust. The moon was in its last quarter, but the night was so clear it threw enough blue light on the beach for her to find her way. She hesitated for a moment—her last opportunity to turn back. And then she recognized the truth: she had given up resisting the moment she had hidden her bike in the backyard.

She allowed herself to be pulled down the stairs. She stepped onto the beach and walked purposefully, her expectation growing, her breath becoming thready and shallow. And now, for the first time, she responded to the call in her mind.

I'm here, she thought. *I'm here.*

She saw him step out of the cave and face her. Her heart pumped so hard she felt each beat thud against the inside wall of her chest. She quickened her pace.

He strode toward her. She began running, to close the distance.

Right before she reached him, his arms opened. It was the most wrenching, welcoming gesture she had ever seen. She launched herself and he caught her. She wrapped her arms around his neck as he spun her around once. His arms held her tightly around the waist, their cheeks were touching, and the electrical sensation had become a magnet, pressing them together.

She heard him suck in air through a delighted smile—and she squeezed him tighter, to the point where she thought she might hurt him. He held her like that, molded against him, delaying putting her down, saying nothing, savoring her. She nuzzled her nose against the cool skin of his neck. He smelled like the sea. He leaned his head back to look at her, examining her, drinking her in. She felt herself blush. She put both hands behind his head and pulled his face close, kissing his eyelids to make him shut his eyes, then the hollow of his cheek, and behind his ear. When she looked at him again, his eyes had pooled with tears. He spun her around again and whispered in her ear.

"I can't believe you're here."

"I came as soon as I could," she whispered back.

He kissed her for the first time, tenderly, gently. "I know you did."

He set her down, still holding her close. She wanted more. She stood on her toes and kissed his lips tentatively. He responded, coaxing her to confidence, restraining his ardor as best he could, giving her time. Soon she felt the streaming sensation she'd felt before. Something flowed from him to her, filled her to full, barely contained by her body, and finally seemed to burst through her in every direction into the night air.

"This could be the death of me," she said breathlessly when their lips parted.

"Don't say that."

As hard as it was, she pulled away from him and faced him,

holding his hands. They were beautifully shaped: masculine, hairless, rough with calluses but with neatly groomed fingernails.

"Why is everything about you designed to make me want you?" she said.

"We are meant to be together, Hester. I knew it when I first saw you in the cave. Until then I had been sleepwalking through a miserable existence. And then with no warning you were there—I still don't understand how it's possible—and I couldn't believe my luck. I couldn't bear it that you walked away before you discovered it yourself."

"It was too dark for you to see me when we met," she countered.

"But we've known each other for ages, don't you feel that?"

She should be frightened by his intensity, she thought. Instead, a part of her—a part deep inside that had nothing to do with her intellect—understood in the profoundest way what he was saying. She gently let go of his hands and said, "I can't think straight when I'm touching you—I'm sorry."

"Let's walk."

He kept his hands in his pockets, strolling with slow, long strides. Hester hugged her chest to resist flinging herself at him.

"Did you finish your research?" he said.

"Yes."

There was a pause.

"Is it as I feared, then?"

She pulled the list of female relatives from her pocket, unfolded it, and handed it to him. "By your criteria it's consistent with a curse."

"I'm so sorry."

"If this is true, how does a person go about fixing a curse? How can I lift it, Ezra?" She didn't say what she meant: *now that it's so important; now that I can't think of anything but you.*

But he understood. "I gather you're abandoning your previous strategy of refusing all lovers?"

She detected the playfulness in his voice. His eyes were focused on the sand as he walked, but he was smiling.

"You're so maddening sometimes!" she blurted. "This is serious, and if there's no solution then I *can't* be with anyone."

"I'm sorry, I do want to help you. However, the cad in me is a bit preoccupied by that kiss just now, and hoping for—"

"If you won't help me I'll have to resort to Pastor McKee, who's probably in the first stages of Alzheimer's already and will tell me to wear garlic around my neck."

Ezra stopped suddenly. Hester took a couple of steps more before she noticed. She turned around.

"Don't talk to McKee," he said. His voice was completely altered: hard-edged, low, and rumbling like thunder.

"What?"

"Don't talk to him, and don't listen to him."

The wind whipped up, and grains of sand stung Hester's cheek. Several pieces of hair ripped out of her ponytail. She clawed them away from her eyes.

"How do you know each other?"

"Trust me, Hester, he has committed acts that would horrify you. You must stay away from him." He looked at the sky and put his hands on the top of his head, tamping down his anger. "How many times should that old fool be allowed to destroy my life?"

"He said the same thing about you," Hester said quietly.

"That I destroyed his life?" He gripped her elbow. "Just what has he told you?"

Her lips tightened. "No, he said that I should trust him . . . and stay away from you." She looked at her arm and said calmly, "You're hurting me."

"Dear God." He let go. And then he crumpled into a seated position in the sand. The wind died as quickly as it had picked up. He rubbed his face with his hands.

"Please forgive me, Hester. Michael McKee's path has crossed with mine in a most painful and permanent way, and when I am forced to recall my bond with him my blood boils."

She sat next to him and sighed. "I'm going to feel free to swear with abandon because of all these riddles."

He gingerly pushed the loose strands of hair behind her ear and said in a voice so low she almost missed it, "You'll understand soon enough . . . and I dread where that will leave me."

She leaned over and kissed him. She pushed him gently to the sand. She delicately kissed every inch of his face, feeling the contours of his cheeks, nose, forehead, and chin with her lips, and each time she came near his mouth he smiled and faintly kissed back.

His shirt was open at the neck, and she slipped her hand inside it. His body was lean, with a hint of ribs showing. She traced his collarbones and then slid her hand down his chest. Near his left nipple she felt a gnarled lump of skin—a scar, as if a hole had been sewn shut. She explored more and found another, longer one along his sternum—a vertical rope of scar tissue running down almost to his navel. Touching it was intensely moving to her. She traced it up and down, and was suddenly overwhelmed by a feeling of utter hopelessness, as if everything that ever mattered to her was lost. She took an anguished gasp and forced her hand away. She searched his eyes, but he shook his head, with his mouth in a thin line. She kissed him, and in a moment felt his lips open and his body relax. He wrapped his arms around her, pulling her on top of him.

She wouldn't press him yet. For now, she'd allow him his privacy. Just for tonight, she would delude herself that everything about him wasn't a complete mystery. After years of deprivation, she would take one night of happiness.

Chapter 31

1873

It was not a short walk down the hill, even for a man who was not carrying his dead wife on his shoulders in the dark, even for a man whose pericardium had not been pierced with a knife.

No amount of breath could satisfy Ezra's need for air. He felt so dizzy and light-headed that his knees threatened to collapse with each step. Lifting his legs was a monumental effort. The stones in the dirt road pierced the skin of his feet. The pressure in his chest was crushing. There was an alarming opacity to his vision that threatened to blind him before he reached the ocean.

"Please," he said almost inaudibly, to himself, to God, to the creatures of the sea. This would be his last act on earth; he must succeed.

When he had reached the beach and waded into the water several steps, he allowed himself to buckle and fall to his knees. It caused searing pain when he slid Sarah off his shoulders—gently, tenderly—into the sea.

She half sank, half floated lifelessly on her back. He pulled her to him and nested her head on his thighs, to keep her face from submerging in the wavelets. He pushed the wet strands of hair away from her face and tucked them behind her ear. He bent to kiss her lips and felt the knife sink deeper. And then he waited for death, hoping her companions would find them and he would see her saved before his last breath.

He must have blacked out for a moment, because he missed their approach. When he opened his eyes he found he could no longer move. His arms dangled by his sides. His breath was shallow. There were two of them—luminescent in the light of the full moon—an achingly beautiful sight.

They took her from him. His chin dropped to his chest, his eyes closed. He heard them tending, fussing, arguing in their own language. His hearing was fading.

And then English, from one of them, directed at him: ". . . can do nothing . . . Ezra . . . Ezra . . . late . . . so sorry . . . too late."

He heard his own voice, a distant whisper: "Can . . . you . . . use . . . me?" The buzzing of a reply in the affirmative.

He opened his eyes but he was blind now. He raised a leaden arm to the knife in his chest. His hands were clumsy, his fingers useless. With his last effort, as his consciousness ebbed into nothingness, he pulled the knife out and fell face-first in the water.

The creatures acted swiftly. One of them flipped him over and slashed his chest open with a single vertical slice of her wrist fin. The other jabbed her clawlike fingernails into his sternum and pried his rib cage apart. The heart was warm and fluttering like a bird, but not pumping. The first creature slit the major arteries and veins to detach the heart, and carefully lifted it out. As the second creature held Sarah's mouth open, the first forced Ezra's heart down her throat.

Chapter 32

HESTER ARRIVED HOME an hour before her father woke up. She left her shoes in the kitchen and padded quietly upstairs past Sam's room, where he was on top of his covers, spread-eagle and belly down, his face nestled, angelic, in the pillow. She tiptoed in and turned his light off. And then she went to bed, but no matter how tired her body was, her mind would not be calm. The three hours of sleep she'd gotten before she biked to the beach were apparently all she would get. It was after five and the sun was rising when she heard the quiet chinking sound that meant Malcolm was unloading the dishwasher. She rose and pulled on her jeans and T-shirt from the night before. There was a pile of sand scattered on the wooden floor where the jeans had been. She used her foot to sweep most of it under the bed.

Malcolm had the local TV news on softly in the background while he made breakfast.

"You're up early," he said.

"You have no idea." Her cheeks got hot.

To avoid looking in his eyes, she walked over to the coffeemaker on the counter behind him. It gurgled and hissed as the last drops of coffee dripped into the pot.

"Did you make enough for me to have some?" she asked.

"Sure."

She took a mug down from the cabinet and poured herself half a cup. She glanced at the TV and saw that the news was showing footage of gravestones.

". . . vandals came sometime in the middle of the night . . ."

She got out a spoon and the sugar bowl and dumped a heaping teaspoon in her mug.

". . . pastor says that youths are often the culprits, not realizing the costs—financial, historical, and sacred—of their actions . . ."

As she sipped the coffee, her ear caught the word "historical" and she looked at the TV again. There was a close-up of a tombstone, apparently ripped out of the earth and planted upside down in the ground, with a clump of moist black dirt and rooty sod dangling where the top of the stone should have been. The camera panned back to show the reporter standing next to a police officer, with Burial Hill in the background. Hester put down the mug.

"Burial Hill is the resting place of several Pilgrims and patriots, including William Bradford, Mary Allerton, John Howland, and James Warren." The reporter was reading this information from a notepad.

"The four graves that were vandalized have no obvious relation to each other and are distributed in different parts of the cemetery."

Which graves? Hester wondered. *Tell us the names.*

The reporter turned to the policeman. "Lieutenant Nicholas Merlino, if you'll pardon the pun it seems like a *monumental* effort not only to dig up headstones weighing hundreds of pounds each but to flip them over, successfully remounting them upside down.

Do you have any idea how someone could have done this without heavy machinery?"

"Yes, sir, it's exactly that difficulty—how hard it is to lift the stones—that's making us think that multiple perpetrators are involved. It's possible that it was a gang of teenagers out drinking."

"But if you'll permit some amateur sleuthing, as far as I can see there are no footprints in the dirt, or evidence that shovels were used. There are no telltale beer bottles or cigarette butts." He let out a laugh. "Given that First Church of Pilgrims has such an infamous history of hauntings, shouldn't your department look into the possibility that this could be—"

Lieutenant Merlino interrupted him. "Look, this isn't a séance, it's a police investigation. And this isn't a joke. Burial Hill has national historic importance." He looked directly into the lens. "If your viewers saw any rowdy bands of teenagers out making mischief last night, they can call anonymous tips in to the station. Thank you." And then he walked off camera.

The reporter wrapped up his piece. "It's certainly a mystery, what happened here—one that's not likely to be unraveled soon if paranormal, rather than teenage, forces were at work. Reporting live from Burial Hill in Plymouth . . ."

"Do you think I can take Nancy's car to work, Dad?" Hester tried to sound natural.

"I'm working from home today—you can use mine."

"Great, thanks." She kissed him on the cheek and put her coffee cup in the sink.

"It's a little early for work, isn't it?"

"It's bread-baking day. I told the foodways manager that I'd

201

help her set up the communal oven." Damn, it was scary how good she was getting at lying.

"You have to eat breakfast," he said.

"After my shower!" She hurried out of the kitchen and up the stairs.

She parked on School Street behind three squad cars, threw her messenger bag over her shoulder, and began to run up the flight of stone steps alongside First Church of Pilgrims. She caught sight of Lieutenant Merlino on the second landing of the steps, huddled with another policeman who was consulting a spiral pad of paper.

"You can't come up here right now," Lieutenant Merlino said to her.

"I just need to see—"

"Nope." He moved to block her way.

"Can you at least tell me which headstones were turned upside down? I have relatives buried here."

The Lieutenant nodded to the officer, who flipped back several pages in his pad.

"Let's see, Eleanor Ont . . . ont . . . tanse," the officer read. Hester's heart tumbled. She bit her cheek to keep herself quiet.

"The second one is Bartholomew Crotty, Mar-jin his wife, and Lucy his wife—that's all one headstone."

Hester nodded impatiently. "Uh-huh."

"Third is Adeline P. Angeln—she was just a kid, poor thing. And the last one is right over there." He pointed with his pen farther up the stairs and to the side, where yellow police tape cordoned off a grave. "E. A. Doyle."

E. A. Doyle? Hester felt dizzy. Not enough sleep? Not enough breakfast? She backed down a step.

Angeln, she thought, her mind racing.

"Did you say Adeline Angeln?" She reached for the railing to steady herself. Peter had mentioned the name Adeline—she was his relative, the one whose doll was on exhibit in Pilgrim Hall. The connections she had missed until now hit her, and she lost her breath: Adeline Angeln was the murdered girl in the *Old Colony* newspaper. Adeline Angeln was Peter's great-great-something-aunt. Adeline Angeln was *Linnie*.

"That's right, Adeline P. Angeln. That a family name?" Lieutenant Merlino asked.

"What? Oh . . . no. Thank you. Sorry . . . I'm sorry to have bothered you." She turned and walked down the stairs. Her knees were wobbly.

She glanced at the back door of the church. It was ajar, inviting her. She looked back up at the policemen, who had their backs to her, stepped onto the landing behind the church, and slipped inside. The lights of the crypt were on, and Pastor McKee was waiting for her at the bottom of the stairs.

"Did you see the graves?" he asked, cackling. "I hope you got t' see 'em. Et was somethen'!"

Chapter 33
1873

SARAH'S BODY SEIZED as she took her first breath. She choked, feeling a sickening bloating in her stomach that she couldn't identify. She was in the water, on her back. Her eyes opened, and she saw Needa and Weeku hovering above her, illuminated by the moon, showing concern, relief, and pleasure. She felt the sand beneath her; she was in the shallows. They were cradling her head above water. How had she gotten to the beach? Her last memory was of losing consciousness in the crypt—the sarcophagus—the knife.

She reached up to feel her neck. The pastor had slashed it open, and she had known it was a fatal blow, but now the wound was sealed. The last thing she saw before she collapsed was . . .

"Ezra," she said. Her voice was raspy. An unease grew in her.

"Where is Ezra?" she said louder. The faces retreated nervously as the hands gently loosed their holds on her.

She lifted herself to a sitting position with her arms. She looked around her. She let out a cry.

Ezra was dead beside her in the water. His chest had been torn open, showing the red raw underside of the skin, splintered ribs, and layers of tissue protruding through the wound. The sight was so unimaginably wrong—they were parts of him that were meant to be protected inside his body, unexposed, for a lifetime. Instinctively, irrationally, she got on her knees and tried to close the wound with her hands, realizing as she did that it was futile. His eyes and mouth were open, his expression empty. His beautiful face had no trace of the feelings and thoughts of the real Ezra.

She took her hands away, and that was when she saw that his heart was missing.

She put her hand to her abdomen. She pressed hard and bent with grief, feeling the bulge in her gut. She was so repulsed she retched, but nothing came up. She knew it was too late.

"What have you done?" She turned on her sister. "*What have you done?*"

Needa approached, supplicating. "He did it for you, Syrenka. He was dying . . ."

Sarah lunged and grabbed her by the hair. "*He* was the one to save, you stupid fool."

"There was nothing to salvage from you," she cried, holding her scalp. "You were gone. He would have died anyway!"

"You should have saved him!" Sarah threw her sister aside and went back to Ezra's body. She closed his eyes and his mouth and flung her arms around him. With his body not yet cool, she could pretend for a fleeting moment that he was alive. Needa laid a tentative hand on her shoulder, stroking her. In that moment of silence, Sarah heard a wail in the distance. She jerked her head up, focusing on the sound. The cry came from the top of Leyden Street, from the direction of the church. It was the vulnerable howling of an infant who had been unattended for too long.

"A baby," she said. She remembered seeing the Ontstaan woman in town on several occasions with a baby in her arms. Yes, that horrible woman had a child.

She knew what she had to do, and time was running out.

"No, Syrenka," Weeku said, anticipating her.

"Don't!" Needa echoed from behind. "Let him go," she pleaded earnestly. "Leave him in peace."

Sarah kissed Ezra's unresponsive mouth. She stood up and pulled him farther into the water.

"Bring his body to the deep and let it wash ashore in three days' time. The townspeople must not find him dead tonight."

"Please, don't . . ."

"Do not fail me," she warned. She stormed out of the water.

Needa desperately slithered onto the sand after her, propelling herself awkwardly with her arms, and grabbed Sarah's ankle.

"This is a mistake that will last for eternity," she gasped, "long after your mortal body has turned to dust."

"I will not live without him," Sarah said. She shook her sister loose and set off up the hill.

The closer Sarah got, the more clearly she heard the baby's cries. She broke into a run.

When she got to the church she was nearly overwhelmed by the sweeping, swirling remainder of emotions of the people who had died that evening, and through it all she could distill the distinct sensation of Ezra: violence and hatred toward the pastor; wildness; confusion; panic; hopelessness; impatience at the little girl; and strongest of all, love for Sarah—tenderness, devotion, and the ultimate act of generosity. The emotions came in waves, plunging in and out of the church, down the road in the direction he had carried her, ebbing and flowing. She knew they would slowly, inexorably dissipate unless she could trap them and pin them to the earth—pin them into a single, beautiful spirit of Ezra. The sensation of him was dizzying. She lifted her face to the air. If she could have breathed him in and held him inside her, she would have. But there was only one way to keep him.

The back door of the church hung open, throwing light onto the gravestone where Adeline had fallen. The baby had rolled onto the ground, facedown, caught in its blankets, and was now screaming with discomfort. Sarah scooped the baby up.

She unwrapped the swaddling layers, and the baby's cries slowed. She looked at the perfect little body in her arms without regret, but clinically, urgently. It was the wretched widow's baby, and it was only right that the Ontstaans should pay for destroying Ezra. Time was running out. Ezra's remnants would soon disperse permanently, reunite with his soul, and be irretrievable.

She hastily rewrapped the baby and held it tight as she moved back and forth in the graveyard—toward the church, away from the church, alongside the church—searching for the spot that captured the strongest sensation of Ezra. The movement soothed the baby, who quieted and began sucking a knuckle. Sarah sensed that the emotions peaked in three locations, and found a spot in the middle that captured as much of each as possible. She laid the baby down on the spot and put her hands on it.

She closed her eyes and reached out to Noo'kas in her mind.

Use this child's soul as the anchor, she drilled her thoughts toward the ocean. *Gather what is left of Ezra and pin his spirit to the earth where he died. I beg you.*

The wind whipped up. Fat drops of ocean rain fell, one by one.

The baby blinked in surprise as each drop hit its face. The drops pattered into a real rain, and then a downpour. The baby squirmed and whimpered, but Sarah did not shield it. There was a sudden, whooshing gust that threatened to knock Sarah over. She steadied herself and held the child in place as the wind swirled and then formed a massive downdraft of air, pressing suddenly, crushingly on top of them. The baby's eyes opened wide in shock as the breath was knocked out of it.

Sarah fell onto the baby. She heard its muffled cry beneath her, already quavering as its life ebbed away, and she knew the magic had been done.

Chapter 34

W<small>HAT THE</small> . . . *HECK*, McKee," Hester blurted, hurrying down the crypt stairs toward him. "All of those graves have a connection with *me*. What's going on?"

"I told you, lass, everything es entertwined."

"Why is Linnie doing this? Is it out of spite? Is it because I don't visit her anymore? How did she know about Eleanor and Marijn?"

"Et does seem t' be a message die-rected a' you. Paerhaps ef you untangle the threads, all well be clear."

"Listen, I have time before I have to be at work." She walked over to the two chairs and put her hands on the back of one. "Sit here with me. Help *me*, if you want me to help her."

"I cannae tell you wha' t' do, Hester," he protested as he shuffled over to the chair. "The decesions you make are yours alone."

"You're getting way ahead of me. I just want information." She held his elbow as he eased himself into the chair. She lowered her bag onto the floor beside her chair, but she remained standing, thinking.

"First of all, how could Linnie be that strong?"

"Adeline es no' a lit'le gaerl anymore, remember. She's inhabiting a *vaersion* of her human body tha's no' real. Och, et feels real to haer, of course."

"And to me," Hester insisted. "I've touched her."

"Aye, you have. But try to remember et's an *earthly fegment*—one that only you and she share."

"Those flipped headstones aren't a *figment* out there! The whole town has seen them on the news. Some real live human being is going to have to get equipment to turn them back over."

"I didnae say she doesnae exest, lamb. Et takes a powerful force to create a spirit like tha'. But she's no' a paerson with a soul. She's a bundle of emotions, pinned to one spot on the earth. She exests without food and water, without feelin' chelled or damp or uncomfortable, without needin' to breathe, even. She's limited to dwellin' where she died, and no human being can see haer or respond to haer. Et's a half exestence—of etaernal isolation—an' she's just a child."

"Oh my God," Hester said.

"What es et?"

"You tried to tell me this before, and I didn't internalize it. I've grown up these ten years—I've lived, and learned, and slept, and eaten—but she hasn't. She has been all alone, always outside, even in the dead of winter, while I've had a home and Sam and my parents."

The pastor sat quietly, looking up at her with narrowed eyes.

"Why did she uproot her own headstone?" Hester whispered to herself with wonder. She finally sat down in the chair opposite him. "Poor thing, she must have been brutally killed." She shook her head to clear it. "It's horrifying to even think about it. No wonder she's a ghost! But what does she want with me?"

"Haer spirit wants the semple thengs she cannae have: to sleep en haer bed, to hear haer mother singin' as she hangs the laundry, to taste peppermint again. Bu' wha' she *needs* es altogether defferent, an' she has no understandin' of et: she needs to be set free."

"I don't know what that means."

"Haer earthly spirit needs to be unpinned so that haer emotions may rejoin haer soul. She desaerves the peace of death. I believe tha' because you can see and speak with haer, *you* can grant et to haer."

"Well, unfortunately my high school doesn't offer a class in Unpinning Earthly Spirits, so do you have more specific instructions?" Hester cringed at her own disrespectful tone.

But McKee was earnest and patient. "I've haerd tell that releasing spirits requires findin' an object from their human lives tha' had strong meaning for them. Spirits weaken en the presence of such an object, because et shows so clearly the detachment between their current existence and their past human lives. En that weakened state, et's possible to banish them or reason them away ef you're paersistent. Et sounds hard-hearted, bu' et's the greatest kindness you could show them."

Hester pushed her hair off her forehead with both hands and thought for a moment. "Linnie had a doll. She told me she lost it, but Peter's family still has one that I'm sure is hers."

"Who es Peter?"

"His last name is Angeln," she said.

"Praise be to God," Pastor McKee whispered, his eyes becoming glassy with tears. "Are you strong enough to do this? Well you use the doll t' help haer?"

"I just show her the doll? And encourage her to leave?"

He bit his lip and nodded. "Haer pinned emotions well rejoin haer soul."

Hester crossed her arms in front of her chest and was quiet. She looked into the middle distance, thinking.

"*Everything is intertwined,*" she finally murmured, repeating McKee's observation to herself. "Ontstaan. Crotty. Angeln. Doyle."

"Wha' are you thenkin', lass?"

She focused on him. "There are common threads, for sure, but I can't get them all to connect. The police haven't figured this out, but three of the vandalized graves are linked. Eleanor Ontstaan was Adeline Angeln's aunt. They were killed on the same night at this church."

He shook his head, as if it were a shame.

"I've read as much about it as I can, but the details just aren't in the *Old Colony* newspaper. I don't know why they were killed, or who did it."

"Wha' d'you make of the Crotty grave?"

"Marijn was my great-great-great-grandmother, and also the foster child of Eleanor. I don't know who Marijn's biological mother was." It suddenly occurred to Hester that this was important information for her family curse, but she had never investigated it. The farther back she could go, the higher the probability that she might unravel the mystery.

"And Doyle?" he asked, encouraging her.

She shrugged, confused. "Doyle is the author of a book I stole from the library last week. Linnie saw it over my shoulder, which might explain why she picked on that grave."

"You stole a book?"

She furrowed her brow. "I'm not in the habit of stealing, you know. And anyway, I blame you! It's a handwritten journal about sea folk in the bay, and *you* set me on that topic. It's the most incredible piece of work I've ever seen."

She resisted the urge to glance at her bag, where the journal was. She couldn't bring herself to share it with McKee. She would never share it with anyone.

"Tell me somethen' you've laerned from et." He sat back, like a child waiting for a story.

"Well here's something fascinating: their leader is named Noo'kas—the Native People call her Squauanit, or Squant—and apparently her realm is horrifying, because she has lived for tens of thousands of years and she's a compulsive collector. Her throne room has deteriorated into filthy squalor."

"Has a human ever vesited this place?"

"I don't know, not voluntarily I would guess. Certainly Doyle hadn't seen it—there were no illustrations. The text said that if a human is abducted by her, he or she almost always drowns. There have been only a handful of instances in which Squauanit has successfully transformed a human into a sea creature, tail and all. They remain mortal and die quickly in her servitude."

"Losh, so escape es empossible," he said with genuine concern.

"There is a way, but it seemed too simple to me: you have to remember your connection to the earth. You have to seek an audience with her and insist that you belong to the land and not the sea."

"She sounds like a deffcult creature," he said.

"Yeah, she's definitely not someone you want to cross."

The church bell rang half past seven.

"I've got to go to work." Hester sighed, standing up.

"Aye, me as well."

"I wish—" Hester said as she helped him to his feet. "I wish I knew more about the circumstances surrounding Linnie's death. I wish I knew who Marijn's real mother was. I wish I knew why the murders took place on this particular spot. Sylvie Atwood was right: these are stories that will be lost forever, because everyone who knew them has died."

He walked her slowly to the stairs. "Only the humans are dead, lamb."

Hester looked at him quizzically.

He glanced at her from the corner of his eye and then concentrated on the floor. "Ef th' Doyle journal es correct, the local sea folk waer alive a' the time. They may yet have the answers tha' you seek."

Chapter 35

HESTER STOOD IN THE PARKING lot of Plimoth Plantation during her lunch break two days later, finishing half a sandwich and waiting for Peter to pick her up. She was wearing street clothes, which made her blessedly incognito to the visitors who streamed under the welcome sign. The bag over her shoulder held the Doyle journal—a gentle hug against her waist reassured her of its presence. She balled up the tinfoil wrapping of the sandwich and tossed it at the barrel, but missed. She frowned. It was unfortunate that she'd have to lie to Peter, but she couldn't see a way around it.

She had been honest over the phone at least:

"I want to see your great-aunt Adeline's doll," she had told him. "And the museum closes at four thirty, so we can't do it after work."

"That's *Great-Great-Great-Great*-Aunt Adeline, to you. But I can't stay long; I'm running the two o'clock whale watch."

"We'll be quick."

She shook her head, dreading the next three-quarters of an hour. He was bound to ask questions at the museum—questions that she had to plan answers for, and quickly. His truck was already pulling in to the lot. She picked up the wadded foil, put it in the garbage, and waved to him as normally as she could.

* * *

The banner for the exhibit said "Childhood in the Old Colony: 1620–1920." The artifacts were books, furniture, clothing, games, and toys. In the toy section there was a glass case with a primitive, hand-sewn doll from 1615 that had belonged to Mary Chilton, a Mayflower passenger. Next to it was the larger, elaborate doll Hester had come to see: *Attributed to Adeline P. Angeln; manufacturer François Gaultier, c.1870, France. Bisque socket head, paperweight glass eyes, jointed composition-and-wood body, bisque arms.*

There was no mistaking it, it was Linnie's doll. It had a serious face with pudgy jowls, hand-painted rosebud lips, lifelike eyes with long painted eyelashes, and tiny turquoise bead earrings. There was a hairline fracture on her cheek, and her left eyebrow was crushed, showing the white, raw porcelain underneath. Her auburn hair was in long ringlets, held back loosely on two sides with black satin ribbons. Her dress was deep violet, just as Linnie had described, with inset lace at the collar, sleeves, and hem. She wore a petticoat with eyelet trim, and antique black net stockings. Hester understood now why Linnie had criticized her own doll, Annabelle, the day they met.

"Even broken, this doll puts her to shame," Hester murmured.

"Hmm?" Peter said.

"I said . . . it's a shame that she's broken."

"Adeline had it with her when she was killed." He pointed to the doll's foot. "The family lore says that's when the little shoe got lost, too."

"You never told me Adeline was killed."

He shrugged. "I only remembered just now."

"Who killed her?"

"I don't think it was ever solved. They found her dead in a grave-yard. There was an orphaned baby involved somehow, and Adeline's parents adopted the baby. That's all I know."

"Peter," Hester said, steeling herself to tell him the real reason she had brought him to the museum. "I need to borrow this doll, just for a day. For a history project."

"I'm sure my parents would let you, but it's on display until May."

She shook her head impatiently before he finished his sentence.

"That's too late. I need it now. If you could persuade the director to lend it to you after they close today, I could get it back here tomorrow—maybe even before they open. It'll be like I didn't borrow it at all, as far as museum visitors are concerned."

He turned his attention from the doll to her; she had protested too much. Behind his glasses his eyes were thoughtful, examining, and for the first time she realized that he did know her better than almost anyone in the world—maybe a little too well.

"This is the first I've heard of a history project. What's up with you lately?"

"Nothing is up! I'm doing some research for a paper."

"A paper for what? The school year is over."

"Ugh! Why are you giving me the third degree?"

A tourist walked up with her two children. They were filling out a sheet for the exhibit—a scavenger hunt provided by the museum, with the promise of a prize at the end. They stopped to look at the dolls and put check marks in two boxes on their papers. Peter waited until the family had moved on before he spoke.

"My dad got a call from the public library yesterday."

Hester froze.

"There's only one Angeln listed in Plymouth, so they called us."

"So . . . what was it about?" She tried to sound clueless. She forced her body to relax.

"They were looking for an Esther Angeln. My dad told them there was no Esther in our family."

"Are you accusing me of something?"

"I didn't think twice about it until now. Was it you, Hester?"

"Was *what* me." Her voice was biting and loud—meant to show that she had nothing to hide. But her face flushed when the other patrons looked over at her.

He waited until they had turned away before responding quietly, "Did you take a book from the special collections?"

She widened her eyes in outrage. "Have you ever known me to steal anything?"

"No, of course not . . ."

"Besides, the last time I checked, my name wasn't Esther."

He stared at the dolls. "I know. It was just a weird coincidence. I'm sorry that I even suggested it."

She was quiet for a moment. The doll was so close to her, it was frustrating that she couldn't just take it. She bit her cheek and scanned the edges of the glass case, noticing that there was no lock. She *could* just lift the lid and take it, if she wanted, right then and there.

Maybe she didn't need Peter after all.

He interrupted her thoughts. "I'll talk to my parents. Maybe we can request to have the doll back for a day or two."

"No, don't."

"There's no harm in asking."

"Forget about it!" Too brusque, she realized. She took a breath and lowered her voice. "Honestly, thanks, but I'll make do without it."

He shook his head, unable to figure her out. "Whatever. I'd better get you back to work or I'm gonna be late."

"That's okay," Hester said, thinking on her feet. "I'm going home to get Nancy's car. I have errands to run later." She swallowed, hoping he wouldn't press her for details.

"Do you want a ride to your house?" He looked at his watch.

"No, thanks, but I'll . . . I'll walk you to your truck."

After he had pulled away, Hester lingered in front of the museum. Finally, she pulled out her phone and called her boss to say that she didn't feel well and wouldn't be returning to work that day. She thanked her for her good wishes and agreed she hoped she'd feel better by tomorrow. Then she sent a text to Nancy and Malcolm, saying she would be home late and didn't need supper.

Inside the museum, she showed her Plymouth ID for free entry, grateful that the volunteer didn't recognize her from half an hour before. She wandered the museum slowly, pretending to look at the exhibits but really examining the security system. It seemed to be based entirely on motion detectors, with no cameras, as far as she could see. She investigated the area surrounding the restrooms, and finally, in the hall near the offices, she found a steel door with a bar handle like some of the side doors at school: *Emergency exit only, alarm will sound*. This was what she was looking for: city code required that sort of fire door to remain unlocked on the inside.

With her plan fixed, she went to the gift shop. She browsed for a while before buying a small battery-powered toy lantern, which she put in her bag. She went to the restroom because she knew it would be a while before she could use it again. While she was in the stall she turned her phone's ringer off and put it in the outside pocket of her bag. Then she made her way through the permanent collection to her chosen hideout. It was a six-sided wooden chest, about the size of a small coffin, under a portrait of Elizabeth Paddy Wensley, 1670. Elizabeth Wensley was wearing a lavishly embroidered dress, but it could not distract from her weary eyes.

Hester stood back, pretending to admire the painting. She looked over her shoulder, right and left. She looked behind her. Nobody was in sight. She lifted the lid of the chest—it was heavy and it creaked with a jittering whine. She gritted her teeth. The hinge was so stiff, the lid remained propped without her having to balance it against the wall—a relief, since she did not want to risk damaging the painting behind it. She hoisted a leg up and climbed in. Her bag clunked against the wall of the chest and she winced. As quietly as possible, she pulled hard on the lid to lower it on top of herself. She spent several anxious seconds getting as comfortable as she could while making as little noise as possible: pulling down her shirt, which had gotten twisted around her torso, lying on her side with her knees tucked in, and placing her bag in front of her with the flap open. It was dark in the chest except for the light that shone through the tiny keyhole, which also allowed her to see whether anyone was in front of the chest. She took her phone out of her bag and looked at the time. It was 1:58. She shut her eyes and concentrated on slowing her heart rate.

She waited like that, to give herself time to adjust to her new setting. The walls of the chest were so thick, she could hear visitors only when they were directly in front of her and speaking in normal voices. All the better that it was so well insulated: no one would see or hear *her*, either. She was free to breathe. When she was confident that she knew the environment, she slowly removed the Doyle journal and the toy lantern from her bag.

For the next hour and a half she read. At three-thirty, with the blood pooling painfully in her hip and shoulder and her legs aching from being folded, she shifted onto her back and propped her head against the wall. At four-thirty, the visitors left and Hester saw someone—the docent?—sweep past the keyhole three times, making sure everyone was gone. At four-fifty the lights went out. Within minutes of each other, two office doors slammed. She decided she would stay hidden until five-thirty to be safe. Besides, the next part of her task—stealing private property, trespassing, and setting off alarms—promised to be much more stressful than waiting in a cramped chest. All at once she was nervous about leaving, after hours of wishing she could.

She calmed herself by reading.

The most extraordinary ability common to all females of this species and of obvious potential temptation to mankind is not only the power to heal wounds, including those dire in nature, but most incredibly, under the proper circumstances and given suitable material to work with, the power to resuscitate the living from near death, or even the newly dead from veritable death.

The little lantern flickered, and the glow weakened as the battery began to die. She shook it, but the light was waning quickly.

Such feats are not achieved without cost, however, as the principle of conservation holds with equal importance in the undersea realm as it does in our own earthbound world. In short, one cannot get something for nothing, and in practical application the exchange proves to be as much or in some cases more of a sacrifice than the original loss, with an added measure of uncertainty regarding a successful outcome, making the use of such powers inadvisable, and their existence something to be concealed from the human race forever, to avoid their misapplication.

The lantern faded completely. Hester stayed still for a moment, thinking. If she had read the passages correctly, they were essentially saying that the sea creatures could raise the dead. But what exactly was "suitable material"? What was "the exchange"?

She thought about her mom, her ashes scattered in the ocean. She felt a heaviness in her chest: there could never be "suitable material" there. Then she thought about Linnie—deprived of growing up, eternally longing for love and warmth, never understanding her half existence—whose bones might still be in a casket at Burial Hill. How might Linnie use the rest of her life if she could live again? Were bones "suitable material"?

She shook her head. Those thoughts were too macabre. She had to stick to the task of taking Linnie's doll to her, of putting her spirit to rest. She felt for her bag in the dark and put the toy lantern and the journal inside, closing the flap but not fastening it. She squirmed to put the strap of the bag over her shoulder. Her legs were asleep now, tingling with pinpricks. She took a deep breath. She rehearsed the steps in her mind, trying to visualize a flawless performance: open the lid (do not hurt the painting); climb out of the chest; close the lid; take a moment to stretch and get your balance; step into the main part of the permanent collection, in view of the electric eye (alarm sounds); move quickly to the childhood exhibit; lift lid of glass case; remove doll; put doll in bag; fasten magnet closure on bag; exit via fire door; walk (do not run) along back wall of museum behind bushes; reach Chilton Street; walk away (casually); police arrive but you are already gone; sneak home for supplies; hide out until dark.

"Showtime," she breathed aloud, and pushed up the lid.

Chapter 36

HESTER SLIPPED A NOTE under Peter's back door after dark, sealed in an envelope with his name written on the front.

> *By now you know I stole the doll, and you're convinced I've lost my mind, which I probably have. Please forgive me for lying to you. My only defense is that I'm using it to help someone. If all goes well I won't damage the doll and I'll return it to the museum tomorrow, taking full responsibility. (Will colleges refuse me admission if I have an arrest record?) If for some reason I haven't returned the doll by morning, look for it in Burial Hill and remember that I am*
>
> > *Your friend always,*
> > *H.*

She put her hand on the back of her head and felt the shell barrette. She bit her cheek. She remembered when Peter had given it to her. He had pulled the perfect gift from his back pocket and handed it to her as if it were nothing. It was the night of the school party. The night she'd met Ezra in the cave—or, rather, the night she'd heard his irresistible voice—without knowing what he would become to her.

"Ezra," she whispered, exhaling.

Just saying his name filled her with the desire to see him.

She looked at her watch under the Angelns' porch light. It was just past ten o'clock. She had promised herself she would stay away from Ezra, at least until she had freed Linnie. Then the hauntings would end, Pastor McKee would be satisfied and stop trying to dissuade her from going to the beach, and Hester could quietly go back to researching her curse with Ezra.

She sighed. Who was she fooling? She knew what she wanted—to hold him, to kiss him, to break all of her rules.

She walked her bike out to the street and felt her resolve weakening. Maybe a short visit with Ezra would actually help? He was an expert in myths and legends, after all. Maybe he could offer some advice that would help her speak coherently to Linnie. McKee had been so vague: Show her the doll, talk her away. But what exactly was Hester supposed to say? Were there ways in which it could go wrong? She nodded her head, having decided: she needed to see Ezra.

She rode to the beach, with the cool night air raising the hair on her arms. She locked the bike to a lamppost and carefully hid her bag inside the dense bushes next to it. With rain in the forecast, she had switched her bag at home for her waterproof backpack; she couldn't risk getting the journal or the doll wet. She rolled her eyes at the irony: she was protecting her precious stolen antique contraband. What was wrong with her? After seventeen years of impeccable behavior, she had tossed ethics aside, along with her once-steely resolve never to fall in love. She ran across the lawn to the stone stairs.

Even in the darkness she could tell that the beach was flooded. "Damn!" she shouted, stamping her foot.

In the two days since she had seen Ezra, the tides had changed. She could see that the water was just beginning to ebb. That meant that low tide would be around three in the morning.

She walked down the stairs to the water. There was barely any beach left. She stepped out of her shoes and left them on the landing with her socks tucked inside. There was no moon yet, only a faint ambient light from the streetlights. She swallowed a sharp pang of disappointment in her throat. Ezra would have helped her; Ezra would have bolstered her for what she needed to do. She could almost see his eyes—caring and penetrating, his attention intense and undivided.

She waded into the black water. It was soft around her ankles, soothing her, calming her, making her muscles relax. She went in up to her knees. She swished her foot, feeling her toes drag in slow motion through the heavy, rippled sand. Her foot passed over a large shell—it felt like an intact knobbed whelk. She was wasting valuable time, she knew. But she didn't want to see Linnie, not just yet. She bent over to pick up the shell, feeling for it underwater. Something stirred in front of her, and from the corner of her eye she thought she saw a flash of white.

Two cool hands grabbed her wrists and pulled her into the water. She barely had time for half a scream before she was plunged under headfirst. Bubbles burst around her face and water rushed up her nose. She yanked her right arm away. She was being pulled hard, and her feet were scrabbling frantically along the bottom. She dug them into the sand, slowing the creature, or startling it. Her face broke the surface for a moment—long enough to take a gulp of air—before she was pulled under again. The water quickly became too deep for her to feel the sand beneath her.

She struggled and writhed as the thing switched positions, easily hooking an arm around her neck and swimming her down—headfirst, faceup, deeper and deeper—in a death-spiral version of a lifeguard rescue. It was a distinctly humanlike arm that held her, and Hester clutched it with both hands, afraid of the speed, and afraid it would strangle her. The rhythmic thumping and pumping beneath her was the unmistakable action of a powerful tail, propelling them to the depths of the bay. Hester kept her eyes closed, but she knew without seeing the creature: it was a mermaid.

They were real.

McKee was right; E. A. Doyle was right.

And Hester was about to be killed.

Her lungs felt as if they would implode from the pressure. She had the sensation of knives stabbing through her ears into her brain. She tried to release small bubbles of air from her nose, hoping it would ease the pain. She clawed at the arm around her neck. She dug her fingernails in, but they bent backward against the tough skin. She pounded on the arm, twisting and turning her body. She had used up the last of her oxygen fighting, and she had been dragged too deep, too fast. She stopped resisting. She felt her body begin to go limp.

Would she take a breath when she fainted? Was that how people drowned?

Her parents flashed into her mind, then Sam. And next a picture of the doll, tucked safely in her backpack with the journal. Who would find them under that bush? And finally she saw an image of Ezra, beautiful Ezra, lying under her in the sand, looking into her eyes with a contentment she'd never before seen on anyone's face.

Her mind clouded with pain. She felt a scorching in her lungs. Even if she could break free, she couldn't swim to the surface in time to save herself. Remaining alive was no longer bearable. She felt herself begin to lose consciousness.

And then she had a vision:

little Peter's feet dangling above her
the hot pink of the underside of his swim-a-ring
the jack somewhere past the sandbar
swimming
the murky depths
searching
deeper
seeing
deeper
there's the jack
forgetting to hold her breath.

Chapter 37

THE WATER RUSHED into Hester's lungs, and her body seized. In the fraction of a second in which she thought she died, she felt the dry cavity of her chest flood with an oddly familiar, merciful coolness. She waited another second, anticipating a death that didn't come. Instead, the scorched feeling had been bathed away. She was still being carried to the bottom by strong arms and those powerful, rhythmic tail bursts. She sucked in more water and closed her mouth. It refreshed her. It oxygenated her. It made the pressure of the ocean around her tolerable.

It was impossible.

The stabbing pain in her ears was gone. She dared to open her eyes, and she could see—at such depths!—a grainy, dark, monochromatic-green vision of another world. A huge fish swam by, the retina of its eye warily glinting metallic in her direction. She breathed again through her nose. It was miraculous. And yet it was a sensation she recognized—that hazy, early memory from childhood. Her muscles became tense with anticipation. If she was going to die, it would not be by drowning.

Her marvel increased with every moment. Not only could she see and breathe, she realized that she could also hear underwater. The bay was full of sounds that her dull ears had never picked up before when she was swimming at the beach: the low-frequency rumblings of distant boats, the high-pitched call of dolphins, the melancholy song of a humpback whale, the sound of rocks and pebbles shifting against each other on the ocean's floor. And then a voice—the voice of the thing that had her in its clutches. It was incomprehensible, with periodic click-consonants.

"S!glaemie tor!ga meelay, Syrenka."

Hester angrily shook her head, but the motion nearly strangled her because of the arm around her neck. "Nng" was the only sound she could get out in protest, clawing at the arm again, which finally loosened. The creature stopped swimming, released her, and turned to face her, holding Hester's upper arms, steadying her. Hester expected to float up, the way a human body should in water, but she remained stationary, neither sinking nor floating.

Why hadn't she died of hypothermia? The water at the surface was sixty-five degrees on a good day, but at this depth it had to be close to freezing.

The creature stared at her. Hester was riveted by her eyes—large and round and nearly clear, with horizontal slits for pupils. She was beautiful . . . and frightening. Hester had a sudden instinct to tuck her legs and arms in, recoiling from danger like an octopus.

"Sno eaer!gla Syrenka?" The creature pointed to herself. "!Gla Needa."

Hester unfolded a little and shook her head to indicate that she didn't understand. The creature reached out curiously to touch Hester's hair, which was floating behind her, still clasped by Peter's shell barrette. The creature's hair was thick, white, and drifting in a halo around her head. Her skin was pale, and Hester couldn't help but notice how beautiful her nude body was, how perfect her breasts were, and how natural it seemed for her to be unclothed. Hester felt clumsy in her shorts, shirt, and underwear.

Syrenka, the creature had said. Where had Hester heard that word before?

The creature moved closer, cocking her head at different angles to study Hester's face, as if she thought she knew her but was now unsure. She touched Hester's chin to lift it. She was gentle and inquisitive, and as Hester grew used to her attention, her body unfurled. When the creature wasn't swimming, her movements seemed deliberate and slow, and they were beginning to have a mesmerizing effect.

"Syrenka," the creature said again, with an odd mix of certainty and confusion.

Then suddenly Hester knew. Syrenka was a person. Ezra had called her Syrenka.

Hester opened her mouth to see if she could speak. "I am not Syrenka," she said, too loud and much too slowly, as if she had a mouth full of caramel. She pointed to herself and said, "Hester." The H disappeared in the water.

"Needa," the creature said, pointing to herself. And then she spoke in English with a lively look in her eye. "I think . . . you are Syrenka."

"No. But you're not the first to say that I look like her . . ." Hester glanced up toward the surface and pointed. "I have to go back."

"You look nothing like Syrenka," Needa said, shaking her head as if it were a silly notion. Her hair billowed gracefully as she did. She touched Hester's chest. "Except inside."

Hester stared at her, dumbfounded. When she found her voice she asked, "Why am I alive?"

Needa understood the question, and a mischievous smile spread across her face, showing razor-sharp teeth. "Because you are Syrenka." She put her arm delicately around Hester's waist. "Come now, Noo'kas wants you."

"Wait!" Hester said, but it was too late. She had been swept up, and with vigorous pumps of Needa's tail they were skimming the ocean floor. She had to close her mouth and duck her head to reduce the drag.

They rose over the hulk of a sunken metal ship, darkly rusted, with a downy sort of sea lanugo covering its surface and fish darting in and out of its many holes. They passed boulders and human debris—an outboard motor, broken lobster traps, and hundreds of bottles and cans. Another sea creature joined them, swimming alongside, unable to resist reaching for Hester's hair. Her fingers had sharp, ridged nails. Hester pushed her hand away, careful not to get close to the fins on her wrists.

They slowed as they passed over an area fenced in on four sides with the intertwined masts of many ships. Inside the pen there were children's toys and mangled parts of playgrounds, including a largely intact but rusted swing set and half of a seesaw. There was a slimy red and yellow ride-in plastic car just like the one Sam had as a toddler, and decomposing wooden cribs and bassinets. The pen was staged as a nursery, right down to baby bottles full of sea glass, dishes, spoons, and dozens of faded, cracked rubber pacifiers. But most unusual were the hundreds of dolls—of every imaginable size and shape. There were plastic dolls, dolls with ceramic heads and stuffed bodies, wooden dolls, homemade dolls, headless bodies with round tummies, loose arms and legs, and many disembodied heads weighted down on the trays of high chairs and the surfaces of a dresser and a table. It seemed that every doll that had ever been dropped overboard by a child, or lost in a stream or storm drain, had found its way to this faux nursery. The creature who had been swimming alongside them lingered for a moment to arrange a bassinet that had been tipped by the currents. Hester looked back as she finished tenderly tucking in an eyeless doll and swam to rejoin them.

Hester wondered what time it was. She had something to do on the surface that she couldn't quite remember. She was about to ask Needa something, but the question eluded her—and now they had come upon an immense shelf of rock on the ocean floor, littered with a mountain of debris. Hester strained her eyes to see what it was composed of as they approached.

They entered a pathway through the mountain, and she saw that the walls of debris on either side of her contained hundreds of thousands of lost human objects—all of them metallic, some still shiny and glittery, others dull and black.

"Noo'kas's treasure," Needa said as they slowed. "If you find anything on the sea floor, you must take it to her. If she does not want it, you may keep it."

"I . . . I can't stay," Hester protested.

The pathway widened into an open-water "room" surrounded by mounds of treasure. Noo'kas was piled in an oversized, elaborately carved, dark wooden chair, which had lion heads on the armrests and lion claws at the end of each exquisitely turned leg.

The seat was upholstered with ragged fabric that had once been luxurious velvet, of a color Hester couldn't see with her monochromatic vision. It had to have been the closest thing to a throne that had ever fallen into the ocean.

Noo'kas was large—taller and broader than the dozens of females that swam in attendance upon her. She had rolls of fat on her body and lumpy, pendulous breasts that hung below her waist, but an oddly skeletal face and head. Her nose had worn away to only vestigial pits where nostrils might have been if she had been human, and her ears had decayed to show three holes on each side of her head—two small and one large. Her eyes had sunk deep into her skull so that they appeared from every angle to be dark and shadowed. Her head was nearly bald, with patches of flaking scales and sparse, stringy strands of hair that sagged lifelessly the full length of her body. She was festooned with blackened silver jewelry: multiple tangled necklaces; long pendants; bracelets; rings on every finger; and four or five Native silver-link concha belts with turquoise and onyx stones, all hooked together to circle her massive girth just once. Something about her seemed vaguely familiar to Hester: she had seen an image of her before but she couldn't quite place it. She closed her eyes for a moment, trying to shape the memory from the clouds in her mind, but it wouldn't come.

Needa deposited Hester before the throne so that her feet lightly touched the ground. She passed her lips by Hester's ear, saying in a low voice, "Bow." She herself lay facedown on the rock shelf, reaching her arms forward in supplication to Noo'kas, and then rose and swam backward into the ring of beautiful attendants.

Hester reached a tentative hand out to Needa as she receded, to keep her from leaving her there alone, but Needa frowned and tipped her head once, coaxing her manners. Hester turned to Noo'kas and bent at the waist, taking the opportunity to pull her shirt down in the front and tuck it into her shorts so it wouldn't float up in her face.

"You might have paid your respects sooner." Noo'kas's voice rumbled at such a low frequency that Hester felt the vibrations burst like bubbles through her body.

"Do you mean me?" She looked around to see if there was anyone else.

"Of course I do, vile creature."

Hester stood up straight and glared at the hag in the shadowed recess of her eyes. "I don't even know you."

"Tell me who you think you are."

"I'm . . . I'm . . ." She looked to Needa for help, but Needa turned away. She had called her Syrenka. Was that her name? Her mind was hazy. "I'm not sure."

"How old do you think you are?"

"I think . . . seventeen?" She looked at the ground, searching her thoughts for something to hold on to. *What day was it?*

"Wrong. You are ancient. Tell me . . ." She motioned to Hester's belly. "Has that human body borne offspring?"

She was dizzy and forgetful, but she knew that she resented the tone of voice.

"What kind of question is that? Why should I answer you? No! I won't—I will never have a child!" *But look, she had answered the question! She had divulged her most private thought. Where was her will?*

"Syrenka yearned to give Ezra a child, and look how you squander her body."

"This is *my* body! I am not Syrenka!" Hester felt an ache in her chest. The name Ezra meant something to her, but she couldn't remember what exactly.

The sea hag raised a single finger. Her attendants surrounded her, lifting her massive form slowly from the throne until, semireclined in their arms, she traveled under their power. They took her to Hester and circled her, while Noo'kas considered her from every angle.

Suddenly the hag burst into thunderous laughter—her own private joke. The fish that were grooming the barnacles and lice from her body darted away. The attendants tittered, chirping like porpoises. They took her close to Hester, so that she could lean her bony face forward.

"Semiramis . . . that's what I'll call you," she said, as if affectionately. And then she announced to the audience, "Semiramis was the daughter of the fish goddess, Atargatis. And the inventress of the *chastity belt*."

There was more chirping, and the sound of thousands of throaty clicks, which had the effect of hearty applause.

"Semiramis! Semiramis!" the attendants chanted quietly.

Hester shook her head, scowling. *Stop*, she thought, but she didn't have the courage to say it aloud.

Noo'kas lifted her open hand, waiting. An attendant hastily swam away and returned with a thin spear, placing it in her mistress's palm.

Hester watched, mesmerized, as Noo'kas raised the spear and

muttered an incomprehensible incantation. She removed a scale from her fin and impaled it on the tip of the spear, forcing it down toward the shaft.

No, Hester thought.

Something shook awake inside her. She had to escape. She turned and tried to push off the floor of the shelf, to swim up and away.

The spear glided smoothly through the water and pierced the back of Hester's right thigh. She curled to the side in agony, her body sinking slowly to the ground. She screamed and reached back to pull the blade out. Blood trailed in smokelike plumes from the wound. An attendant retrieved the spear.

"Semiramis! Semiramis!" the attendants chanted.

"Why . . . ?" Hester cried. She half crawled, half floated using her hands and her left leg, trailing her right leg behind her, which felt both dead and on fire. The blood was in a cloud around her now. She saw Needa among the attendants and reached her arm out, pleading. *Help me,* she mouthed. Needa shook her head, but her brow was furrowed with something like pity. The attendant put the spear in Noo'kas's waiting hand. She plucked another scale from her tail, secured it to the spear, and with obvious pleasure, took aim.

Hester pulled herself frantically along the sea shelf, looking for an opening in the mountain of treasure. Even as she did, she knew it was hopeless. She was incapacitated, and the attendants could swim like dolphins. Escape was impossible. She was going to die on the ocean floor, with hundreds of sea women watching the sport.

The spear entered her left calf like a hot iron. She fell flat, and as her cheek hit the floor, a cloud of silt and blood mushroomed around her. Before she blacked out, before her body mercifully took her conscious pain away, her eyes rested on an object at the base of the treasure. It was a hip flask, sterling silver once, but now overgrown with green-black algae. The engraved monogram was not quite obscured: MMM. Something stirred inside her—a memory of her past, a connection to her life on land. Through the swirling cloud of sand she reached out a trembling hand and gripped the flask tightly, bringing it to her heart.

Chapter 38

W HEN SHE AWOKE she was lying on a bed of kelp. Needa was applying an ointment of gelatinous mucus to her wounds, which were inexplicably closed. Scar tissue had formed around the holes—the skin looked thin and striated and white, as if she had been burned. The scab in the center of each wound had almost disappeared. Another creature hovered nearby, watching critically, or perhaps standing guard.

"How long have I been here?" Hester asked.

Needa smiled at her. "Hello, Hester. Do not be anxious; you have just arrived."

The guard said to Needa, "Noo'kas prefers the name Semiramis."

Needa's lips tightened. She motioned to the other. "This is Weeku."

"But . . . the wounds have already healed," Hester said. "It should take weeks . . . or . . . or *never* while they're in salt water. I should be bleeding to death!"

"I am sorry you were frightened. Truly I am. It is against the rules to explain the process ahead of time. If you had known how easily we can heal the wounds, perhaps you would not have fought to save yourself. Noo'kas has so little to entertain her now . . ."

Hester couldn't believe what she was hearing. "She could have killed me! And it hurt like hell."

Weeku spoke up. "Death was unlikely; Noo'kas has excellent aim. You will soon forget the pain—it lasts for almost no time."

Time. "What time is it?" Hester blurted. She pushed onto her elbows, trying to sit up.

Weeku said, "Time means nothing. Soon it will mean nothing to you."

"I'm supposed to be somewhere . . ." She had forgotten where, but it felt urgent.

Needa eased her back down. "Here. Noo'kas requires you to stay here."

"My legs are tingling. They've fallen asleep."

"They have begun their transformation. It is slow. It does not hurt. We will bind them to complete the process. The skin will fuse, and then the bones. But first, now that you are awake, Noo'kas wants you. She has never asked to see an initiate before the transformation is accomplished. She is quite taken with you."

Hester shook her head. "Are you saying . . . Are my legs becoming . . . ?"

"Yes."

"I can't! Needa, I'm not—"

"You belong here," Weeku said sternly.

"I belong here?"

"Yes."

It made sense—it all made perfect sense—and it was wrong at the same time. She lay back down, vaguely uncertain. The pressure of the water surrounding her body was comforting, but shouldn't it be deadly to her? The kelp felt luxurious, but shouldn't its slimy, tentacled touch disgust her? She closed her eyes. Her muscles felt loose. Her thoughts pleasantly escaped her. She rested.

Needa finished her work and turned to Weeku. "Tell Noo'kas we arrive presently." The guard bowed her head and swam quickly away.

Needa reached under the bed of kelp and removed the silver flask that she'd found in Hester's hand. She studied it, not quite sure what to do, and then finally she stroked Hester's cheek once. Hester's eyes opened at the touch.

"What is this?" Needa asked gently, showing her the flask.

Hester was ashamed. "I don't know. I took it from Noo'kas's pile. It reminded me of something. It felt important to me."

"From your life on land?"

"Yes."

"Can you fit it in your pocket?"

"I should give it back, shouldn't I?"

Needa thought for a moment. She shook her head. "Keep it for now. We will trust your instinct. But take care: do not allow your mind to wander to it while you are in her presence, or Noo'kas will sense that you have stolen from her."

She rose up and said, "I am to take you to her. There is not much time to tell you what you need to know, but I will try. You must not reveal it to Noo'kas, or Weeku, or anyone, do you understand?"

"Why are you helping me, Needa?"

Needa smiled wistfully. "I want you to live with us—so dearly—but unlike Noo'kas, I believe it must be your choice. Oh!" She covered her mouth. "I am speaking treason!"

She rose up and swam in a graceful figure eight, pacing. "But I cannot leave you defenseless. She is treating you unfairly, out of jealousy. I owe it to my beloved sister." She stopped pacing, swam to Hester, and offered her hands. Hester reached out to grasp them. Needa turned Hester's right hand over.

"Look at your palm. Look carefully."

Hester examined it. "It's just my hand."

"Look at the pattern."

"Wrinkles—I see lines and wrinkles."

"Look again, there." Needa touched the skin lightly with her fingertips.

Hester's hand burned. She looked closely—her vision was coarse, but she saw that some of the smaller, fainter wrinkles seemed to form crackled letters. "Peter," she said after a moment. She looked up at Needa. "How did you know this name?" She made a fist with her hand, opened it, closed it, and opened it again. The letters remained. "How did you do it?"

"You called the name while you were sleeping."

"While I was unconscious," Hester corrected.

"I never spoke as well as Syrenka." Needa smiled. "You must think hard while you are in Noo'kas's realm. Try always to remember where you came from, and if you cannot, look at your palm to remind yourself. She wants you to forget everything—your family, your friends, who you are. She never wants you to know your real connection to Syrenka."

"Who *is* Syrenka?"

"Syrenka was one of us. She was my dearest sister. She became human to be with her lover. They were happy for a time. They were married, but then it went wrong. He was killed, and

Syrenka—she was always so passionate, so determined!—she desperately wanted to save a part of him. It was a mistake. She did a terrible, impulsive thing: she bound his emotions to the earth using the soul of a baby. To do that, she needed Noo'kas's help. But Noo'kas was jealous. She had always been jealous of her. Syrenka was smart, powerful, and headstrong—never obedient enough. Noo'kas could have mercifully refused to help, knowing what poor Syrenka would discover as soon as the deed was done. But she didn't refuse her, because she selfishly wanted those last, lingering pieces of Ezra for herself, and because she wanted to punish her."

"Ezra," Hester said, disquieted by the name of Syrenka's husband. "I know an Ezra."

"Just so. Tell me about your Ezra, Hester."

"The Ezra I know . . . he's lovely," she said with heat building in her face. And then she felt the distinctive knife of longing and suddenly remembered him clearly, as if he were standing in front of her. "In some ways I know him as well as myself. In other ways I don't know who he is at all."

"Think on it, Hester, I entreat you. Remember your past. But there is more to the story. I shall tell you on the way—we must leave now or Noo'kas will punish us for dawdling. Can you stand?"

Despite her relative buoyancy in the water, Hester struggled and failed. "I'm all numb and tingly. I'm afraid of losing my legs, Needa."

Needa scooped her arm around Hester's waist. "It is because you still feel a connection to land. Listen carefully, Hester. If you leave the ocean, the spell will be interrupted, and you may keep your legs. Noo'kas does not want you to leave, so you will have to be clever and determined. If you choose the land over the sea, I cannot help you."

As Needa swam, she explained that for mischief's sake, Noo'kas had deliberately fouled Syrenka's magic. She had entangled the emotions of others who had also died that tragic night.

"It entertained her to know they would always suffer, trapped halfway on the earth, neither truly living, nor freed by death."

"Ghosts—do you mean ghosts, like Linnie?"

Needa nodded. "Yes, I believe that is what you call them. And until now Noo'kas had also delighted in the misery created by the stolen soul of the infant, because it had become a debt that generations of Syrenka's family would pay, over and over again. For Noo'kas that was an unexpected benefit that she came to feel was her biggest achievement: a deliciously recurring punishment. She believed the cycle would continue forever: love, birth, suffering, sacrifice. And she thought she would always have Ezra as her plaything. She calls on him as she wishes, when the tide is high and he is trapped in the cave. Then you came along, trying to break the cycle, discovering important pieces of your curse, causing Ezra to know real love again."

They passed the doll nursery, and Hester knew they were almost at the throne room.

"I haven't discovered a thing," Hester said. "Help me, Needa! Why is the baby's soul a debt?"

"Because it is contrary to nature for a soul to exist on earth without a body, as the baby's soul does. It is also not possible for a human body to live without a soul . . ."

Weeku appeared in the distance, swimming toward them.

Needa swore under her breath in her own language. And then she said in a low voice into Hester's ear, "Do not speak in front of her. This is the last thing I can say to you. Commit it to your memory: as long as the infant's soul is selfishly detained, there is one soul too many on earth, and one will be taken from Syrenka's family."

"But I don't understand," Hester said. Needa squeezed her powerfully around the waist, scolding her. Hester clamped her mouth shut. *A fucking riddle.*

They traveled in silence, with Weeku escorting them. A part of Hester didn't want to understand the story Needa had begun to tell her. She tried instead to concentrate on what it would take to free herself. But her mind would not let go.

The Doyle journal contained detailed, intimate knowledge of the sea folk. Syrenka's lover was named Ezra. E. A. Doyle was Ezra. He had died generations ago, and yet he was still Noo'kas's plaything—until Hester came along, until Hester caught his attention. E. A. Doyle's headstone was upended, along with Linnie's. Hester had no doubt that Linnie had been sending her an angry message. *Why do you want to be with Ezra more than with me?*

Hester felt a film of warm tears bathe her eyes, and the cold ocean wash them away. She breathed in water and felt the sting of the salt against a suddenly raw throat. Ezra, her beloved Ezra, was a ghost like Linnie.

Ezra.

Once it entered her mind, she couldn't erase it. She had deliberately disregarded everything that was unusual about him: that they'd met only on the beach or in the cave; his handmade clothing that was always clean; the outdated language and references; that he never seemed to feel cold; that she'd never seen him speak to another person. Pastor McKee had said that no one could see or hear Linnie but Hester. If she were honest, couldn't the same be said of Ezra? She remembered the couple who passed him on the sand—the fraternity boy and his girlfriend, who both looked bemused when she motioned in his direction. She recalled him standing unnoticed in a sea of people on the Fourth of July.

But what about Joey Grimani? He had heard Ezra's voice in the cave that first night, hadn't he? She replayed the incident in her mind. *You're a crackpot*, Joey had said to her before she shoved him out of the cave. She suddenly recognized that he'd never responded to Ezra's voice at all, he'd only responded to her own perception of a voice.

Even Ezra had seemed taken aback when she spoke to him. *Whom are you speaking to?* he had asked her. She had thought the comment was strange, but she had tucked it away into the recesses of her mind after she got to know him better. Now she wondered, could she have been the first person to speak to him in generations? The first human being to touch him and hold him with love? If it were true, good God, how lonely had he been until then? How could someone so sensitive survive that deprivation? Suddenly Hester was thinking critically again. The lulling effect of Noo'kas's undersea spell was fading.

The mountain of treasure grew before them, and Hester clamped her lips tight, preparing to face Noo'kas.

Her mind asserted itself defensively: why shouldn't she have ignored the warning signs about Ezra? It was an understandable, protective reaction. He was made for her. He was intelligent, he was odd and old-fashioned, and he knew her well—he knew her to her core. He had crushed her resolve with that crooked tooth and his maddening, endearing verbal playfulness. He sparred with her; he made her happy; he filled her with desire. Her connection to him was something they'd both felt, almost instantly. It defied time and space. He had been waiting for her, he'd said once, and now she knew he meant it literally. She knew that she was somehow inextricably linked to him through Syrenka.

This realization was followed quickly by another, more painful one: all the time he'd waited he had been enduring Noo'kas. He'd been trapped on the beach; trapped in a cave that filled with water every twelve and a half hours, exposing him to that hag on her whim; trapped for all eternity, with no control over what happened to him. What horrors had Noo'kas inflicted on him— Noo'kas, who was so selfish and cruel? She wanted to roar in frustration for him. And then, with her thoughts so discomposed, she found herself in front of the sea queen again.

Chapter 39

NEEDA AND WEEKU PLACED Hester on her numb feet in front of Noo'kas, who was sitting in her throne like a giant slug. Her flesh spilled both over and under the armrests, and the tiny fish that groomed her formed a cloud of movement. Needa and Weeku genuflected—which reminded Hester to bow—before they retreated to the phalanx of attendants.

"Ah, Semiramis," Noo'kas said, obviously pleased. "Thank you for coming; I did so want to see your legs one last time before your confinement."

Hester wanted to retort that she'd had no choice in the matter, but quickly felt a rush of warm water bathe her—a current, swirling past every crevice of her body, soothing her and lulling her. She felt a wobble in her self-confidence, and the fog of forgetting.

"Please don't call me Semiramis," she said uncertainly. "My name is Hester." She looked at Needa, who stared with determined blankness at Noo'kas.

"But Semiramis suits you so well, now that you belong to the sea."

The attendants clicked welcomingly.

Just a moment ago Hester had been seething with anger. But what had caused her rage? It escaped her now, and she felt the first winding threads of a cocoon of belonging.

"We want you," Noo'kas said.

"We love you," the attendants echoed.

"Be with me."

"Stay with us."

Noo'kas smiled broadly. Hester felt herself smile back. And then her eyes gravitated to Noo'kas's teeth. They were sharp like Needa's, but yellower. Hester stared, mesmerized, until she realized that something else was different: Noo'kas had multiple rows of teeth, like a shark. Hester blinked.

Something was not right. Something was clouding her judgment. She found herself squeezing her hands into fists. And then, as her fingernails dug painfully into the palm of her right hand, she remembered that it contained a secret. She opened her hand. She pretended to rub one of her fingers thoughtfully with the other hand, and then she glanced at it.

Peter.

So kind.

Peter.

Her loyal friend.

Her home was on the surface.

"I want to go back on land now."

Noo'kas's smile evaporated. She pushed her skeletal face forward.

"*What you want* means nothing in my world. Do not defy me, Semiramis. You will lose."

"Hester, please. It's *Hester*. I belong on land. I'm not one of you. I don't want to be one of you."

There was a disapproving murmur among the attendants.

"Come closer," the hag said.

Hester looked at her legs. She knew that if she moved them, she'd collapse. "I can't."

Noo'kas waved a hand. Needa swam over at a quick clip, picked Hester up under her arms, and deposited her in front of the throne. She held her in place.

Noo'kas lifted Hester's face with something that was more claw than hand and looked into her eyes, penetrating her.

"Mmm. So many unfortunate traces of Syrenka. Perhaps I should have killed you." She reached back behind Hester's head to stroke her hair. She drew a handful forward and then sniffed it through the pitlike nostril holes in her face. "Such a gloriously rich shade, like a sea otter—sleek and much too lovely."

"I need to go back to the surface," Hester said, in as controlled a voice as she could. She had something urgent to do, an errand, or a favor . . . she was on the verge of remembering.

Noo'kas's voice exploded so unexpectedly that Needa's hands clenched involuntarily and pinched Hester's skin:

"SILENCE."

She let Hester's hair slide through her crooked fingers, as if affectionately. "You are one of us now. It is impossible for you to leave."

She petted her again and then held tight to a section of Hester's hair behind her head.

"Did he love this hair, so thick and full of color? Did he stroke it like this?" She yanked it down, forcing Hester's chin up. Needa held her fast.

"Look at that neck, Needa, slender and sensual. Do you think she offered him her neck? And those lips—did they beg for a kiss?"

She leaned her face forward, with her wide, fishlike mouth nearly touching Hester's. The aroma of rotting mackerel bathed the inside of Hester's nose.

"Did you really think you could triumph over me with simple, youthful beauty? It will disintegrate as you age—you cannot escape thin hair, thin lips, sagging flesh, spotted skin—and before you had blinked your eyes, you would have lost him. That is what it means to be mortal. Now that I think on it, I have spared you that pain—spiriting you away from the surface—the pain of being rejected by him when your mortal body becomes decrepit."

Ezra. The witch was talking about Ezra, and Hester suddenly remembered that *he* was the reason she had held such rage for Noo'kas. Hester reached back to brace her stinging scalp. She could hear a crackling inside her skull as Noo'kas pulled her hair out at the roots.

She gritted her teeth. "Let. Me. Go."

"I, on the other hand," Noo'kas said in a repulsive, seductive way. "I will always want you, even as your body fails you. And it *will* fail you, even living among the immortals. You see, I can make you look like one of us, but I cannot make you live forever." She used her other claw to lightly trace an S shape down Hester's chest. "Not with that pesky soul of yours."

The hag tilted her bony head to the side, and Needa forced Hester's face forward. Noo'kas kissed her then, and a tongue as rough as sandpaper sliced its way into Hester's mouth. Needa held Hester in place to prevent her from thrashing away.

Hester fought uselessly. Needa was too strong. Needa, who had pretended to be her friend! She closed her eyes, trying to endure the kiss. The tongue was so long, it caused a gag reflex, which only seemed to ignite Noo'kas's passion. Hester remembered the illustration in Ezra's journal—he had written that she was the longest-living sea creature, so old she was physically eroding—and although the shadowy image resembled her, it couldn't capture the horror of the living monster. Was this what the ghost of Ezra endured at high tide?

Noo'kas sat back in her throne, licking her own lips. "Delicious," she said in a low voice. Needa relaxed her grip.

Hester tried to remember what Ezra had said in the journal. He'd explained how to get away from Squauanit: insist on your connection to the land; insist on leaving. She'd done both of those, hadn't she? And it hadn't worked! Soon they'd bind her legs and a tail would form in their place. The others would call her Semiramis, and her human identity would fade away. Her family and friends would wonder forever what had happened to her, unable to mourn her properly. Linnie would continue to exist in torment. Ezra would endure Noo'kas's repulsive visits for all eternity. She had let them all down, including Pastor McKee.

Pastor McKee. How had he known of Ezra's connection with the sea folk? Why had he sent Hester off to investigate them? Did he know she would become trapped in this godforsaken underworld? He'd warned her away from Ezra . . . why hadn't he told her Ezra was a ghost, like Linnie? She suddenly remembered the flask in her pocket. Michael Morangie McKee's flask: MMM. He'd longed for that lost flask, and taken such care to describe it to her. It was almost as if he'd willed her to find it.

The understanding hit like a physical force against her chest: Pastor McKee was a spirit, too. *He* was the pastor whom Sylvie Atwood had mentioned among the dead that tragic night in the crypt, and whom Hester had read about in the archived newspaper. She teetered on her numb legs, and Needa gently, surreptitiously righted her.

It was so clear to Hester now: McKee wanted her to set him free, along with Linnie, and the flask was the beloved object from his past that had the power to do so.

Noo'kas snapped to attention. "What is that you are hiding from me, my dear Semiramis?"

Hester stood straight, pushing her shoulders back even while Needa held them.

"My name is Hester Goodwin, and I'll be returning to the surface now."

But Noo'kas was obsessively focused on Hester's pocket. "It is a piece of my treasure. You have been stealing from me!"

Noo'kas gestured to Weeku, who swam over to pull the flask out of Hester's pocket. She sneered at her as she did. Noo'kas received the flask from Weeku without looking at it.

"That's not yours!" Hester said to Noo'kas, fighting against Needa's grip, reaching futilely into the space between them. "It belongs to my friend, and I'm taking it back to him."

"Everything that falls into the ocean is mine." She held up the flask. "Pretty bottles, and pretty girls."

"I didn't fall in." Hester pointed her finger at Noo'kas. "You kidnapped me. You sent Needa to drag me under. I was drowning, until your magic took over!"

"You did not drown," Needa pointed out. "You have always been able to breathe underwater, your whole life."

"Shut up!" Noo'kas snapped at Needa. "You reveal too much, you prattling fool."

"I am sorry, Mistress." She hung her head.

"No one takes treasure from me," Noo'kas bellowed.

Hester remembered the barrette in her hair. She shook Needa's hands off her arms and reached back to unclasp her hair, which loosened into a shifting halo around her head in the thick water.

"I'll trade you for the flask, then." She held up the barrette. "It's a shell. A silver shell."

Noo'kas sat forward, grunting as she did, eager to see it.

"It's like nothing else in your collection. I will exchange it for the flask—which is merely a dark, dull lump—plus safe passage to the surface."

"What is that object to me?" Noo'kas said irritably. "I have no use for it!" She combed a stringy clump of her hair with her fingers and then lightly pulled on it—it released from her head with no resistance and left a raw patch of scales beneath it. She became enraged. "You know I cannot use it in my hair. You insult me, offering it to me."

Hester impulsively tried to escape then—tried to swim clumsily, up and away, out of the walls of metal debris, with only the power of her arms because her legs were useless. Needa did not follow.

Noo'kas shouted, "You, with your hateful lush hair! You mean to mock me in front of my attendants!" She pushed her blubber out of the throne purposefully, inching one hip and then the other to free herself. Her silver jewelry tinkled like underwater bells. She grabbed a spear from Weeku and swam toward Hester, alarmingly quickly for such a massive being.

"You belong to me! You will stay here!"

Hester stopped swimming and curled herself into a protective ball. She was trembling, but her will was intact.

"I'm my own person, and I'm leaving!" She held out the palm of her right hand with the barrette resting on it. "Take the shell, or live forever with the filthy flask in your collection. It's your choice!" Noo'kas dropped the flask, which tumbled onto the sea floor, and greedily snatched up the barrette to examine it. In that fraction of a second, her eye caught on Hester's palm. Hester saw the look and snapped her hand shut, drawing it in to her body.

Noo'kas reached with the reflexes of a shark to seize Hester's hand. She wrenched Hester's fingers open, clawing wounds with her sharp nails and drawing blood.

"*Who did this?*" She turned on Needa. Needa, who had her head bowed, dropped to the sea shelf, prostrate. Noo'kas raised the spear.

"No!" Hester shouted, trying to grab the weapon. "She's defenseless!"

But it was too late. The spear sliced unerringly through the water, and Needa did not attempt to escape. The spear pierced her heart. She turned silently on her side, until she rested in a curled position on the ocean floor with wisps of dark green blood around her.

"Needa!" Hester screamed. She swam awkwardly toward her— back down into the horrific throne room that she had tried to escape just moments ago. Needa had endangered herself to allow

Hester to stay connected to the earth. She had protected her from Noo'kas as much as any being could.

Hester hadn't gotten far when Noo'kas caught hold of her hair. Her head jerked backward, snapping her neck painfully.

"Why could you not simply go about marrying and dying like the rest of the women in your family?" Noo'kas thundered. She began to shake her back and forth, the way a wolf shakes small prey, with whiplashing strokes. "Why were you so determined to end my beautiful cycle of pain by not having a child? Why did you find Ezra and awaken his feelings? Why are you ruining everything?"

You're our hope. At long last. You're here. Hester heard Pastor McKee's words in her mind.

"Let me go!" Hester screamed.

Noo'kas swung her by the hair into the pile of silver objects, and one wall of the mountain began to shift and fall. Hester scrabbled with her hands and feet, trying futilely to get a foothold. If she couldn't free herself, her neck might break.

Noo'kas pulled her away from the pile, still by the hair, just as Hester spied a dagger. She reached for it but missed as Noo'kas yanked harder.

Hester flung herself stubbornly forward, like a dog on a leash, knowing the pain she would inflict on her own neck and scalp. She strained for the dagger. The fingertips of her left hand caught the handle, and she passed the knife to her right hand, slashing blindly behind her head with a speed and strength she didn't know she had, slicing off her tethered hair. She fell forward, crashing into the mountain of treasure, and Noo'kas rolled backward into the throne room, still holding Hester's hair in her hand.

Hester tried to drag herself out, but the mountain was like quicksand—the objects shifted with every struggling movement. The attendants hurried to set Noo'kas right, but she shoved them away.

And then Noo'kas began to laugh. It was a low, quaking laugh, and it seemed to shake the very floor of the ocean. It vibrated through the water, and the mountain of metal objects trembled, clinking and shifting, causing Hester to sink deeper. Through the debris she saw Noo'kas look at the glossy clump of hair in one hand and the silver barrette in the other, and laugh again, even more deeply.

Weeku swam over to Hester and pulled her out of the wreckage, throwing her in front of the throne. Then she swam to Noo'kas and eased her into her chair, gently tucking the blubber around her.

"You are hideous now," Noo'kas bellowed at Hester, holding up the disembodied hair.

Hester's head felt light and free, but she made herself look miserable to satisfy Noo'kas's narrative.

"I have decided I like this trade," Noo'kas said. She held up the barrette for all to see. "You have even less use for this trinket than I! It shall remain forever with your amputated hair!" She boomed with laughter at her own joke. The attendants tittered and clicked their tongues in applause.

Hester reminded her, "The trade was for the flask and safe passage to the surface."

"Oh, go, you hateful thing." Noo'kas was instantly deadpan. "Go and live your pathetic mortal life. It will be over in a heartbeat. You will die and Ezra will be all mine again." She tilted her head toward Weeku. "Get her out of my sight."

Weeku swam over to Hester and lifted her by the waist. As she circled up and out of the throne room, she passed the spot where the flask had dropped. She slowed down almost imperceptibly. Hester understood the gesture and reached out to scoop the flask up.

They traveled at such a speed, Hester could only close her eyes and mouth tightly and wait until it was over. They broke the surface of the water at Ezra's beach, and Hester was surprised to see that it was still dark out, with only the waning crescent of the moon. The tide was receding, and the cave was still partially submerged. The entire event had happened in just a few hours.

Her legs were tingling but functional as her feet touched sand. Weeku released her to stumble ashore. Hester coughed forcefully, and a spray of water came out of her mouth. She turned to see Weeku watching her.

"Thank you for this," she choked, showing Weeku the flask, "and for bringing me to shore."

"I did it for Needa only. She thought of you as her sister. And now I am done with you."

Chapter 40

HESTER WAS DRENCHED, but the night air was warm. She looked wistfully at Ezra's cave, knowing she could not visit him just yet. Time was running out, and in an hour or two the town would come alive. She put the flask in her pocket.

At the base of the stone steps she pulled her socks onto gritty, salty feet, and forced her feet into her running shoes without unlacing them. In the dim light of the old lamps above, she could see that the scars on her legs had healed to barely visible. She took the steps two at a time, ran to the bushes, and pulled out her backpack. She left the bike locked, knowing that she would be back to see Ezra when she finished her task. And then, taking a deep breath to prepare herself, she jogged up to the churchyard.

Before she had a chance to look for Linnie, she saw that Pastor McKee was waiting in the back doorway of the church, his dark body silhouetted by the light behind him.

He motioned to her, and then slipped inside and down the stairs. Why wasn't he waiting for her? Hester wondered. She flipped on the crypt lights and followed him.

Halfway down the stairs she heard his nervous laugh. "You've found my flask, haven't you? You claever gaerl."

"Yes, how did you . . . ?" She pulled it out of her pocket.

He reached the bottom of the stairs, turned to face her, and walked backward with each step that she took, until he was touching the far wall. He seemed frightened of her. She set her backpack gently on the floor, taking care not to hurt the doll or the journal inside.

"I'm ready. I know I am. The Lord knows I've wai'ed long enough." He laughed again. "Where ded you find et?"

"You'll never believe the things I've seen tonight, Pastor. I hardly believe them myself. I've been underwater, in the bay. For hours—although it felt like a lifetime. Noo'kas—Squauanit—had your flask in a mountain of found objects. She has a penchant for shiny things. I traded it for my silver barrette." She held up the flask as she walked toward him.

"Wait," he said, expelling air. He put his hand out. "Wait, just a moment, lamb. Dinnae hand et to me yet."

She stopped walking. She saw his hand was trembling. She looked at the flask—the treasure from his past, a gift from his mother, and judging by its weight, still full of his beloved McKee family scotch. It must be a powerfully sentimental object, she thought, to affect him even at this distance.

"I know you wanted me to find this—you guided me to it," Hester said.

"Aye," he said, again laughing nervously.

"You're the pastor who died in the crypt."

"Aye."

"You're a . . ."

"A pinned spirit. I'm sorry tha' I didnae tell you sooner, lass. Truly I am. One might assume I'd have had a plan en place, having

260

had nearly one hundred forty years to think about it—hopin' for someone to come along who could see me an' hear me, waitin' for you, tryin' to trick and entice you here."

Hester went back and sat on the bottom step to keep the flask far away from him.

"How did you know I would come?"

"I knew ten years ago that you exested because Adeline could speak with you. I tried to catch your attention with the hauntings, to make you understand there was magic en the waerld, an' tha' you waer special; I was hopin' to draw you in, tha' you'd become curious an' speak to me."

"But the silverfish were terrifying," Hester said. "Why scare a child?"

"Och, the selverfish waer an accident, plain an' semple. I cannae leave the chaerch, an' so I charged Adeline with drawin' you enside, so I could speak to you. Poor lass doesnae know haer power. Because of the selverfish we lost you for a decade. Et was a heartbreak for us both."

"I'm sorry."

"She also helped me with the overtaerned stones. I had t' get you back the mornin' after . . ." He stopped, flustered.

"The morning after I spent the night with Ezra."

"Adeline doesnae understand why I asked haer t' do any of et, Hester. She jus' wanted t' see you again." He spoke in a low voice. "Be kind to haer, please, my dear—unpin haer as gently as y'can. I know tha' you will."

Hester looked at her backpack, bulging with not only Linnie's doll, but also Ezra's journal. Somehow, through cleverness and uncanny luck, Pastor McKee had maneuvered her into collecting the three objects she needed to release each of their pinned spirits. She scowled. She felt manipulated—by him and by fate.

McKee said, "When we spoke for the faerst time en the crypt, wha' a miracle tha' was. You'd come to me at last. But et was defficult for me to fegure out wha' to tell you, an' at wha' pace. I had t' get you to believe the unbelievable. I knew that guidin' you to descovery was the surest path, bu' a dangerously slow one. I worried tha' you might fall en love with Ezra en the meantime, and then you wouldnae be able to let hem go."

Hester stared him in the eye, unflinching.

"And now y've fallen." His face was more tired than ever. "And all may be lost."

She said, "You should have told me that he was a spirit."

"He'd have sensed my betrayal, and he would have kept you from me. I'm so sorry, lamb."

"How did you know I would fall in love with him?" Her voice cracked, although she didn't want it to.

"I suspected, because of somethen' I saw en you." He looked as if he wanted to comfort her, but thought better of it and pressed his back into the wall.

"He'll never age?"

The pastor shook his head solemnly. "I'm afraid no'."

"He'll never leave the beach?"

"Et's where he died."

Died. The word was so final. And yet Ezra was so alive, so animated, so present.

"I could visit him every day . . ." Hester said, staring at the dirt floor. "High tide or low—now that I know I can breathe in the water, it will make no difference what hour it is. I could live out my days with him."

"Dinnae make the mestake tha' Sarah made, Hester, I beg you."

"What mistake?" she said.

"Thenk, Hester. When you're dead an' gone, he'll stell be here. When the human race es gone, he'll stell be here. As lovely as you are, en mind and body and spirit, from hes point of view you're a cut flower—you're dying already. He'll have no connection with humanity when you're gone. He'll be alone. Sarah should never have pinned hem. *Fex* haer mestake, Hester, for only you can do et—let hem go. Let Linnie go. Let me go."

"I can release you and Linnie first, and him later—"

He interrupted her. "Na, lass. You mus' release us all together. We are pinned by the same soul."

Something boiled up and exploded from inside of her. "Then you'll have to stay in limbo a little longer! It's not asking much—according to you it's the time it takes a cut flower to die!"

He looked stunned. She could see him reassessing. Where had he gone wrong? How had he misjudged her character?

Her voice was suddenly weak. "Yes, it's selfish. I'm being a jerk. I just want *a little time* with him."

He sighed. "Et was to be expected. Et's a powerful soul you have there, Hester. I cannae blame you for wha' you want."

"I promise I'll release you someday . . ."

"Wha' ef you die, love? Everythen' depends on you. What ef you walk out of here and you're struck by a carriage?"

"By a car," she mumbled.

"Aye." He nodded, smiling at her. "A car."

Hester's mind raced through the possibilities. She could release them before she got old. She could write a will, requiring the unpinning, in case she died unexpectedly. But how could someone else carry it out, without seeing or hearing or touching them? Her instructions would seem to be the ravings of a lunatic.

"You're forgettin' about the sea hag." He broke into her thoughts. "Do you truly thenk she'll wesh you and Ezra happy, and go on haer way? Do you thenk you've won? Thar's no winnin' with Squauanit, and you know that. But thar's more, Hester. A connection—an explanation—tha' I hoped you would find yourself, but I dinnae think y'have. You see, I suspect your own caerse depends upon freein' us. Tha's wha' I meant when I said everythen' es entertwined."

"How do you know about my curse? I've never mentioned it to you."

"I know et drove you to the crypt the faerst time we met. You waere searching for a link to your past. You knew tha' a tragedy happened here—you knew the sarcophagus meant somethen' to your family. But more than all tha': you looked into my eyes and I recognized your soul."

"What does that mean?"

"Et means—an' I dinnae know why—that you're carryin' the soul of another paerson—one I've met before. Hester, my darlen', you have the soul of Sarah Doyle, Ezra's wife."

"The soul of Syrenka," Hester murmured. She lifted her feet onto the step below her and hugged her knees. She concentrated on breathing.

Needa had insisted she was Syrenka. Noo'kas had chastised

her for having too much of Syrenka in her. Ezra had called her Syrenka the first time they had touched. And now Pastor McKee said he saw Sarah's soul in her—Sarah, who was Syrenka.

Pastor McKee said, "I dinnae pretend to understand how et happened—I never was a brillian' man, even when I was alive. But somethen' on that horrible night caused Sarah's soul to pass t' you, though you waeren't yet born. I cannae fegure et . . ." His voice petered out to nothing.

Needa's cryptic comments swirled in Hester's head: she had mentioned a recurring punishment for Syrenka's family; a cycle of sacrifice that would last forever, all because of a stolen soul. *As long as the infant's soul is selfishly detained, there is one soul too many on earth,* Needa had said. Hester knew that it was the soul of the baby that Syrenka had used to pin Ezra's and McKee's and Linnie's emotions to the earth. But who was the baby? And why did Syrenka's soul pass intact to Hester almost one hundred forty years later? Where had it hidden until then?

All of the deaths in her family had happened within days of giving birth, as if each mother was giving her life to pay for that one soul. But why did they *all* have to die, for one baby?

Who was the baby?

Her head ached, and she felt a little woozy. Did it really matter if she figured out a connection to her own curse? After all, she could end the cycle of deaths in her family merely by remaining childless, which had been her plan all along. No, the real consideration was this: three spirits she had grown to love were experiencing an eternity of pain, and Hester was the only person in the world who could end it.

"There has been so much suffering because of that single night," she said, her voice muffled by her knees.

"Aye."

"And that witch Noo'kas has enjoyed watching the suffering continue generation after generation."

She looked up at Pastor McKee. He was staring intently at her.

Hester went on, "Noo'kas wanted me safely under the ocean, lulled into forgetting, to keep me from Ezra. What she didn't realize when she let me go was that I know how to take Ezra from her forever. I can spare him the horror she's inflicting on him—and you, and Linnie."

"Aye."

She felt chilled in her wet clothes in the damp crypt. Her flesh was raw with goose bumps, and she was trembling. She worried she would soon collapse from exhaustion—from lack of sleep and the physical and emotional trial Noo'kas had put her through. The night had ended, and morning was near. She stood up.

"I have to release you now, Pastor. I have to save Ezra."

Pastor McKee heaved a choked sob that had been held back for more than a century. Tears came to his eyes, pooling above pink lids. "Tha's right—brave, kind gaerl. Tha's right."

Chapter 41

HESTER'S SHIVERING INCREASED, but she wasn't sure if it was just the chill. Unpinning Pastor McKee's spirit meant ending what little life he had. Was it the same as murder? It was so final. She didn't know if she had the strength to do it.

"I thenk et's time you tried your faerst nep of scotch, Hester," he spoke up. "Et will do you good. Et will calm your naerves and warm you up."

"Alcohol makes your core body temperature go down," she mumbled. Her jaw quivered so violently that her teeth chattered.

"Ah . . . well . . . no' en my day. But et will give you fortitude, and you need tha' now." He was somber—more subdued than she had ever seen him.

She nodded in agreement. At the very least, she could call it the first step in her miserable task. Maybe subsequent steps would follow, if she just took the first one.

She flipped the flask over and over in her hands. She rubbed it against her shorts—with all of its recent handling, it had regained most of its shine. It was a beautiful little thing, and it showed its age in its fine workmanship. Hester imagined its journey through time: from the silversmith who crafted it, to McKee's mother, to McKee, to America, to almost a hundred forty years under the ocean, and now to her. Lifetimes had come and gone in the meanwhile. She pulled out the stopper, which was a cork embedded in a decorative silver cap. She sniffed it and suppressed the urge to wrinkle her nose. It might as well have been lighter fluid, as far as she understood scotch.

"It smells good," she lied, looking across the room at him. He smiled broadly.

She knew enough science to know that there could be nothing poisonous about it: silver is inert; alcohol is itself a preservative; it had been tightly sealed in a dark, cool place. It would be as healthy for her as the day it had been distilled in Morangie, which is to say, not very.

She took a gulp. An instantaneous, piercing burning gripped her throat. It was impossible to swallow and cough at the same time, but her throat tried to make her do it. When she finally did let out a single sharp, spraying bark it was too late: the liquid was already on its way down, making her aware of every inch that it traveled. She felt it coating, burning, easing its way through her insides. By the time it reached her stomach, it was warm and genuinely lovely.

She forced another gulp, and this time she was able to swallow without coughing by holding her nose until the scotch was safely down her throat. And then she stood up, with her heart blazing fire, her face flushed, and the acrid smell of alcohol in her nasal passages.

"Here we go, my friend," she said.

"God's grace upon us."

Pastor McKee walked toward her, and she walked toward him. He grimaced as they got close.

"I only ask, dinnae try to save me," he blurted.

He extended his hand, trembling. She held out the flask. She tried to think of what she might say to talk him off the earth.

He grasped the flask and collapsed on the spot, as if he had been shot. Hester gasped. She knelt at his side.

He opened the bottle with monumental effort. His entire body began quaking with tremors. He managed to get the flask to his lips. It spilled, but some of it went into his mouth. He swallowed. He closed his eyes, in what Hester thought was either agony or ecstasy. The cork dropped to the ground and rolled on its side in an arc on the floor, landing next to her. In his seizure, he held the flask out to her, with the liquid splashing out of the narrow opening. He wanted her to have it. She took it from him and threw it down, lifting his head and shoulders onto her lap.

"What's happening?" she asked him.

He looked at her with wide, frightened eyes. She saw bruises forming on his neck, and she gasped. He wheezed at first, and the sound got tighter until a high-pitched whistling barely escaped. His lips began to turn blue. She heard a rattling gurgle as his windpipe closed. She saw the bony structure of his throat collapse, as if an invisible hand had crushed it, and then—worse than the rattling—she heard eerie silence. His eyes bulged until she could see their ball shape protruding from the sockets. His face was bright red, and his body writhed as she held him, but not a sound escaped his mouth. His head shook wildly back and forth, as if saying no, no, no. He didn't want to die!

"You said I had to talk you away!" she cried. "You lied to me!"

His eyes rolled into his head.

"Not like this, Pastor!"

His face was blue. The spasms of his body subsided. She wrapped her arms around him, leaned her cheek against his head, and held him tightly. Within a minute, he was absolutely still.

"You lied to me," she whispered into his ear. "It wasn't supposed to be like this."

Chapter 42

Hᴇꜱᴛᴇʀ ᴇᴀꜱᴇᴅ Pᴀꜱᴛᴏʀ McKee's body down. She closed his eyelids, put his arms by his sides, and smoothed his wild white hair away from his face. And then she remembered that she was the only one who could see his body or touch it, and the full weight of his aloneness hit her.

She got up slowly with aching knees. She picked up the flask and stopper. He had given it to her as a memento of their friendship, and she would treasure it. Making sure the stopper was in tight, she tucked the flask into the pocket of her shorts. She walked on wobbly legs back to the stairs, where she had set down her bag, and gingerly pulled the doll from the main compartment. She fixed the doll's hair and hugged her to her chest.

Now she knew what unpinning a spirit entailed. Pastor McKee hadn't had the heart to tell her. And maybe he was right not to: she might not have agreed to it. It meant causing her friends to experience their deaths again, with all the pain of the original event. It meant being helpless to ease their suffering.

She walked up the crypt stairs and outside. It was not yet dawn. Linnie was waiting for her—a waif of a shadow, huddled behind a tombstone in the dark. Hester put the doll behind her back.

"Hi, Linnie."

"Where is Pastor McKee?" Linnie's voice was puny.

"He's inside—in the crypt."

In the faint light streaming out of the doorway, Hester could see Linnie shaking her head.

"I don't feel him."

"He's there, I just left him."

"He's not there!" Linnie shouted.

"Linnie . . ."

"Call him to the doorway!" And then she crouched again. "My head hurts."

Tears came to Hester's eyes.

"I know it does. I'm sorry. Please believe me that I'm so sorry."

"What are you holding behind your back?"

"It's . . . I found something for you, Linnie. Something you lost. My friend had it all along, and I didn't know it."

She brought the doll out from behind her back.

"Poppet," Linnie whispered. She stepped around the gravestone.

"Wait," Hester said. She wanted to explain. She wanted to say something that would make what was going to happen easier. But Linnie was already running toward her. And how could she make death easier for a child with just words?

Instead, when Linnie grabbed the doll Hester scooped her up in her arms before she fell to the ground. The doll was wedged between them.

Linnie let out an inhuman wail of agony.

"Forgive me, Linnie," Hester said.

But Linnie began to thrash wildly. She wrenched herself out

of Hester's arms and started pounding on her with the power of a grown man, all while clutching the doll. She grabbed Hester by the shirt, ripping a sleeve partly off, and threw her to the ground several feet away. Hester crawled to a granite tombstone. She instinctively rolled into a ball, tucking herself into a fetal position facing the tombstone, with her arms protecting her head. Linnie stumbled over like an injured bear and began kicking her with massive blows, screaming in pain.

"Drop the doll, Linnie!" Hester shouted, not knowing what else to do to end Linnie's pain. She would be killed herself if Linnie kicked in her head, or decided in her rage to use a stone as a weapon. But Linnie wouldn't drop the doll, and all at once she fell in a heap on the ground next to Hester. The attack had ended as quickly as it had begun. She had fallen face forward, and Hester saw that the beautiful thick rope of a scar—the scar Hester had secretly coveted as a child—had opened into a gaping, bloody gash the size of a man's hand. Her skull had fractured, and the bony plates had cleaved open, exposing the brain underneath.

"Linnie!" Hester cried. She crawled to the little girl's side and rolled her over. A fluorescent burst of lightning revealed Linnie's open and lifeless eyes. Poppet was still clenched under her arm.

A clap of thunder made Hester jump. She kissed her old friend's cheek—plump with youth.

"Rest now, Linnie."

She closed Linnie's eyes. Fat raindrops began to fall. She gently wiggled Poppet from Linnie's grasp, whispering "I'm sorry," and carried the doll inside the church, out of the rain. She leaned Poppet against the wall, away from the door, so that Peter would find it in the event that—she didn't know what. The skies opened, and the rain came down in beating sheets. The wind picked up with a hurricane-like, swirling burst, soaking the floor at the threshold. And then she went down the stairs toward the crypt to retrieve her backpack, and the journal that would destroy the spirit of the man who had become everything that mattered to her.

Compared with the darkness of the graveyard, the light was harsh as she descended into the crypt. Hester squinted and put her hand up against the glare of the bulbs. She kept her eyes down to avoid looking at the pastor's body. She concentrated on her next worry: Ezra's death and the form it would take. The long scar she had discovered on his chest flashed through her mind, and she remembered the feelings of loss that had coursed through her when she touched it. How unbearably cruel was it to inflict that injury on him again? How long would he live after it opened? What pain would he be in? Would his spirit react with the same violence that Linnie's had?

As she came down the last step she decided she didn't care if he raged. It would be an understandable reaction, and she had no choice but to face it. She wasn't frightened of dying anymore. Her only concern was for the pain it would cause Malcolm, Nancy, Sam, and Peter if she were killed.

Even from the crypt, she could hear the howling of the storm outside. She realized now that it was Noo'kas: the hag finally understood that Hester was two-thirds of the way through her grisly task, and on her way to taking Ezra. Hester wondered if the storm could become strong enough to prevent her from unpinning

Ezra's spirit. She had little physical strength left, and faced with losing Ezra, her conviction was as fragile as it could be.

As she bent to pick up her bag, she saw movement out of the corner of her eye. Before she could react, she was tackled to the ground and being clawed and punched by a raving madwoman.

Chapter 43

Hᴇsᴛᴇʀ ᴛʀɪᴇᴅ to roll away, but the woman had straddled her. She was not only strong, she was stout, too, and Hester was hopelessly trapped.

"Stop! Please!" Hester shouted as the woman smacked her face once with the back of her hand.

"You hateful sea monster!" the woman said, lifting Hester's torso by the shoulders and shaking her. "I have waited too many years to avenge Olaf."

"I'm not a sea monster," Hester cried, realizing at once that she sounded as crazy as her attacker.

The woman pushed her face into Hester's, and spittle flew out as she said, "I won't grace you with the name 'mermaid.' You are no maiden—you whore!" She pointed toward Pastor McKee's lifeless body. "Your legs fool only the feebleminded, like that useless idiot, McKee. I see what you are! You killed my husband, and I know how you did it. It is divine justice that I have been given, by your own act in murdering me, the physical strength now to do the same to you."

She thought Hester was Syrenka! But where had Hester heard the name Olaf?

The woman slapped her face with each hand, one after the other.

"You're Eleanor!" Hester blurted at last. "Eleanor Ontstaan."

Mercifully, calling her name had the effect of stopping the beating, as least for the moment.

"You're not a *stupid* monster then, are you. Just a vicious, heartless one."

Panic rose in Hester. Another pinned spirit! Why hadn't Pastor McKee warned her? How could he have left her so defenseless? She had nothing to use against this ghost—no object from the past. Her heart raced, and her breath became quick and shallow. Why hadn't she thought of it on her own? It was right there, in the *Old Colony* newspaper: Eleanor Ontstaan died in the crypt. Eleanor's drowning was the reason Hester had met Pastor McKee to begin with. Why had she embarked on this plan to unpin them without thinking it through?

"You took a good Christian man from this earth—nay, the best. At long last God will punish you, and He shall use me as His weapon."

"Oh, God, why didn't McKee tell me?" Hester screamed, turning her face away from Eleanor's horrid mouth, which, unlike the other three ghosts, spilled putrid fumes of over a century of rot.

"He forgot about me, the old fool. It is as simple as that. They all forgot about me after they suppressed me. They cowered from my wrath in those early days—though I was justified in my anger—and they pushed me down, the three of them together. If he hadn't been senile, that worthless man might have recalled that it took them all to hold my spirit down. *One* is not enough, not even one as clever as your heathen lover." She grabbed Hester's chin with her left hand and forced her to face forward, raising her right fist to strike her. "Look at me while I kill you!"

"I'm not who you think I am," Hester pleaded. "I'm not Sarah Doyle. Sarah is long dead."

"Your magic does not blind me. It never has. I see your soul, monster."

"But mermaids have no souls!"

It was pointless to argue logic with a furious spirit. The blow came down hard, and Hester felt her nose break as her head was slammed to the side. Blood spattered and beaded on the dusty floor beside her. She felt as if her face had exploded.

She was going to die here. Killed by a ghost that no one else could see, no one could even imagine. It would be another tragedy to compound the one so long ago. Her parents would spend the rest of their lives trying in vain to find her killer. Ezra would be tormented for all eternity by his isolation, and by Noo'kas. The spirits of McKee and Linnie would never be freed. She had failed.

"I know how you got your soul, witch," Eleanor said. "You got it when you tore out my husband's lungs, which is how you are going to die now."

She grabbed the front of Hester's collar and ripped open her shirt. The buttons popped off and flew in every direction. Hester felt a burning sting across the back of her neck, as if she had been slashed with a knife.

Eleanor paused, with wide eyes. She hovered above Hester, teetering for an agonizing moment, and then fell to her side, crumpling half on the floor and half on Hester's torso. Hester shoved her off and scooted wildly away, kicking her legs frantically to disentangle herself. What had just happened?

Still lying on her side, Eleanor looked at the necklace in her hand, which she had ripped off Hester's neck. She pulled it to her heart.

"Marijn," she gurgled, with her body going into convulsions.

Water began pouring from her mouth, as if from a spring. She gasped horribly between gushes in the flow, trying to get air, aspirating the water, choking, and then unable to make any noise as a geyser of water spewed from her mouth. Her body shook with spasms for more than a minute. Then they slowed, the flow of water ebbed to nothing, and soon she was completely still.

She had drowned on dry land.

Great clots of blood oozed from Hester's nose. She put her hand up and pinched the bridge to stanch the flow. Her nose had already swelled, and it was throbbing with every heartbeat, but she didn't care. She was alive. She counted in her head to one hundred twenty, her entire body trembling violently. Two minutes was all she could devote to recovering her wits, catching her breath, and, she hoped, slowing the bleeding. She did not take her eyes off Eleanor's body. It remained still and lifeless.

When her time was up, she stood and approached the body cautiously. The necklace dangled from Eleanor's closed fist. It had saved Hester's life. Now she knew that Eleanor, Marijn's first foster mother, had given the necklace to baby Marijn, beginning the tradition of women in her family passing the necklace to their daughters, until Hester's own mom had given it to her before she died. There was no way she was leaving it behind.

She reached out and tugged on the heart and the chain together. To her relief, the necklace slid out without her having to touch the body. The clasp was broken, so she put the necklace safely in her pocket, in case she survived the next step. She didn't worry that the body would attract any notice; no one but her could see it or touch it.

She secured her backpack as well as she could to keep the rain out and walked up the stairs. No matter how tumultuous the storm was, it was time to go to the beach.

Chapter 44

THE RAIN PELTED HESTER, and the wind was so strong she had to lean her body against it to make progress down the hill. Thunder rumbled—she knew it was Noo'kas threatening her, but she didn't care.

She felt Ezra reaching out to her, and she could hardly bear it. He must know why she approached. He must have felt the loss of the others. And still he wanted her.

How could she live without him?

She held the wall as she went down the stone steps. It should have been low tide, but the waves crashed onshore, making the beach treacherous. She saw Ezra waiting, seemingly oblivious to the storm surge, his eyes locked on her. She slid her backpack off her shoulder and tucked it on a top step, close to the wall. She wanted one moment with him—one last moment—without harming him. She left her shoes on to protect her feet. She ran down the rest of the steps, plunged into the waves at their base, and ran into his arms.

"Your face," he said over her shoulder, holding her close, his voice heavy with concern. "You're bleeding."

"It's nothing," she said. And it was just that: nothing. Nothing compared with anything that had happened to her that night. Nothing compared with losing him.

A large wave knocked into them, but Ezra held her and stood firm. When it passed, he loosened his hold to look more closely at her face. He lifted her chin, looked at her injury with furrowed eyebrows, and softly kissed the space next to her nose, where it wouldn't hurt. He understood everything.

"Eleanor did this."

Hester nodded.

"I'm so sorry, Hester. I had forgotten about her spirit until to-night. We all forgot. I suspect it was a corollary to suppressing her. But you might have been killed—and I would never have forgiven myself." He touched her cheek. "Does it hurt terribly?"

Another massive wave came, and he picked her up to protect her. It broke against them and splashed over their shoulders. She tucked her face into his neck to block out the salt spray.

"I'm fine," she murmured. And it was true, as long as he held her.

They stayed like that through several cycles of waves, pressed together, stopping time. If only. When the water had retreated, he set her down.

"Your hair . . ." he said.

"Noo'kas."

"You are a remarkable woman." He shook his head. "But I'm sorry that you've crossed paths with her. It colors your decision about me."

"I don't care about her. I don't care about my hair. I don't care about anything but you."

"And yet you are here to destroy me." His lips were tight, his eyes penetrating.

She knew him well enough to know that he was confronting

her, and yet he was so calm. She lifted onto her toes and kissed him. He scooped her up and returned the kiss with impatient desire. And then he put her down and shook his head. He took a step back, flustered.

"Let me stay a little longer, Hester."

It stabbed her to hear him say it. Her eyes filled with tears. Thunder clapped. The largest wave yet came with such force, she saw it crest over their heads before she was knocked over. She felt Ezra grab her just as she lost her footing and her body threatened to somersault underwater. He held her solidly in place as the wave retreated with a strong undercurrent, sucking at her clothing. His arms were firmly around her waist and she was on her feet again. She turned to look at the stone steps. The bag was gone. Her eyes darted frantically in the blue, predawn light until she caught sight of it floating in the water, bobbing out to sea. The journal would be lost!

She pushed away from him and ran after it through the high waves and into the ocean.

"Hester!" Ezra called. He was anchored by his curse to the beach. He could not follow.

She dove onto the bag and looped her arm through the strap. She struggled to her feet and ran across the sandbar toward shore until a wave caught her. It flowed over her, pulling her feet out from under her and dragging her down. Noo'kas aimed to have it all— the journal, Hester, and her favorite trinket, Ezra.

The wave tugged Hester backward. She clawed at the sand underneath her, trying to resist the swirling retreat of the water. The next wave came, forcing her briefly toward shore. She staggered and then tumbled, rolling submerged for a moment until she could right herself. When she came up, she could see Ezra, knee-deep in the waves, reaching out for her. She stood again and tried to run the rest of the way to him through the seething water, which held her back until another wave knocked into her. Hester tripped and fell forward.

Strong hands grabbed her under her arms and hauled her ashore. It was Ezra. Her torso, at least, had fallen into his territory. He pulled her out and carried her effortlessly away from the water.

After several steps he began to weaken. He staggered, seeming to will himself to reach the bluff where the land met the beach, and finally collapsed there, holding her. The sea churned so roughly that the leading edge of the storm surge still licked over their bodies, even at this distance.

"Ezra!" Hester said. He was clutching his chest.

"Take it away, please," he begged her. She knew he meant the journal—it was in the backpack, and too close to him.

By rescuing her, he had exposed himself to the instrument of his death.

She kissed him. Her throat was hot and tight as she said, "I'm so sorry." She began to cry as she opened the backpack and removed the journal.

"Syrenka made a mistake all those years ago because she loved you." She pressed the journal to her heart as hot tears mixed with rain and blood on her face. She had to do this before she lost her courage. "Now I'm fixing her mistake because I love you."

She kissed the book. He cried out in agony as she pressed it into his hand.

She fell on top of him and sobbed into his ear, "Forgive me."

"I waited so long for you," he whispered.

"I know. Me, too."

She sat up. A bloody spot had bloomed on his white shirt, wicked by the wet linen like a watercolor painting. She unfastened the buttons. The small scar had opened and was bleeding. The long scar down the middle of his chest was still intact. She put her hand on the smaller wound; it was a clean piercing, from a knife. Touching it made her own heart ache. He had died from the smaller wound all those years ago. His breathing became shallow and quick. She gently moved wet strands of hair away from his eyes.

"Why did you not live out your life with me?" he gasped. His skin was ashen. Until this moment she had never seen him appear to be anything but perfectly healthy.

"Oh, Ezra," she choked, "I would never have said goodbye." She kissed his temple tenderly, feeling the coolness of his skin beneath her lips. She kissed the beautiful hollow of his cheekbone. She kissed near his ear and said softly, "A lifetime with you wouldn't have been enough."

With a grimace he lifted his free hand and draped it on her back.

"I think . . ." he started. He could hardly speak.

"Don't," she said.

". . . I have solved your curse," he finished.

Hester leaned her head in the crook of his neck. "I don't care."

"That is—" He breathed in, and she heard his chest rattle horribly. "*You* have solved your curse. Just now." She put her fingers on his lips. He shook his head, making her drop her hand.

"I missed the obvious. You have her soul. To gain a soul, she had to have had . . ." He couldn't finish. He grunted in pain.

Hester stayed nestled against him. Soon he would be gone, and every joy in her world would be gone with him. She would return to her solitary life. She would never love anyone after him.

". . . a baby," he finished.

He stopped speaking, but with her head against his chest she heard that his breathing had become irregular. There was an agonizing moment when he drew in no air, followed by a deep, gurgling gasp.

What had he said? *She had a baby.* Syrenka had a baby. She lifted her face to look at him. His eyes were closed.

"What does that mean, Ezra? Why is it important that she had a baby?"

He opened his eyes, looking at her with such pained affection, it pierced her with longing for what they would never have together.

His hand pulled her against him one last time. "Little Adeline held a baby that night." His voice was barely audible. "Eleanor's baby. *Syrenka's* baby." His arm seemed to relax and slid off her back.

"Marijn!" Hester cried. "Marijn was Syrenka's baby."

He closed his eyes and nodded almost imperceptibly, with a grimace of satisfaction on his face. He trusted her to figure out the rest.

Hester's mind raced. Her great-great-great-grandmother Marijn was the baby from that tragic night in the graveyard. It was Marijn's soul that Syrenka had used to pin Ezra's emotions to the earth, entangling Linnie's emotions and Pastor McKee's and Eleanor's in the process. But Marijn had not died that night, even though she had lost her soul. She had gone on to have a daughter of her own.

And then Hester remembered what Needa had said: it would have been merciful for Noo'kas to refuse to help Syrenka pin those spirits, knowing what she would discover "as soon as the deed was done."

"Syrenka didn't know that Marijn was her child until after she had sacrificed her! And so she gave her own soul to the baby to save her," Hester cried. She lifted herself up to look at him. "Is that right, Ezra?"

His eyes were closed, his face relaxed. He seemed at peace— even contented. He exhaled one long, shuddering breath. And then he didn't move again.

"Ezra," Hester whispered.

The scar on his chest began to peel open at the edges. As she watched, the seam burst, revealing a broken rib cage beneath. The rib cage slowly spread apart, and between the ragged edges of the bones she could see he had no heart.

The skies opened and the rain poured down in sheets, as it had the first day she met him in the cave. One last wave washed over them, and the journal was swept out of Ezra's hand into the sea. Hester let it go. She flopped back down on him and sobbed into his cheek.

"Thank you," she said. "Thank you for figuring it out."

At last she understood what he had pieced together in his final moments. She understood what the debt of the baby's stolen soul meant, and why the curse had passed from generation to generation in her family. She understood what Syrenka—and every woman in her family after her—had sacrificed, for love of a daughter. Because even though Syrenka had given her own soul to save her baby, Marijn's soul was still selfishly detained on the earth. *There is one soul too many on earth, and one will be taken from Syrenka's family*, Needa had said. Which meant that Marijn's first child was born without a soul, and Marijn was faced with the agony of watching her daughter die in her arms.

Each new baby in her family had arrived without a soul. Each innocent, soulless infant had begun to fade away within days. And faced with the prospect of losing a child, each mother had willed her own soul to her baby, giving up her life so that her daughter might live.

By unpinning Ezra and Linnie and Pastor McKee and Eleanor, Hester had finally released baby Marijn's soul, and the debt was paid. Hester would die with her soul intact—Syrenka's soul, she knew now—which had passed from Syrenka to Marijn, to Nellie, to Grace, to Carolyn, to Susan, and finally to her. If she married and had a daughter, Hester would *live*, and with a bit of luck and good health she might be blessed to know her grandchildren and great-grandchildren someday as well.

She looked at the body of her beautiful lover. In the end he had accepted death so gracefully, knowing what she would gain. She kissed his lips for the last time.

"Goodbye," she whispered, wishing it might not be forever.

Chapter 45

THE STORM EASED, and within minutes the rains stopped. Noo'kas had lost her playthings, but her consolation prize was Ezra's journal. Hester took comfort in knowing that within days or weeks it would disintegrate, and the hag would own no part of him for the rest of time.

She folded Ezra's hands on his chest. She touched his cheek and his lips with her fingertips.

She stood up and tried her best to close her torn shirt by fastening the one remaining, dangling button with trembling hands. Her socks and sneakers were full of wet sand. She ran her fingers through her short hair. She was covered with blood, salt, sand, and bits of ocean debris, and she felt more drained, in every way, than she would have thought possible. Her insides had been scooped out, her head had been emptied. A battered, fragile shell was all that remained. There was no way she could be remotely presentable, but she didn't care. It was almost dawn, and she had a life to live—for Ezra and Syrenka, for Linnie and McKee, and for all the women in her family who had died too young. The first thing she was going to do was take Linnie's doll back to the museum. Then she'd have a hot bath, a long nap, and maybe see a doctor about her broken nose.

She took one last look at Ezra and forced herself to walk away from him. At the top of the stone steps she noticed that the sun was rising. The horizon was on fire with oranges and reds, and above that the sky was full of the gnarled gray and black remains of heavy storm clouds. After billions of years, she thought, the earth was still passionately creating another new day.

Something caught her eye: at a distance it seemed as though shimmering figures were walking on the water, toward the sun. She wondered whether she was seeing things. She squinted against the glare—there were four of them, one much smaller than the rest, one much taller. The taller one lagged a step or two behind the others and seemed to turn, hesitating. She looked back at the beach where Ezra's body had been; it was gone. She looked out at the horizon, searching for him. The procession had disappeared.

She walked up the lawn and retrieved her bike from the post. She did not have the energy to ride her bike up the hill of Leyden Street, so she walked alongside it. A fisherman passed her as he drove up Water Street. She saw his brake lights brighten; his pickup truck slowed to a stop. He craned to see her through the passenger window, calling, "Hey, are you okay?" She nodded, and put up her thumb with such conviction that he waved and drove on.

It took her several minutes to walk up the hill. The church seemed to be quiet, finally resting. She dropped her bike in front and walked around the back. As she turned the corner of the building, she was startled to see Peter come out of the back door with Poppet in his hand. He saw her and his face was instantly shadowed with a worried frown. He rushed toward her, and she fell into his embrace. She let him hold her up as she cried into his shirt.

"I've been searching for you all night," he said. "When I got home I found your note. What the hell is going on?"

"It's a long story," she said, sniffing through a throbbing nose. The story was generations long, she realized. But it was a secret she needed to share with him . . . after a good long sleep. "Can I tell you later?"

She rested in his arms for a minute before she pulled away.

"I lost your barrette," she said, her eyes pooling up again.

"Your hair seems to be too short for it now."

She reached back to feel her hair—strawlike and hacked.

"That length suits you." His smile was tinged with concern. "But I'm not sure about your nose."

She laughed, in a half-crying way. "Come with me for a second," she said.

She took his hand and walked the few yards to the graveyard stairs. She guided him past the spot where she and the police detectives had stood and then ducked under the iron railing onto the grass. He followed her.

Ezra's gravesite still had yellow police tape around it. The headstone was no longer upside down, but had been laid flat until it could be set properly.

She couldn't see for the tears in her eyes. "Read it to me?" she sobbed.

Peter put his arm around her and hugged her shoulder.

"E. A. DOYLE
1853–1873
Death is the privilege of human nature
And life without it were not worth our taking
Thither the poor, the unfortunate, and Mourner
Fly for relief & lay their burdens down."

Hester's throat was too tight to say anything.

Peter tipped his head to look at her. Her cheeks were soaked with dirty tears. He squeezed her to him.

"Let me take you home."

She nodded. "Please."

Epilogue

1873

THE DOWNDRAFT FROM NOO'KAS'S MAGIC had knocked Syrenka onto the baby in the graveyard. She heard its muffled cry beneath her and pulled back onto her knees to examine it. She had not injured it, but without a soul it would not live long. She intended to rush to the beach to see Ezra, but something about the baby kept her there for a moment, transfixed.

It was crying weakly and growing pale. Its skin was beginning to wrinkle, as a plum does when dried in the sun. It was as if the baby were desiccating before her eyes. The legs were exposed through the bunting opening, and flakes of dry skin had loosened on them. In a moment the flakes seemed to be forming into scales.

Scales.

Syrenka's chest tightened, as if an invisible hand squeezed her heart.

She slowly unwrapped the baby's blanket. The scales began layering themselves—growing, shingling. The legs kicked feebly, pitifully. The cotton diaper had come loose, and Syrenka saw that she was a girl.

A little girl.

She was the right age. She was pale, with beautiful green eyes. The vestigial scales, reappearing as her life faded, were unmistakable.

At once she knew it was her child. And she knew that she had killed her.

"No!" she cried, with tears welling in her eyes for the first time in her ancient life.

Syrenka had learned much from Ezra's gentle devotion, and from her own responsive mortal heart. The grief over her error was immediate and profound. It spread through her like flames consuming a dry forest. Every selfish thought for herself disappeared. Every care for her own life and happiness dissolved. There was only the urge to protect her child.

She scooped the baby onto her lap. She enveloped her with her body. She pressed her cheek against the baby's delicate scalp and whispered a plea, with every part of her: "Take me, instead."

Marijn's thirsty body reached out for Syrenka's warm soul. Syrenka released it willingly. From the ocean, Noo'kas provided the magic, with pleasure. The baby took a deep breath and cried lustily as her mother collapsed.

Syrenka's unanchored life began to ebb away. With her face pressed to the ground, her thoughts turned back to Ezra. He had died at the beach. If Noo'kas had dealt fairly with her, his pinned spirit would be there. She might see him one last time. She might say goodbye.

She willed herself to her knees, and then to her feet. After a thousand years of physical strength she was overwhelmed by what it felt like to be frail. She swaddled the baby as best she could and lifted her, staggering to the threshold of the church door. She kissed the baby and laid her gently on the stone floor. Her legs buckled. She clung to the doorjamb, resting. Time was running out.

The journey was downhill, but her steps were short and faltering. Twice she crumpled to the ground, and twice she rose through determination alone, until she was nearly there. She crossed the grassy lawn to the stone steps, fell to her knees, and descended backward, like a child. The tide was high, and the last step was submerged. She turned to push against the iron gate and let herself fall onto the flooded sand. She lifted her head, trembling. She searched the beach north and south.

Ezra was not there.

She wanted to call out to him, but she had no voice.

As her head dropped and her vision clouded to black, she saw her sister pulling herself through the shallow water to reach her. Needa gently tugged Syrenka into the ocean and swam her body to the depths, where it belonged.

Syrenka's final breath escaped slowly from her lungs in a slim stream. Minutes later, the last evidence of her human existence danced up through the ocean as air bubbles, softly breaking on the moonlit surface of the water.

2/13, 11/14, 9/15, 1/17, 12/17